KU-512-004

MURDER OF A
BEAUTY SHOP QUEEN

MURDER OF A BEAUTY SHOP QUEEN

Bill Crider

CHIVERS

British Library Cataloguing in Publication Data available

This Large Print edition published by AudioGO Ltd, Bath, 2013.
Published by arrangement with the Author

U.K.   Hardcover   ISBN   978 1 4713 3440 5
U.K.   Softcover   ISBN   978 1 4713 3441 2

LP

Printed and bound in Great Britain by
MPG Books Group Limited

In memory of David Thompson,
one of a kind

CHAPTER 1

THE BEAUTY SHACK.

The red sign painted on the big window on the front of the little white building bothered Sheriff Dan Rhodes. The words "beauty" and "shack" didn't seem to belong together.

The wooden building had been sitting there on a concrete slab for twenty years or more, about two blocks from what was left of Clearview's downtown. While the building was a little the worse for wear, it wasn't a shack. There was nothing wrong with it that a new coat of paint couldn't fix.

Rhodes got out of the county car. The early morning air smelled fresh and clean. The pea gravel crunched beneath his feet.

Two other vehicles were parked in front of the building. One was a red Chrysler Sebring convertible with cat tracks on the windshield and dew on the top and hood. Beside it was a black Suburban that was coated with dirt and dust. Someone had written WASH ME with a wet finger on the side near the back.

Rhodes looked toward downtown. Deputy Ruth Grady's cruiser was headed in his direction, its light bar flashing. No siren, though. Ruth knew better than to attract too much attention this early in the morning, or any time of day for that matter, though it was hard to say just whose attention she might attract. The downtown area was deserted, and many of the old buildings had fallen down or been demolished. The bricks had been hauled away, and now only gaping openings remained. Businesses had migrated out to the highway where the new Walmart was, and the old central business district was like a ghost town.

The early morning sun threw a long shadow from the decrepit building across the street from the Beauty Shack. Fifty or sixty years ago the front half of the building had housed a Buick dealership, and a Studebaker dealership before that, or so Rhodes had been told. The second floor had been a hotel, respectable at one time, then a flophouse, and then nothing except vacant rooms.

The glass show windows on the bottom floor had been replaced with plywood, now dark with age and covered with fading graf-fiti.

Brush and trees grew thickly around the faded brick walls and hid most of the amateur artwork, which was as faded as the bricks except for one or two halfhearted recent attempts that had been partially foiled by the bushes.

In the window frames of the old hotel above, some panes of glass were missing entirely, and most of the rest were cracked. In one window a bedraggled bird's nest drooped between a broken pane and the frame.

Rhodes heard the hum of an air condi-tioner as it kicked on behind the Beauty Shack. It was going to be a hot day. Rhodes brushed his fingers across his damp fore-head and wiped them on his shirt. Ivy, his wife, wouldn't have liked that, but she wasn't there to see.

Ruth Grady drove into the little parking area and stopped her cruiser next to Rhodes and got out. She had a camera and some evidence bags in one hand.

"Ready to go in?" she asked.

Ruth was Blacklin County's youngest deputy but one of the best qualified. Rhodes had never doubted her abilities or judgment until recently, when she'd begun dating

9

Seepy Benton, a math teacher at the local community college branch. Benton was a bit odd. Ruth's personal life was none of Rhodes's business, however, so he kept out of it. So far her work hadn't been affected.

"I'm ready," he said.

He went up the two concrete steps that sat in front of the Beauty Shack and opened the door. As soon as he did, he smelled the peculiar beauty shop smell. Even with the air conditioner running all night, the smell remained. Rhodes had never known exactly what it was, other than that it had to be some combination of permanent wave solution, blow-dried hair, shampoo, perfume, ointments, creams, dyes, nail polish, hair spray, mousse, and other things he couldn't identify.

Ruth was right behind him as he stepped inside. Thanks to the air conditioner, it was cooler there than it had been out in the parking lot. Both of them pulled on polypropylene gloves.

The shop had only one room other than the restroom. On the wall opposite the door were four chairs backed up against sinks with mirrors above them. Near the mirror on his left was a large rack that held bottles and jars of beauty products. Two big chairs with dryer helmets above them were on the right. A price list was thumbtacked to the wall between them.

A woman sat in one of the dryer chairs. She got up when Rhodes and Ruth entered, but Rhodes hardly glanced at her. He was looking at the other woman, the one who lay on the floor near the wall to his left, the one who wasn't moving.

Her name was Lynn Ashton. Young, blond, and pretty. She was the owner of the convertible. Or she had been. She was too dead to own anything now. The usual wave of melancholy at the waste of a life passed over Rhodes. He couldn't help the young woman, and it made him feel old and ineffective.

"I found her just like that, Danny," said the woman who'd been sitting in the chair. She was Sandra Wiley, the owner of the shop. "I saw her soon's I opened the door. Scared me half to death. I called you soon's I got hold of myself. I got that dispatcher of yours instead, though."

Rhodes shook himself and took a deep breath. Sandra was his own age, almost exactly. He knew that because they'd been in the same class in school, when her last name had been Rankin, and, thanks to the fondness that many of the teachers had for alphabetical order, they'd sat next to each

11

other in homeroom and classes for twelve years. Only people who'd known Rhodes in those long-gone days called him Danny.

In the years since their graduation, Sandra had gained a bit of weight, and the skin of her face drooped a mite. Rhodes thought he was the same, at least as far as the weight gain, but while his hair was thinning at the crown and turning gray, Sandra's was still as dark brown as it had ever been, maybe darker. Rhodes figured it had some help from the beauty shop. It was cut short and held firmly in place by some kind of spray. She had a wide face, thin lips, and sad brown eyes.

"I probably touched some things," Sandra said. She nodded at a counter just to the right of the door. It held a cash register and an old push-button landline phone. "I know I should've used my cell."

"Don't worry about it," Rhodes said. He didn't think the killer would have used the phone.

Sandra wore a pair of navy blue slacks, a white shirt, and white canvas shoes with rubber soles. She reached into the shirt pocket and held up a cell phone as if Rhodes might want to inspect it. When she saw that he didn't, she put it back in her pocket.

"Did you call anybody else?" Rhodes asked.

"I called Abby and Lonnie and told them not to come in to work today. I didn't say why. They'll think the air conditioner's gone out or something. It's happened once already this summer. Was that all right?"

"Sure," Rhodes said. Abby and Lonnie wouldn't be spreading the word about what had happened, not yet, anyway.

"That Hack Jensen, the dispatcher who works for you, said he'd call the hospital," Sandra said.

Hack was the dispatcher, all right, but he worked for the county, not for Rhodes. Rhodes didn't think this was the time to explain the distinction to Sandra, however.

"That Hack said you'd call for an ambulance," Sandra said. "I didn't think it was any use to call the EMTs. They couldn't help her."

With that, she started to sniffle. Ruth put the camera and evidence bags on the counter and went to her. She spoke quietly, and Rhodes couldn't hear what was being said, but he knew Ruth was offering more comfort than he could. He walked over to look at the body of Lynn Ashton.

She wore the same color of slacks, shoes, and shirt that Sandra did, but she also had

13

on a green smock. Rhodes knelt down and touched her neck. It was cold, and he could feel no pulse. He stood up and walked back to Sandra.

"When's the last time you saw Lynn?"

Sandra sniffled into a handkerchief that had appeared from somewhere. She looked at a small gold watch on her wrist.

"About fifteen minutes ago."

"I mean before that," Rhodes said.

"Oh. Sure. Yesterday afternoon about five. Lonnie and Abby had left, and I was ready to close up. Lynn said she had a client coming in for a late appointment and she'd lock up." Sandra started to sniffle again. "What am I going to tell Lonnie and Abby?"

"Did she say who the client was?" Ruth asked.

"No, and I didn't ask. We stay all the time if one of our clients needs to come in late. Everybody has a key to the door so they can lock up. It was nothing unusual."

Rhodes looked at the body. A silver blow-dryer lay nearby. It wasn't plugged in. Rhodes knelt beside the body again. He saw an indentation in Lynn's temple. There was only a little blood around it clinging to the blond hair. There didn't have to be much.

Not far from Lynn's fingers lay a pair of scissors. The points weren't particularly sharp, but they could've done some damage.

Rhodes stood and looked around the shop for signs of a struggle. The chairs in front of the sinks weren't aligned perfectly, but nothing had fallen from the shelves. If there'd been a fight, it hadn't lasted long.

"That's Lynn's dryer on the floor," Sandra said. "Everybody has their own. Their own scissors, too. I'll provide what they need, within reason, but I won't pay the price for some of those things. That dryer's a little heavier than most, but it's a good one. Ceramic heating element. Cost nearly a hundred and fifty dollars. The scissors cost almost that much, too."

Rhodes noticed quite a bit of hair on the off-white vinyl floor and asked about it.

"We always sweep up after every client," Sandra said, "but it's just impossible to get it all. I have someone come in on the weekends and do a real cleaning."

"Let's you and me go outside and talk," Rhodes said.

He planned to let Ruth work the scene. She was good at it, better than he was, and she'd need some time alone with the body before anyone else messed up the place.

"I need to tell you something," Sandra said.

15

"Tell me outside," Rhodes said.

"That's what I have to tell you about. Something outside."

Rhodes opened the door and held it until Sandra had walked down the steps.

"You need anything?" he asked Ruth.

"Not that I can think of. Hair evidence won't be any good, but I'll collect it if you think we need it. There'll be fingerprints all over everything in here."

"Just do the best you can," Rhodes said. "Then start on the car." He went out and closed the door.

Sandra stood beside her Suburban, smoking a cigarette. When she saw Rhodes, she said, "I know these things are bad for me. I just smoke about two a day."

She tossed the cigarette to the gravel and ground it out under the sole of her canvas shoe. She picked up the butt and put it in the pocket of her slacks.

"I like to keep the place clean," she said.

Rhodes nodded. "You said you had something to tell me."

Sandra looked over at the dilapidated building across the street. The sun was just above the top of it now, and Rhodes shaded his eyes with his hand as he turned to look. There were times when he wished he wore a Western-style straw hat in the summer like

16

nearly every other sheriff in Texas, but he'd never liked hats, and they made him uncomfortable.

"I think there's somebody over there," Sandra said. "On the second floor. I thought about reporting it last week, but it slipped my mind. It's some kind of tramp, I'll bet. Maybe he killed Lynn. If he did, it's all my fault."

"It's not your fault," Rhodes said. He pulled off his gloves and stuck them in a back pocket. "Unless you killed her."

Sandra lit another cigarette and sucked down some smoke. She let out a white plume and said, "You know me better than that, I hope, Danny."

Rhodes could've told her that nobody ever knew anyone that well, but he didn't think it was a good idea.

"I should've reported that tramp," Sandra continued. "I did the last time somebody was there."

Rhodes thought back. It had been nearly three months, but he remembered the call. Buddy, one of the deputies, had checked it out. He hadn't found anyone, but he did see signs that someone had been living there: an old mattress on the floor, some empty bottles and cans. Buddy had checked on the building every day for a while after that, but whoever had been occupying the place had moved on.

Maybe he'd come back, or maybe someone else had moved in.

"I think he was there this morning," Sandra said. "I thought I saw someone moving around up there when I got here."

"Where was he?" Rhodes asked.

"Up there on the second floor." Sandra pointed. "The first window on this end. He might still be there." Sandra shivered. "I'm afraid he killed her, Danny."

Rhodes stared up at the window she'd indicated. It was the only window along that side with all the glass panes intact. Rhodes thought he'd better take a look up there before whoever Sandra had seen took a notion to leave, never to be seen again. If he hadn't left already.

Rhodes went to the door of the beauty shop, opened it, and told Ruth what he was going to do. She nodded, too engrossed in her examination of the scene to do anything more.

Rhodes closed the door.

"You can stay here," he told Sandra.

"You don't have to worry about me," she said. "I'm not about to go over there. You be careful."

"I will," Rhodes said.

18

"Ivy says you aren't, not always."

Rhodes looked at Sandra. His wife had her hair done at the Beauty Shack.

"What can I tell you?" Sandra said. "We talk about everything here. It's not gossip. Just sharing information."

"I've heard that before," Rhodes said.

"I'll bet. You be careful, anyway."

"I will," Rhodes said. "Trust me."

"I've heard that before. It usually means things won't turn out so good."

"They will this time," Rhodes said. He hoped it was the truth.

CHAPTER 2

Rhodes crossed the street. The old building was alone on the block. Years ago there had been other things near it. A church at one time. An auto repair shop at another. Houses. Now the nearest house was a block away. The ground was mostly hard-packed dirt, though in a few spots blades of brownish green grass poked through in discouraged clumps. Old tire ruts, hardened into near-permanent trails, crisscrossed the lot. On the corner to Rhodes's right an old mesquite tree leaned toward the street, its tiny green leaves barely moving in what passed for an early morning breeze. Long green beans hung among the leaves, and Rhodes remembered a day long ago when he'd been pulling a few of those beans and accidentally rammed a mesquite thorn into the heel of his hand. He'd been wary of mesquites ever since.

The door to the hotel was in the middle

of the building, or it had been. Now there was a big sheet of graffiti-covered plywood over it. Rhodes gave the edge of the plywood a pull, but it was nailed to the door frame and didn't budge. He walked along the side to the other end of the building, the part that had housed the service department of the auto dealerships. The two wide wooden doors to the service bays were pulled down and nailed shut. Rhodes tried both of them, but all he could do was wiggle them a bit in their frames.

Rhodes walked around the far corner of the building, but there was nothing at that end except a brick wall covered with more graffiti. It was easy enough to read because there was gravel all along that end of the building and no bushes grew there. Rhodes looked at the initials and slogans that had been spray-painted on the bricks. LARRY LOVES SUZIE. A red heart with an arrow through it. SENIORS '99. BEAT THE GOATS. The last one had nothing to do with animal cruelty unless you believed that football rivalries fell into that category.

Rhodes turned the corner and looked around the neighborhood. The Clearview city hall and post office were a couple of blocks away on his left. They were on the edge of the old downtown, and they were both well-kept buildings. A couple of cars were parked in front of the post office, and another drove by down the street. That counted as a busy morning in Clearview.

Rhodes turned to look at the side of the former car dealership. The sun brightened the bricks and graffiti, and there was a rusty fire escape attached to the wall. It led up to a cockeyed door on the second floor. Rhodes looked at the door for a couple of seconds. It had been painted at one time, but the constant exposure to the sun and weather had stripped it bare. No one had bothered to cover the half-open doorway with plywood.

Rhodes put his foot on the first step of the fire escape. It seemed solid enough, and he started to climb.

Then he thought better of it. Going up there alone could be a bad idea, and Rhodes had said he'd be careful. He might need backup. Ruth was busy, but Buddy, the other deputy on duty, should be available. Rhodes went down the two steps he'd taken and walked back to his car.

Sandra leaned against her dirty Suburban, smoking another cigarette. "You find anybody?" she asked.

"I haven't been up there yet," Rhodes said. He opened the car door, got in, and called Hack on the radio.

"You got a murder on your hands?" Hack asked as soon as he heard Rhodes's voice.

"Could be. Send Buddy out here. I'm going to check out that old building across the street from the Beauty Shack, and I want him for backup."

"He's headed down to Thurston to patrol."

"How far away is he?"

"Couldn't be far. He just left. Maybe five minutes."

"I'll wait for him," Rhodes said.

"Did you call the ambulance yet?"

"No," Rhodes said. "Ruth's still working the scene. I'll have her take care of it, though."

"Don't forget to call the justice of the peace."

The JP would have to make a declaration of death.

"She'll do that, too," Rhodes said.

He racked the mic and got out of the car. He might as well ask Sandra a few questions while he was waiting.

"You see anybody move around up there while I was gone?" he asked.

Sandra took a deep drag on the cigarette, inhaled, and blew out smoke. She tossed it to the gravel and stepped on it. This time she didn't pick it up.

"I didn't see anything. I guess I was watching you most of the time. You still look like Will o' the Wisp Rhodes from a distance."

In his one moment of high school athletic glory, Rhodes had run a kickoff back for a touchdown. The reporter for the local paper, long since deceased, had tagged him with the nickname that Sandra had recalled. A few plays later, Rhodes had gotten the injury that ended his season, and the Will o' the Wisp was no more, though the nickname wasn't entirely forgotten.

"The greater the distance," Rhodes said, "the more I resemble that kid."

The truth was that it was hard even to remember those days now. They'd been a long time ago.

"Tell me about Lynn," he said.

Sandra looked down at the cigarette butt. She bent over and picked it up. When she straightened, she said, "I guess I know what you mean. You've probably heard the stories."

"A few," Rhodes said.

"People talk," Sandra said. "When a woman's young and pretty." She gave a rueful grin. "I guess they never talked much about me."

24

Rhodes grinned, too. "Jimmy did."

Jimmy was Sandra's husband, James Ray Wiley, whom everyone had called Jimmy and still did. He'd been on the football team with Rhodes, but he'd played in the offensive line and had been a considerably better player. He'd even made all-district his senior year, and because of that he'd had a college scholarship. A broken leg his freshman year ended his football career. He'd dropped out of college and come home to open a car repair shop, but he'd gotten cancer and closed it a couple of years previously. The cancer was in remission, but he still wasn't up to working.

"Jimmy was the only one," Sandra said.

"I wouldn't let that worry you," Rhodes said. "Nobody talked much about me, either."

"Now, Danny," Sandra said. "Don't sell yourself short. All the girls went for you in a big way."

"Maybe for the fifteen minutes that I was a hero," Rhodes said. "After that, it was all over. But we weren't talking about me and you."

"I know." Sandra shaded her eyes and looked at the building across the street. "I don't like to say anything bad about somebody who's dead."

"She won't mind," Rhodes said.

"Lynn didn't mind when she was alive. People talked about her even in the shop. They knew she could hear them. They wanted her to. She just laughed, and that made them mad. They never quit coming, though, most of them. One thing about us here at the Beauty Shack, we can sure cut hair."

She pulled a cigarette pack from the pocket of her shirt and took a butane lighter from her pants.

"I know what you're thinking," she said. She returned the pack to its place, lit the cigarette, and slipped the lighter back into her pants pocket. "I'm just nervous, that's all. Anybody would be nervous if they came in to work and found a dead person."

Rhodes nodded. "You were going to tell me about her."

"We all liked her." Sandra puffed on her cigarette. "Me and Lonnie and Abby, I mean. She was funny, always joking around, and she didn't act like she was prettier than me and Abby, even if she was. Younger, too, at least younger than me." Puff. Puff. "A lot younger."

Rhodes knew the feeling. He often thought that everybody was younger than he was these days.

26

"She even joked about running around with men," Sandra said. "Married ones, single ones, she didn't care, she said, as long as they were fun to be around. Lots of women in town wouldn't like that."

A car drove by. The driver slowed down and looked out the window when he noticed the county cars and the sheriff standing there. It was Billy Lee, who owned a small pharmacy, on his way to work. Rhodes lifted a hand in a wave. Lee nodded and drove on. In a little while the news that something was going on at the Beauty Shack would be all over town.

"Did any of them dislike it enough to kill her?" Rhodes asked.

Sandra drew so hard on the cigarette that it burned down to her fingers. She exhaled such a cloud of smoke that Rhodes had to wave it away with his hand as she tossed the butt to the gravel and crushed it.

"I couldn't tell you that," Sandra said. She pointed. "Is that somebody moving up there?"

Rhodes looked up at the window of the old hotel. He didn't detect any movement, but that didn't mean there hadn't been any. He looked down the street and saw a county car.

"That's Buddy coming along," he said.

27

"Send him over when he gets here."

Rhodes trotted across the street and around the building. He didn't want anybody to sneak down while he wasn't watching, and he hoped they hadn't done it already. Maybe he shouldn't have called for backup, after all.

Nobody was on the fire escape, and nobody was in sight other than the drivers of a couple of cars that passed a block away. Rhodes stood at the foot of the fire escape and waited for Buddy, who hustled up in a minute or so.

"What's going down?" Buddy asked.

Buddy was short, wiry, and a bit fidgety, not to mention addicted to out-of-date clichés. He didn't like crime and criminals, and he sometimes acted as if he had a personal mission to straighten out the morality of the entire county, an attitude that led to a certain overeagerness.

"Maybe nothing," Rhodes said. "Sandra says there might be someone upstairs."

"I should've kept on checking the place," Buddy said. "Those dadgum squatters come in all the time."

"Also, somebody killed Lynn Ashton."

Buddy's face turned red. He shook his head. Crimes upset him, and this was a bad one.

"She's over there in the Beauty Shack," Rhodes said.

Buddy's voice was choked. "She . . . had a bad reputation."

"She did, but we don't know that's why she was killed. Could've been a robbery. Could've been something else."

"We'll find out who did it," Buddy said, without hesitation or doubt. He pointed up the fire escape. "You want me to go up there?"

"We'll both go," Rhodes said. "Me first."

Buddy's fingers twitched above the butt of his revolver. "Think we'll need our side-arms?"

"Not yet," Rhodes said, and he started up the iron steps.

The fire escape squealed a little, but it didn't pull away from the wall. When he got to the top, Rhodes started to push aside the crooked door.

Almost as soon as his fingertips touched it, it whipped open and two men exploded through it. They crashed into Rhodes and sent him back against the railing, fast and hard. Rusty rivets popped under the sudden strain, the thin top bar fell away, and so did Rhodes.

CHAPTER 3

Agility had never been Rhodes's strong point, not even in his Will o' the Wisp days, but gravity and momentum allowed him to do an acceptable flip over the low bars of the fire escape. Flailing with both hands, he managed to catch hold of the top landing. He was even able to hang on, though his arms were nearly jerked from their sockets. He had a good view of the two men who'd bowled him over as they plunged down the stairs, trampling Buddy, who lay stunned on the steps as the men pounded past him.

Rhodes didn't have long to contemplate his options. Maybe there'd been a time when he was young and slim and nimble enough to pull himself back onto the landing, but that time was long gone. How far could it be to the ground, anyway?

He let go.

He hit the hard ground and let his legs go limp as they absorbed some of the impact, though not enough of it. He wound up in a heap. He would have liked to spring catlike to his feet, but instead it was something of a struggle to stand. He did stand, though, and began to run after the fleeing men.

"Running" was something of an exaggeration. Rhodes wasn't sure of the right word. "Shambling," maybe, not that it mattered. The two men were gaining on him.

They passed the mesquite tree and turned toward the railroad tracks that were only a block away. Rhodes heard a train whistle and looked to the north. Sure enough, a freight train was barreling along the tracks. It had two more crossings to make before it got to the one on the street the two men were running down, but it wouldn't take long for it to get there. Rhodes kept going.

So did the two men. It was obvious that they were going to try to make it across the tracks before the train arrived. It was going to be close, and while Rhodes thought they could do it, he knew he couldn't.

The engineer must have seen the runners at about that time, because the whistle shrilled without a break. The engineer didn't try to stop the train. It was far too late for that.

Just then, Buddy passed Rhodes, waving his revolver.

"Stop or I'll shoot!" Buddy yelled, though the men couldn't possibly hear him. They kept right on going and crossed the tracks not ten feet in front of the train as it rumbled by, the whistle still screaming.

Buddy stopped and holstered his revolver as Rhodes caught up with him. Rhodes was glad to stand and catch his breath as the boxcars whipped by, the wind of their passing rushing over him as the ground vibrated under his feet.

The train was a short one, only ten or twelve cars, and as soon as it was past, Buddy took off.

"Hold on," Rhodes called, because the two men had disappeared.

Buddy stopped. He might not have heard Rhodes, but he didn't have anyone to chase now. He looked back, as if waiting for Rhodes to give him an order.

Rhodes walked to meet him. On the left side of the crumbling street was a long-abandoned warehouse that had once been used to store cotton bales. A railroad siding beside the building had allowed the dropping-off of boxcars to be filled, but there hadn't been a bale of cotton made in Blacklin County in more years than Rhodes could remember.

On the other side of the street there had

once been a cotton gin, one of many in the county, but they were all gone now. The property was currently being used by a business known as the Blacklin County Environmental Reclamation Center, which Rhodes thought was a mighty fancy name for a junkyard.

Behind a rust-stained sheet-metal fence some of the old gin buildings still stood, but the entire block was covered with scrap metal of all kinds, old auto bodies, defunct washing machines and dryers, stoves, engines, lawn mowers, air-conditioning units, and things Rhodes couldn't begin to name. It looked a little like the set of some post-apocalypse movie, just before the rise of the machines. Rhodes wouldn't have been surprised if some of the seemingly inanimate components had reassembled themselves and gone off in search of Sarah Connor.

Outside the fence were several big metal Dumpsters, some of them overflowing with bagged trash. Junk cars took up most of the rest of the space, but Rhodes also saw an old tractor and a hay-bailing machine.

The warehouse was an extension of the junkyard, but Rhodes had no idea what was inside it. Nothing valuable, he supposed, since the big doors were wide open. Outside sat more junk cars and pickups and an oil well pump. The side of the center facing the railroad held a jumble of large rusted metal tanks big enough to hold two or three cars' worth of thousands of gallons of oil or gas.

"Where do you think those two fellas went?" Buddy asked.

"Your guess is as good as mine," Rhodes said. "You want the junkyard or the warehouse?"

"Sure is dark in the warehouse," Buddy said, "and you don't have a flashlight. I do." He touched a small Maglite LED flashlight dangling from his belt. "So I'll take the warehouse."

"You be careful in there," Rhodes said, "and don't shoot anybody you don't have to."

"Don't worry about me. I can handle myself."

"I know you can," Rhodes said, and Buddy went across the street to the warehouse.

Rhodes went to the gate of the recycling center. Nobody was around in the yard, but that was no surprise. It was still early. The gate was open, however, and so there was probably someone in the office, a low building that had seen better days. It looked so old that it could very well have served as the office for the cotton gin.

Rhodes walked up to the door and knocked. The man who opened the door was about three inches taller than Rhodes and twice as broad. He looked so hard that he might have been carved out of some of his own scrap metal. He wore a khaki work shirt with the name AL stitched in red on the right side.

"Yeah?" Al asked.

Rhodes showed his badge. "Sheriff Dan Rhodes. I'm looking for two men. Did you see anybody come inside here?"

"I've been looking at the books, not out the window."

Al wasn't a friendly sort, then, and not prone to introductions, but Rhodes didn't mind. Liking the local sheriff wasn't a requirement to live in the county.

"I'm sure you're busy," Rhodes said. "Mind if I look around?"

Al stared over Rhodes's head and didn't say anything for a while.

"I guess it's okay," he said at last.

"Got a deputy checking across the street," Rhodes said. "That all right, too?"

"Long as there's no shooting."

"I don't plan to shoot anybody," Rhodes said.

He couldn't speak for Buddy, but he hoped the deputy didn't get carried away.

He couldn't speak for the men he was chasing, either. He didn't think they were armed, but it would be a mistake to assume they weren't. Rhodes figured it was best just to keep quiet about that kind of thing.

"Go ahead," Al said. "No shooting, though."

He went back inside and closed the door. Something was bothering him, for sure, but he wasn't the type to unburden himself to an officer of the law.

Rhodes had paid more than one official visit to that office, though he'd never encountered that man before. Maybe there was something going on that Rhodes should be interested in, but he'd worry about that later, if ever. Right now he needed to find the men he was looking for.

There were plenty of places to hide in the junkyard, but Rhodes wondered if the two men had bothered. They could just as easily have worked their way through the scrap and headed in any direction. The place wasn't even fenced on two sides. If the run had tired the men out as much as it had him, however, they'd have found a place to hole up and rest. They were younger than Rhodes, but they'd run faster, too. He was betting they'd need the rest.

Rhodes looked at the ground, but the

trails that led through the junkyard maze were too hard to take footprints. He looked up. The stacks of metal all around offered plenty of concealment, but if Rhodes had been the one choosing a hiding place, he'd have picked the big metal building that loomed over everything else. He didn't know what purpose it had served, but it had a tower on one end that was several stories high. The top of the tower was stained dark, as if it might have been burned, or as if something had been burned inside it. The discoloration was more likely just corrosion, though.

Rhodes walked over to the building to see if it had an open doorway. Sure enough, it did. At one time a big sheet-metal sliding door had covered the opening in the building's side, but the door now lay on the packed earth outside. It had been there a long time and was rusted through in spots. A droopy weed poked through one of the spots, looking as if it had taken a wrong turn at Albuquerque.

Rhodes bent over, pulled up his pants leg, and got the little Kel-Tec .32 out of the holster. Rhodes had carried a .38 for a long time, but it was too evident and bulky, so he'd looked around for something smaller. The Kel-Tec was what he'd come up with.

It was like a little Glock, but with a better trigger. It was light, it held seven hollow-point bullets, and as long as Rhodes wasn't involved in a serious firefight, it would do just fine. It wouldn't stop a charging rhino, but it would stop most anybody Rhodes was likely to encounter.

He'd said he didn't plan to shoot anybody, but he remembered some poem he'd read in high school about how plans sometimes, or maybe it was often, went wrong.

With the pistol at the ready, he looked around the edge of the doorway. Thin shafts of sunlight came into the building through holes in the walls and roof, and dust motes drifted through the light. Scrap metal was heaped all around, but no one was in sight.

Rhodes stepped inside. The place smelled of oil and gasoline. The concrete floors, where they weren't covered with scrap, were stained by petroleum products and rust.

A couple of yellow jackets buzzed around a nest that they were starting just above the door. If the men were in the building, they were going to be hard to find, and it was going to be dangerous to look for them. Rhodes glanced at the yellow jackets. They were dangerous, too.

Danger is my business, Rhodes thought. That was why they paid him the mediocre bucks, so he started down the snaky aisle to his left. In places the metal was higher than his head, with piles of engine blocks, car fenders, refrigerators, air conditioners that had been gutted for their copper, metal lockers, army surplus ammo boxes, and anything else that was made of metal. There were a couple of piles of plastic and paper. Rhodes saw plastic buckets, bags of bottles, cookie containers, and even some flowerpots in huge clear-plastic bags. The back wall was lined with batteries from trucks, cars, and tractors.

Rhodes stood still and listened. He didn't hear a thing, not the sound of the yellow jackets, not the clink of a shoe against a tie rod, nothing. Maybe the yellow jackets had been frightened by his pistol.

"I guess there's nobody here, Deputy," he said, a little too loudly. "Let's check the outside."

It was an old trick, one that had been used since long before Rhodes was born, but it had been around for so many years because sometimes it worked.

Rhodes started for the door, but just before he got there he stepped behind a couple of refrigerators without doors and stopped. He squatted down to wait, thinking about the two men he'd chased. He hadn't had a good look at either of them, but they were both Hispanic and both young. Odds were that they didn't have green cards and were just passing through town on their way to somewhere else. Otherwise they'd have found better accommodations.

He could understand why they'd run. They wouldn't want to have any dealings with the law, whether they'd had anything to do with Lynn Ashton's death or not. Rhodes thought it was likely that they hadn't. If they'd killed her, they wouldn't have stayed around, and they certainly wouldn't have stayed right across the street.

They might have seen something, however, if not a person, then a car or a pickup. Any information would help.

Rhodes thought about Buddy, searching the dark warehouse. It seemed to Rhodes that the men wouldn't have gone there. They wouldn't have been familiar with it, and they wouldn't have wanted to stumble around in the dark. They were in the junkyard, all right, either in the building where Rhodes waited or nearby, if they hadn't already gone on somewhere else.

A bird that Rhodes hadn't seen earlier fluttered near the roof and flew out a broken window. Something must have spooked it, and just as Rhodes had that thought, he heard a soft noise that sounded like the scrape of a shoe on concrete. He straightened a bit but not far enough that his head showed above the refrigerator.

Someone whispered, but Rhodes couldn't make out the words. He waited. The seconds stretched out. Someone whispered again, closer. This time Rhodes could hear enough to know that the language was Spanish.

Two men edged into sight. "*Buenos días,*" Rhodes said as they passed by the refrigerator. He held his pistol so they could see it. "*¿Cómo están ustedes?*"

"*Mierda,*" one of the men said, which wasn't the polite answer that Rhodes had hoped for.

The speaker was the taller of the two men. His black hair was mostly covered with a Texas Rangers baseball cap, and he wore a T-shirt emblazoned with the Rangers emblem. The other man also wore a T-shirt, but it had a faded Bugs Bunny on the front.

Both men looked at Rhodes as if they couldn't quite decide whether to run, jump him, or just give up.

They didn't appear to be impressed with his pistol, but Rhodes thought they would have given up anyway, if the shooting hadn't started.

41

CHAPTER 4

The shots came from the direction of the warehouse, and Rhodes was distracted just long enough for one of the men to snatch the handle of a five-gallon heavy-duty plastic bucket from the pile of scrap beside him and swing the bucket at Rhodes's head.

Rhodes dodged aside, but not far enough. The bucket made a hollow *clonk* when it connected with his skull. The bucket split down its side, and Rhodes was staggered. He slumped against the refrigerator as the two men bolted out the door.

Rhodes saw blackness and pinwheeling sparks, and he had to lean against the refrigerator for a short while until the wave of dizziness passed. When it did, he kicked the bucket aside and walked out the door. The sun dazzled his eyes, and he saw nothing of the two men.

He did hear two more shots from the warehouse, however, so he started to walk as fast as he could in that direction. Running was out of the question.

When he arrived at the office building, the man he'd spoken to earlier came out the door.

"Dammit, you said there wouldn't be any shooting," he yelled.

"My plans didn't work out," Rhodes told him and went on by without stopping.

Rhodes walked out of the junkyard and smelled something that might have been a load of dead chickens. He thought for a second that the air from Mount Industry had become fouled again by the chicken farms out there and blanketed the town, but the odor came from one of the Dumpsters.

As Rhodes crossed the street, two more shots boomed in the warehouse. Rhodes saw a muzzle flash through the doorway, and he hotfooted it over there.

He flattened himself against the wall and yelled, "Are you all right in there, Deputy?"

Rhodes had hoped for an answer, but none came.

"Buddy?" he called. "Let me know if you're all right."

"I'm okay!" Buddy yelled. "I'm coming out!"

Rhodes waited, and it wasn't long before

43

Buddy backed out of the warehouse door, stepping down carefully so he wouldn't fall. He held his revolver in a two-handed grip as if ready to fire it again at any moment.

"Who's in there?" Rhodes asked.

"I didn't see anybody," Buddy said. He didn't lower his pistol and continued to stare into the dark warehouse.

Rhodes noticed that he was still holding his own pistol. "Then what are you shooting at?"

"Rats," Buddy said. He shuddered, though the day was quite warm now. "Giant ones."

"How big would that be?" Rhodes asked.

Buddy held his hands apart. "About the size of a cat. There's a lot of 'em in there."

"How many is a lot?"

"Maybe a dozen. That I could see. Might be more hiding around in there. Probably are. They were coming at me. I could see their little beady red eyes in the flashlight beam." Buddy shuddered again. "I don't like rats."

Rhodes didn't like rats, either, but he wouldn't shoot at them with a gun the size of the one Buddy carried. A .38 would splatter a rat over a wide area if the bullet hit it right. Or wrong, depending on your point of view.

"It's dangerous to shoot in that warehouse," Rhodes said. "A bullet could ricochet off some of the metal and kill you."

Buddy gave him a look that seemed to say that when it came to rats, he considered the risk worth taking.

"The floor's wood," Buddy said. "I shot at them when they were on the floor."

Bullets couldn't hurt the floor, Rhodes knew. It had been built to hold hundreds of bales of cotton. It was as solid and thick as the walls of a frontier fort.

"When I was a kid," Buddy said, "my grandmother read me a poem about rats. It was in some old book she had."

" 'Three Blind Mice'?" Rhodes asked.

"No. I wouldn't have minded if it had been about them getting their tails cut off. This one was about some old-timey guy who did something wrong. Hatto was his name. Anyway, he tried to get away from the rats by hiding in his tower, but they came after him and got him." Buddy paused and shook himself. "They whetted their teeth on the stones. I remember that part. Then they picked him clean like a chicken. I sure wish she hadn't read me that poem. I've never liked rats since then, and I didn't like 'em any even before that."

"I don't blame you," Rhodes said.

"It's the garbage that's attracting those

devils," Buddy said. "I can smell it from here."

"Right," Rhodes said.

"They probably come out and scrounge around in it at night," Buddy went on. "They don't like the daylight. They're like vampires."

"You mean like Dracula?"

"It's not funny," Buddy said.

"And I'm not laughing," Rhodes told him. "Those two men we were chasing got away from me."

Buddy lowered his pistol and looked at Rhodes for the first time. "How'd they do that?"

"Hit me in the head with a bucket."

Rhodes reached up with his free hand and felt the left side of his head. He could feel a small knot, but it didn't hurt much. Maybe nobody would even notice it.

"Now we can get 'em for assaulting an officer," Buddy said. "Plus murder."

"I wouldn't be too sure about that last part," Rhodes said. "I don't think they're guilty of that one."

"They ran, didn't they?"

"Sure, but so would you if you were squatting in an abandoned building and the law came calling."

Buddy gave a last look into the warehouse

and holstered his pistol. "They didn't know we were the law."

"I expect they'd been looking out the window," Rhodes said. "They must have seen us in the parking lot across the street."

"Maybe so. They're probably not in the country legally, either."

"We don't know that."

"I guess not." Buddy didn't look convinced. "What do we do next?"

"We go see what Ruth's found out."

"Clues," Buddy said. "What if she didn't find any?"

"We do what we always do," Rhodes said. "We start asking questions and hoping we can find some answers. In fact, you can get started on that as soon as we get back across the tracks."

"You have some suspects already?"

"Not a one, but somebody in those houses up the street might have seen or heard something that will help us. You can ask them."

Across the street from the big lot where the hotel building stood were three houses. All three had been there for generations, and while Rhodes had known some of the owners at one time or another, he had no idea who lived in the houses now.

"Let's go, then," Buddy said. He looked

toward the houses. "I don't even know if anybody lives in those places."

"You'll find out," Rhodes said. He put his pistol back in its hidden holster, straightened up, and started walking.

"Sure is a sorry excuse for a street," Buddy said just before they got to the railroad tracks. "I can remember when it was fairly smooth."

Rhodes looked down. The pavement was crazed with cracks, and in some places the bare ground showed through. He didn't know how long it had been since the street had been paved, but he knew it was a long time. All the life had been sucked out of the downtown, and the nearby areas and the businesses had moved out to the highway, trying to get as close to the Walmart as they could. Paving the streets anywhere in the older areas of town was no longer a priority.

They crossed the tracks and went down the incline. Rhodes noticed that walking downhill seemed to jar his bones more than it had a few years earlier.

When they got to the cross street, Buddy went over to the houses to begin his questioning, assuming he could find anybody at home. Rhodes walked on back to the Beauty Shack, where Ruth Grady was putting something into the trunk of her car. Sandra

Wiley stood by the Suburban, smoking a cigarette and watching Ruth.

"Find anything?" Rhodes asked the deputy.

"Nothing that's going to help us. There are prints on the hair dryer, but I'd bet they're Lynn's. I'll check. There's not much else."

"Did you check the car?"

"I haven't had time," Ruth said. "I'll get on that right after you tell me what you've been up to. Sandra says you and Buddy went tearing off after a couple of squatters from that old building across the street."

Rhodes gave her the short version.

"And they got away?" she said.

"They got away. On the upside, Buddy didn't get his bones picked clean by the rats."

"Was there any danger of that?"

"There was if you ask Buddy."

Ruth laughed. "Maybe I'll do that. Do you think those men you chased had anything to do with Lynn?"

"I doubt it," Rhodes said. "They were just scared of getting picked up."

"They could've had another reason to be scared."

"Maybe. Was Lynn's purse in the shop?"

"No. You think this was a robbery?"

49

"I don't know what to think yet. You go ahead and look over the car. I'll talk to Sandra for a minute." He started toward the Suburban, then turned back. "Did you call for an ambulance and the JP?"

"They're on the way," Ruth said.

Sandra lit a cigarette as Rhodes approached.

"You're going to smoke up the whole pack before noon," Rhodes said.

"I guess I'm nervous," Sandra said. She brushed at the corners of her eyes with the hand not holding the cigarette. "I still can't believe this happened. I can't believe Lynn's dead."

Rhodes didn't have any comforting words for her. He didn't think there were any.

"Remember what it used to be like here in Clearview, Danny?" she asked. "Back when we were in high school? Remember how quiet and peaceful the town was?"

"It wasn't all that quiet," Rhodes said. "We just didn't know what was going on. Kids never did, not in those days."

"At least there was a town then," Sandra said. "Stores and drugstores, and things going on. Cars on the street. It's quiet as a graveyard now." She paused and looked at her shop. "I guess I shouldn't have said that."

"Lynn won't mind."

"No, she won't, and the quiet's not real, anyway, not when somebody can come here and kill a girl like Lynn." Sandra puffed her cigarette, not looking at Rhodes. "It's a terrible thing, just terrible."

"You said you don't have any idea who might have killed her."

"Not a single one, but I'll think some more about it. I heard what your deputy said about the purse. I'll bet it was a robbery. I'll bet those two men across the street killed her for her money and her credit cards."

"I doubt it," Rhodes said. "They wouldn't have stuck around."

"You don't know what that kind's like."

"What kind is that?"

"Those illegals. That's another thing that's different now. They come here and take our jobs and send the money back home. It doesn't do the town any good."

Rhodes would have said something about that, but he saw the ambulance coming down the street.

"We're going to have to keep people out of the shop for a while," he said. "A few days, probably."

"I'm closing for the week," Sandra said.

"People will just have to put up with bad hair."

The ambulance parked by the Suburban, and the justice of the peace parked next to the ambulance. The parking lot was getting crowded. Rhodes spoke to the ambulance crew and the JP. Then he told Ruth that he was going to have a look inside the hotel building. "Maybe those men left something behind that will help us find them."

"You don't really believe that," Ruth said.

"No, but it never hurts to be sure."

Rhodes started across the street just as a car pulled into the parking lot. The driver, a woman Rhodes didn't know, rolled down her window and asked what was going on.

"Sandra can tell you," Rhodes said, and he went on his way.

CHAPTER 5

The room was cluttered with paper, and it smelled of cigarette smoke, dirty laundry, and fast food. Empty chip bags, candy wrappers, and jerky coverings were scattered all around, along with plastic sandwich containers and hamburger wrappers. Plastic soda bottles lay all over the place, and they would provide some fingerprints. So would some of the empty cigarette packs. Rhodes knew the men must have eaten real meals at some time or other, but there was no evidence of it in the room.

A couple of thin mattresses lay on the floor. A mound of clothing filled one corner, and a couple of roaches skittered out of it when Rhodes kicked it. Where there were two, there were hundreds more, Rhodes had heard, but he didn't look for them.

He didn't see anything that looked like a woman's purse anywhere in the room. He'd have Ruth go over everything again, but he didn't think she'd find any clues to Lynn Ashton's death.

Rhodes left that room and took a look in the others. They were even more depressing than the one where the men had stayed. Rhodes wondered if there were any rats in the building. He wouldn't be surprised if there were. Maybe he could have Buddy come and investigate.

The floor in one room was rotten. A hole near one wall made walking inside dangerous, so Rhodes didn't bother to enter. It was time to go.

He went back down the fire escape and back to the Beauty Shack. The ambulance was gone, and with it the earthly remains of Lynn Ashton. The JP was gone, too, and so was Sandra. Ruth had put the crime-scene tape around the building and was waiting for Rhodes by her car.

"She's coming back with a sign to put on the door," Ruth told Rhodes. "I'm supposed to turn the customers away."

"Have you found anything in the car?"

"Not if you don't count the things that belong there. No sign of the purse."

"We'll impound the car," Rhodes said. "You'd better go over to the hotel and have a look at the room where the men stayed. When you're finished, call Carl Evans. He can secure the door."

Evans was a carpenter the department had used before. He'd have to put in a new door with a lock. That wouldn't keep a determined person out, but it might be enough to hold things for a while.

"Who owns that building, anyway?" Ruth asked.

"Well," Rhodes said, "that's the problem. Nobody knows for sure. The owner of record at the courthouse is Dill Reynolds, but he died twenty years ago. His will's on file, too, and he left the building to his cousin. I can't remember the cousin's name, but he lives in Kentucky. Or he did. Nobody's been able to locate him, as far as I know."

"That building should be pulled down."

"I agree, and so does the mayor, but the city council members are a little skittish about doing it. Some of them are afraid that as soon as it's demolished, that cousin will show up and sue the city for damages."

"It's a public nuisance," Ruth said. She looked over at the building. "Not to mention an eyesore."

"Sure it is, but so far it's not bad enough to get anything done. Besides, it's not as much of an eyesore as the reclamation center up the street."

"That's a business operation, so at least it's paying taxes. This building's not doing anybody any good. What about the taxes, anyway?"

"I'm sure they haven't been paid in years," Rhodes said.

"So it could be auctioned off by the county."

"Who'd buy it?" Rhodes asked. He waved an arm around. "It would have to be torn down, and this isn't what you'd call a thriving business area."

"I can see that," Ruth said. "You want me to fingerprint that room?"

"Just bring in some of the evidence, bottles, wrappers, whatever you think will take good prints. You take the prints later."

"They won't be on file anywhere."

"Nope, but we'll have them if we need them."

Ruth didn't have a chance to remark on that because Sandra's Suburban pulled into the lot, tires crunching on the gravel. Ruth went on across the street.

Sandra parked, got out, and showed Rhodes the sign she'd made. It was white posterboard with black lettering that read CLOSED FOR THE WEEK. She'd also found a black wreath somewhere.

"I'm going to put these on the door," she

said. "Is that all right?"

Rhodes said it was, and Sandra got a hammer and some tacks from the back of the Suburban. Ruth went to check out the hotel, and Rhodes watched Sandra tack up the sign and the wreath. When she'd finished, he asked if she'd thought of anyone who might have wanted Lynn dead.

"I'm still thinking," she said.

She walked to the back of the Suburban and tossed the hammer inside. Then she got out a cigarette and lit it. Rhodes noticed that she'd started a fresh pack.

Sandra blew out some smoke and said, "There were some women who quit coming here because of Lynn. I hate to name names, but if you think it'd help, I will."

"It might help," Rhodes said.

"All right. Marian Slayton and Johnnie Allison. That's all I'm going to say about that."

"That's fine," Rhodes said. "I'll talk to them."

"Okay." Sandra took a couple of puffs. "I guess there's something else you should know."

"Tell me, then."

"You know how it is in a place like this, I guess," Sandra said.

"I'm not sure what you mean," Rhodes said.

"What I mean is that for some reason people talk in a beauty shop. They tell their hairdresser things they wouldn't tell their best friends. People let their hair down in here."

Rhodes must have given her a strange look, because she said, "I mean, sure, they let it down for us to wash it and fix it up, but they let their feelings out, too. A trip to the beauty shop is a lot cheaper than a head doctor, and it's just as good. People feel like they can say anything. We hear all kinds of stuff."

"What kinds of stuff would that be?" Rhodes asked.

"Like I said, all kinds. We hear about who's running around on who, who's sick, who's having surgery, who's in financial trouble, who's getting a divorce, whose kids or grandkids are giving 'em trouble, whose house is being foreclosed. Stuff like that. You know."

Rhodes didn't know, but he was going to find out. "What you're telling me is that somebody might have said something to Lynn that she shouldn't have heard, right?"

"Something like that, but there's more to it. What if Lynn heard something that she

58

shouldn't have heard and decided to use it some way or the other? Like they do in the movies. Blackmail." She looked over at Lynn's car. "You think she made enough money to buy that just from cutting hair?"

Rhodes thought about how much a haircut cost. He thought it was possible, all right. He also thought Lynn could've gotten the car another way.

"Maybe somebody gave her the money to buy the car without being blackmailed," he said.

"You mean one of her men friends?" Sandra snorted out smoke. "I guess it could be like that, but who's got that much money? I hope you find whoever it was that killed her, Danny, whatever the reason was."

"I'm going to need a list of her clients," Rhodes said.

"I knew you'd ask about that, so I put her appointment book in my car before I left."

She tossed down her cigarette and got the book from the car. "Lynn said she was going to start keeping her appointments on her phone, and I think she'd started doing it. She might have had one from yesterday on it. I don't have me one of those smart phones, but Lynn's had one for years." She handed Rhodes the book. "This doesn't have the walk-ins written down, so I can't help you there."

"This will do for a start," Rhodes said. "I might need to talk to the customers that Lynn didn't work on, too."

"You can ask Abby and Lonnie about their clients," Sandra said. "I just don't know how I'm going to tell them about this. They're going to take it real hard. They both liked Lynn a lot."

"Better tell them before somebody else does," Rhodes said.

"I guess so, but I sure do hate to."

Rhodes thought she might be hinting for him to tell them, and he'd be glad to if they were next of kin. They weren't, though, and it wasn't his job. He wondered who was. Lynn had grown up in Obert, a little town about five miles away, and her parents had died a few years ago in a car accident in another county. They'd been on vacation, Rhodes remembered. He'd have to get Ruth or Buddy to check on the next of kin.

"I have to get back to the jail," Rhodes said. "You need to stay out of the shop. Call Lonnie and Abby on your cell."

"I guess I'll have to," Sandra said, and Rhodes left her there in the parking lot, smoking another cigarette.

Lynn Ashton had lived in one of Clearview's

60

older housing additions. It had been built sometime in the 1950s, but even now it was outside of the main part of the town, just across a state highway. The town had never grown in that direction, though the community college building and strip center and a restaurant had been built along the road. All the buildings had their backs to the housing addition. Since it was separated from the rest of the town, the addition wasn't a place that people visited casually. They had to have a reason for going there.

Rhodes went there to be sure that Lynn Ashton's house was secure. He planned to come back later that day and go through it to look for something that might give him a hint as to who might have killed Lynn. Before he did that, however, he had to make some reports and ask some people a few questions.

The house had two doors, front and back. Both were locked, which would be a slight problem since Rhodes didn't have the keys. They were probably in Lynn's purse.

Rhodes went to the car and called Hack. He told him to have Buddy patrol the house for the rest of the day to be sure nobody got inside.

"Neighbors'd prob'ly do that for you," Hack said. "Prob'ly doin' it right now."

"I know, but let's keep it official," Rhodes said.

"Sure thing," Hack said. "You comin' back here now?"

"I'm on the way," Rhodes said.

The Blacklin County jail was old, but it was in good repair. The county commissioners kept talking about building a new one, a state-of-the-art affair with cameras in the cells, everything computerized, air-conditioned throughout, electrical doors controlled from a big console in front, the works. They would've built it, too, except for the money problem. The economy wasn't exactly booming, and there was no way the voters would pass a bond issue.

Rhodes didn't mind. He liked the jail just the way it was, and it was adequate for the county without having it expanded. It might not be as comfortable as a new one, especially for the prisoners, but Rhodes thought it would do just fine.

He went inside. Hack, the dispatcher, and Lawton, the jailer, didn't even look up. Rhodes saw that they were both reading books. He looked again and saw that both books had the same title: *Terrorist Terror.*

Uh-oh, Rhodes thought.

A few years earlier a couple of women,

Claudia and Jan, had been in Blacklin County attending a writing workshop. They wanted to write nonfiction, but there'd been a murder at the workshop, and they'd met Rhodes. They immediately decided that their chance at becoming published lay not in writing the truth but in writing about a sheriff like him.

Well, not exactly like him. Their character's name was Sage Barton. Barton, who'd trained as a Navy SEAL, had retired and gone into law enforcement in a small Texas county, the typical kind that was infested with serial killers, terrorists, and others of that ilk. Barton fought them all with a pair of pearl-handled Colt Peacemakers that were a far cry from the pistol Rhodes carried, which Rhodes was pretty sure Sage Barton would think of as a sissy gun.

As different as Rhodes and Barton were, however, there were some people who insisted on thinking that the two were one and the same or at least that they were very similar.

Hack and Lawton, who seemed to believe it was their mission in life to have as much fun as possible at Rhodes's expense and to drive him crazy in the process, were two of those people. Rhodes could have told them that it was against the rules for them to be reading on county time, but he knew it wouldn't do any good and that they'd just use it against him sooner or later.

He went to his desk, put on his reading glasses, and turned on his computer so he could do some of the paperwork relating to Lynn Ashton's death. As if Hack and Lawton would let him. Well, he could at least try.

Hack, who was sitting at his own desk, put a piece of paper in his book to mark his place and looked over at Rhodes.

"You know somethin'?" he asked.

Rhodes didn't answer.

"Sheriff?" Hack said. "You too busy to talk?"

Rhodes gave up. Sure enough, they weren't going to let him ignore them. He shouldn't have bothered to try.

"I can talk," he said.

"Good," Hack said. "Me and Lawton, we been readin' this new book. It's by those two women that know you so well."

"They sure do," Lawton said. "Why, readin' this book is just like havin' you in the same room with me."

"I am in the same room with you," Rhodes said.

"That ain't what he means," Hack said. "What he means is —"

Lawton interrupted Hack with a glare. "I can tell him what I mean my ownself. What I mean is, Sage Barton is so much like you that readin' this book is like readin' about you."

"Sure is," Hack said. "It's you to the life."

"I don't have pearl-handled revolvers," Rhodes said. "I don't fight terrorists, either."

"You would if any was around," Hack said.

"How'd you know this book was about terrorists?" Lawton asked.

"I've taught myself to be observant," Rhodes said. "Like Sherlock Holmes. The title was a clue."

"Oh," Lawton said. He turned the book over and looked. "I shoulda noticed that."

"Where'd you get those books, anyway?" Rhodes asked.

"They come in the mail this mornin'," Hack said. "Signed with autographs and ever'thing. Hot off the presses."

"I know what he's wonderin' now," Lawton said.

"What's that?" Hack asked.

"He's wonderin' where his copy is. Prob'ly has his feelin's hurt because we got copies and he didn't."

"I'd be wonderin', too, if I was him. It's not like Claudia and Jan to forget him. After all, if it wasn't for him, there wouldn't be any Sage Barton."

"Sure enough wouldn't," Lawton said. "Why, Sheriff, Sage Barton is you to the very life. He's the spittin' image. It's like you got a twin. It's like —"

"Just a minute," Rhodes said. "Is Sage Barton married?"

"Nope," Lawton said.

"Does he need reading glasses?"

"Heck no. He's got twenty-twenty. Maybe even better. He can shoot a squirrel out of the top of a tree a hundred yards off. With a pistol."

"A pearl-handled .45," Rhodes said.

"That's right," Hack said. "He sure don't need any glasses. Could prob'ly do it with both eyes closed."

"I don't doubt it," Rhodes said. "Does he have a little bald spot in back?"

"I wouldn't call what you got a bald spot, exactly," Hack said. "More like a thin spot. Ain't that what you'd call it, Lawton? A thin spot?"

Lawton nodded. "That's what I'd call it. A thin spot. Prob'ly be entirely bald in another year or two, but right now, just a thin spot."

"Getting back to Sage Barton," Rhodes said. He wished he hadn't brought up the hair, but it was too late now. "Does he have a thin spot in back?"

"Got more hair than a go-rilla," Hack said. "That guy could probably stuff a pillow ever' time he gets a haircut. Two pillows, maybe, but then he doesn't get many haircuts. He likes to look a little shaggy. The women like it, too."

"So let's get this straight," Rhodes said. "He carries Colt .45s, he sees like an eagle, he's single, he has a lot of hair, and he doesn't have a bald spot."

"That's right," Hack said, and Lawton echoed him.

"Yet you say he's like me."

"To the life," Hack said. "The very life. When they make the movie, they'll have to get you for the part. Couldn't nobody else possibly do it."

"Less it was Tommy Lee Jones," Lawton said. "Tommy Lee Jones can do just about anything."

"Got a thin spot in back, though," Hack said. "Wouldn't work."

"Hold on," Rhodes said. "I thought you said Sage Barton was just like me."

"Well, sure," Hack said, "except for the thin spot and some other little things like that, he's just like you."

Rhodes gave up. He should have never

gotten started. He turned back to the computer.

"Sheriff?" Hack said.

"Yes?"

"What about Lynn Ashton?"

"She's dead," Rhodes said. "Murdered."

"That's a shame," Hack said. "Everybody liked her."

"Not everybody," Rhodes said.

While he filled in the forms, Rhodes tried to make sense of things. One thing he knew for sure, besides the fact that Lynn was dead, was that her purse was missing. Was it robbery, or did someone hope Rhodes would think it was a robbery?

There were other reasons the purse might have been taken, of course. One of them would be to get rid of the cell phone that must have been inside it. Sandra had mentioned that Lynn had one, and a smart phone, at that.

Rhodes could get access to the phone records easily enough, but first he had to find out which company Lynn had her service with. While the records might be helpful, Sandra had also said something about Lynn's having planned to put her appointments in the phone rather than in the book Rhodes had been given. What if she'd kept some appointments on the phone, the ones she wanted to keep off the books, so to speak? The killer might not want the phone to fall into the hands of the law if that was the case.

Or maybe the phone held the names and addresses of some of Lynn's male friends. If it did, their numbers would be among those she called. Or maybe not. Maybe she'd been told not to call. Or not to call on that phone. Rhodes sure wished he had it to check.

He looked through Lynn's appointment book. Some names showed up more often than others, and Rhodes put them on a list. He made a second list of the ones who showed up less frequently. There were more women than men on both lists, but not many. Rhodes wasn't surprised. It must have been pleasant for some men to have their hair cut by someone like Lynn.

Ruth Grady came in and interrupted Rhodes's thoughts. She had a box of bags that she took to the evidence locker, and when she came back, she sat down in the chair by Rhodes's desk. Before she could say anything about Lynn's murder, Hack got her attention.

"Got somethin' for you," he said. He took a padded envelope from his desk and held it up. "Came in the mail this mornin'."

Ruth got up and took the envelope. She sat back down and opened it. Rhodes wasn't surprised that it was another copy of *Terrorist Terror*. He had to admit that the cover was eye-catching. It showed Sage Barton, both guns blazing as he raced across the top of a long concrete dam. He appeared to be chasing several heavily armed men.

"Is it any good?" Ruth asked Hack.

"You bet," Hack said.

Lawton had gone to check on the cell-block, so Hack had the floor to himself. That was the way he liked it, Rhodes thought.

"You remember the last one?" Hack asked.

"The one about the terrorists attacking the nuclear plant?" Ruth asked.

"That's the one. This time they're after a big hydroelectric dam."

"Hold on," Rhodes said. "You're always saying how Sage Barton is like me, but there's no hydroelectric dam around here. I don't think I've ever seen one."

"Well, you ought to have," Hack said. "There's twenty-three of 'em in the state of Texas." He patted his own copy of the book that lay on his desk. "These books are real educational."

"I don't know about Sage Barton being so

70

much like the sheriff," Ruth said. "The way I remember it, old Sage has all kinds of personal troubles. His sister is dying of some strange lingering disease, his father's some kind of spy for a foreign government, and Sage is always thinking about how his only sweetheart took a bullet that was meant for him."

"Well, sure, he has a lot of anxiety and stuff," Hack said. "That's why people like to read about him. A hero with no troubles ain't much of a hero at all."

"I don't have any troubles," Rhodes said.

"That's what you think. You might act like you don't, but you got plenty."

"Name one."

"You got an unsolved murder on your hands, for one thing," Hack said.

"You got that right, and I'd better get busy solving it," Rhodes told him.

Hack looked as if he had a response ready, but the phone rang and distracted him. He answered it, and Rhodes turned to Ruth.

"I'm going to talk to some of the people involved with Lynn," he said. "I need for you and Buddy to talk to a few of them, too. I've made some lists. I'll need you to get the phone records, and then we'll probably have a lot more names."

He gave Ruth the list with the more

71

frequent customers. He'd withheld one name, but Ruth didn't need to know that.

"Phone records won't be easy," he said. "I don't know which carrier she used."

"I'll keep calling until I find out," Ruth said.

"You know what to ask when you talk to people."

"I know," Ruth said.

"People will lie to you."

"I'm used to that, and I'm getting better at knowing when they do."

"All right. You can get started anytime."

"Now is good," Ruth said. She picked up her book to take it with her.

"No reading on the job," Rhodes said.

She laughed and left. As she went through the door, Hack hung up the phone.

"Call Duke Pearson and tell him to drive by the old hotel building across from the Beauty Shack a few times tonight," Rhodes said. "Tell him we're looking for two men who were staying there. They might have seen something that'll help us with the Ashton case."

"How's Duke's mama?" Hack asked.

Pearson had worked in law enforcement in West Texas for more than ten years. He'd moved to Blacklin County to help his wife take care of her mother, who was in the early stages of dementia. He'd been hired as a deputy only days after he'd applied for the job.

"She's no better," Rhodes said. "No worse, either."

"I guess that's a good thing," Hack said. "What happened to the men who were staying in that old building?"

"You'll have to ask Buddy about that," Rhodes said.

He waited to see if Hack would ask for details. If he did, Rhodes planned to make him suffer. Hack and Lawton spent far too much time talking around anything Rhodes needed to know. It was another way they had of getting his goat. They'd finally tell him, but in their own time. Rhodes liked to deal them a similar hand when he could.

Hack, however, didn't cooperate. He said, "Don't you want to know about that phone call?"

Rhodes knew then who the dealer was going to be, but he might as well get it over with. "Do I need to?"

"Sure," Hack said.

"All right. Tell me."

"Now you got another case to work on."

Rhodes waited.

Hack didn't say anything. Rhodes knew there was no use trying to outwait him.

"Well?" Rhodes asked.

"Well, you're gonna love this one."

"Why?"

Hack didn't answer that. He said, "It's just a good thing Milton Munday's left town, that's for sure."

Milton Munday was a muckraking talk-show host who'd made a brief stop in Clearview on his way up the radio ladder to a better-paying job in a much bigger city. He was on the air in Waco now, and he was likely to go higher. He'd given Rhodes a hard time for a while, but Rhodes had won him over after a personal appearance on a remote broadcast of his show.

"Jennifer Loam's still around, though," Hack said. "This is right up her alley."

Loam was a reporter for the *Clearview Herald*. She was a good one, too, and Rhodes had thought she was destined for bigger things. Given the current state of the newspaper industry, however, she was probably lucky to have a job on even a small-town paper. The *Herald* had recently undergone a number of cutbacks. It was also no longer a daily as it had been for something like a hundred years. It was now a weekly, and Jennifer was one of the few employees left.

"She'll be interested in the murder, I'm sure," Rhodes said.

74

"This is different," Hack said, "but it'll get a lot of play in the paper. Trust me."

"Trust you?" Rhodes asked. "I don't even know what you're talking about."

"Wild hogs," Hack said.

CHAPTER 6

Now that the cat, or the hogs in this case, was out of the bag, Hack broke down and gave Rhodes the story.

"Jackie Bradley was riding his four-wheeler out in his pasture, right along the edge of the woods, when a bunch of hogs charged out of the trees at him," Hack said. "Somethin' must've spooked 'em. They ran right into his four-wheeler and knocked him off on the ground. He was lucky he didn't get trampled."

Feral hogs were a serious problem all over Texas. Their numbers had tripled in the past few years, and they were multiplying faster than rabbits. They destroyed crops, tore down fences, and rooted up fields. Recently they'd even started coming into town on occasion. The county commissioners had talked about various ways of getting rid of them, but nobody had come up with a solution.

Not so long ago, Rhodes had been involved with some hog hunters. Shooting the hogs wouldn't control the population. There were too many hogs for that. Trapping didn't work, either. Rhodes wished he had an answer, but he didn't.

"What does Jackie want me to do?" Rhodes asked.

"Natcherly he wants you to come out there and kill all them hogs."

"He should know better than that. We can send Alton Boyd and have him set some traps, but that's it."

Boyd was the county's animal control officer. The traps wouldn't do much good, but they might catch a few of the hogs. That is, they might if the hogs didn't tear up the traps first.

"I'll get him on the radio right now," Hack said.

While he was doing that, Jennifer Loam came in. She was young, blond, and entirely too smart to suit Rhodes. She seemed to know more about what was going on in Clearview than he did.

"Hello, Sheriff," she said. She glanced at Hack's desk. "I see you have the new book. I got mine this morning, too. I can't wait to see what Sage Barton's up to now."

"Terrorists at hydroelectric dams," Rhodes

77

said. "There are twenty-three of those dams in Texas, in case you were wondering, but I don't think there are any quite as big as the one on the cover of that book."

"I wonder if dealing with terrorists is harder than dealing with murderers," Jennifer said.

"I'm sure it is," Rhodes said. "You know about Lynn Ashton?"

"I do." Jennifer sat in the chair by Rhodes's desk. "I don't know enough, though. Why don't you fill me in."

"You probably know more than I do. Do you have your hair done at the Beauty Shack?"

"Yes, but Lonnie does mine. I don't . . . didn't know Lynn very well."

"You know her reputation?"

Jennifer nodded. "Let's just say there are things I won't be putting in my article."

"I'll have more for you after the autopsy," Rhodes said. "We don't have a time of death, a motive, or any suspects, but you can always say that we're expecting to make an arrest any day now."

He thought he was pretty safe in saying that, at least as far as the newspaper was concerned. It was published on Sunday and delivered on Monday so the sports section could have up-to-date information on the

Clearview Catamounts during football season. Since today was Thursday, people wouldn't read the article for a few days. Then they wouldn't see anything again for another week. If Rhodes hadn't caught the killer by then, he probably never would.

"What about Lynn's family?" Jennifer asked.

"She didn't have any that I know of," Rhodes said.

"So you don't know about services?"

"Maybe she'd made arrangements. If she hadn't, Sandra might do something. I don't know any more than that."

"All right, then," Jennifer said. "You'll let me know if you find anything out?"

"Sure," Rhodes said, but they both knew he was lying.

Buddy came in not long after Jennifer left. Hack didn't even let him sit down before he gave him his copy of the new Sage Barton thriller.

"The sheriff's jealous 'cause he didn't get a copy," Hack said, "but he's tryin' not to let on."

"I'll bet it's a humdinger," Buddy said, sitting in the chair Jennifer had vacated.

"You bet it is," Hack said.

"Never mind that," Rhodes said to Buddy.

"What did you find out?"

"From those people you sent me to interview? Just about what you'd expect. Nobody saw a thing or heard anything. They all thought that old hotel was deserted as Death Valley. They had a few words to say about that junkyard, though."

That was about what Rhodes had expected.

"They complained about trucks tearing up the street," Buddy went on. "I guess some of the ones hauling scrap metal are pretty heavy, and that street's sure a mess."

"No laws against trucks, though," Rhodes said. He'd heard the complaints before. "Nobody remembered seeing anybody come and go at all?"

"That's right. Couple of 'em said they saw people walking along the street now and then, but they didn't know where they came from or who they were or where they went."

"And they didn't see anybody parked at the Beauty Shack late yesterday afternoon?"

"If they did, they don't remember it. It wasn't anything unusual for a car or two to be in that lot."

"That reminds me," Rhodes said. "Excuse me for a second."

He picked up his phone and called the towing service the county used and told the man who answered where to pick up Lynn's car.

"Just take it to the impound lot," he said. "You know where it is."

He hung up and turned back to Buddy. "Here's something for you."

He handed him the list of customers and told Buddy what to do.

"If you run into any trouble, just call Hack," Rhodes said.

"I can handle trouble," Buddy said. He looked sheepish. "Long as it's not rats."

"You won't have to worry about that," Rhodes said.

Buddy shook his head. "I sure hope not. Once a year or so is about all I can take."

Rhodes had saved Lonnie and Abby for himself. He was sure Sandra had had time to call them or visit them by now, so he left the jail and drove to Lonnie Wallace's house, which was in one of Clearview's newer residential neighborhoods, if "newer" meant twenty or so years old. There hadn't been a lot of building in Clearview lately.

Lonnie's house was the neatest on the block. The walks were edged; the grass was green, watered, and clipped. Rhodes thought about his own lawn, brown and shaggy, and felt a twinge of envy.

81

Lonnie's driveway looked as if it had been pressure-washed only days ago, the house trim had been painted within the last year, and the flower beds in front looked like something out of a gardening magazine. In fact, the whole place looked a little like a photograph.

Rhodes parked the county car at the curb and walked to the door, which was just as clean as everything else. He almost hated to touch the doorbell button and soil it, but he did.

Chimes rang in the house, and Lonnie came to the door. He was about thirty-five and had lived all his life in Clearview. In fact, he'd grown up only a couple of blocks from Rhodes's house. Rhodes knew his parents and had occasionally seen Lonnie around when he was a kid. He'd read articles about Lonnie in the newspaper when Lonnie was in high school, where he'd been a good student and had won some prizes at the local science fair.

Lonnie was tall and heavy, and he wore jeans cinched with a wide leather belt that sported a big silver buckle. With Lonnie, boots were still in style for manly footwear. His eyes were red, as if he'd been crying. The crying hadn't disturbed his hair, which was dark brown, thick, and werewolf perfect,

82

combed with a clean white part on the left.

"Hello, Sheriff," Lonnie said. "I guess I should have been expecting you. Come in."

He opened the door, and Rhodes went inside. Lonnie led him down a short hall to the den. If the house itself was only about twenty years old, the den looked like something from a much earlier era. The 1950s, Rhodes guessed, though he didn't know a lot about furniture. A heavy sofa and matching chair were covered in green fabric with a geometric pattern woven in. Vases on a couple of end tables held cut flowers, and copies of *Newsweek* lay on the coffee table.

"Nice place," Rhodes said.

"Thank you," Lonnie said. "I decorated it myself. I bought everything secondhand, well, except for the flowers. Have a seat, Sheriff."

Rhodes sat on the sofa, and Lonnie sat in the chair.

"You don't think I did it, do you?" Lonnie asked.

"I haven't formed an opinion yet," Rhodes said. "You have a reason for asking it?"

"I just wondered," Lonnie said. "I didn't, you know. Kill her, I mean. Lynn and I were the best of friends." He took a tissue from the pocket of his Western-cut shirt and dabbed at his eyes. "We shared everything. I knew all her secrets, and she knew mine."

"Then you're just the man I want to talk to," Rhodes said. "Tell me her secrets."

Lonnie looked at Rhodes with exaggerated surprise. "You can't mean that."

"Sure I can."

"Sheriff, Lynn trusted me, and I trusted her. We promised we'd never tell. Why, if some of the things she knew about me got out . . ." Lonnie looked at Rhodes. "I don't want to talk about that."

Rhodes had a pretty good idea what Lonnie was thinking, but he wasn't sure how delicate he had to be in discussing it. He decided that the direct approach might be best.

"Lonnie, I'm pretty sure I know what you mean. It's no big deal."

Lonnie clutched his tissue. "What's no big deal?"

"Everybody in town knows you're gay."

Lonnie nearly jumped off his chair. "Who told you that? It's not true. It's malicious gossip. It's slanderous. It's vicious and mean. It's unconscionable."

Rhodes had to admire the man's vocabulary.

"Lonnie," he said. "It's okay. Nobody cares."

Lonnie dabbed at his eyes. "It's because

84

I'm a hairdresser, isn't it. People think a man who's a hairdresser must be gay, like I'm some big cliché out of a bad fifties movie. I should've been a damn truck driver!"

"It's not because you're a hairdresser," Rhodes told him. "It's not because of anything."

"Yes, it is. It's because I'm not married. That's it, isn't it. Just because I'm thirty-five and not married, then I must be gay. People can be so mean."

"Nobody's being mean," Rhodes said. "Nobody cares. You're just you."

"Lynn told you, didn't she. She promised she wouldn't, but she did. That bitch. I ought to —"

The sudden flash of rage surprised Rhodes, and for the first time he wondered if Lonnie might indeed be a suspect.

Lonnie stopped short. "I shouldn't be talking like that. Lynn would never tell anybody. I'm really sorry I said that. I didn't mean it. I'd never do anything to Lynn. You got me all worked up by saying I was gay. I take it all back."

It was too late for that, but Rhodes nodded in what he hoped was sympathetic agreement. "So you told Lynn?"

"We shared things," Lonnie said without

specifying. "She had problems, too, you know."

"She did?"

Lonnie got up and went out of the room. When he came back he had a box of tissues. He put it on the coffee table, pulled one out, and dabbed his eyes.

"You know Lynn had problems, Sheriff. Men. She thought I could understand, and I could. So we talked."

"Now we're back to the secrets," Rhodes said.

"Are you going to keep mine?"

"Lonnie, it's not a secret. Believe me."

"I thought it was. I tried to be like everybody else. I thought I had to."

"Well, you don't."

"My parents," Lonnie said.

"They probably know, too," Rhodes said. "You might want to talk to them about it."

Lonnie didn't look eager to do that. He said, "Maybe you could talk to them and find out. They're your neighbors."

"And they're your parents. You're the one to talk to them. They'll be glad you've confided in them."

"I doubt it."

"Only one way to find out," Rhodes said.

"Do you think they know about . . ."

Lonnie stopped and looked at Rhodes.

86

Rhodes waited.

". . . about Jeff?" Lonnie finished after a long pause.

Jeff Tyler owned the building near downtown that had once been the biggest and best hardware store in Blacklin County and probably in the entire area surrounding it. Walmart had come into town, and before too long the hardware store had closed. Rhodes remembered the time some years previously when Elijah Ward, the original owner of the hardware store, had chained himself to the exit doors at Walmart, telling the customers that they could get in but they couldn't get out. Things hadn't ended well for Ward, but that hadn't been Walmart's fault. Not entirely, anyway.

Tyler had bought the old building, done a lot of work on it, and opened an antique store there, selling his own items and things he held on consignment. He wasn't getting rich, by any means, and Rhodes wondered how he managed to stay in business.

Come to think of it, the hardware store was only a couple of blocks from the Beauty Shack. Easy walking distance. It was something to check on later.

"Maybe some people know about Jeff," Rhodes said.

"We've been very discreet," Lonnie said.

"We never see each other anywhere around here. I don't even cut his hair. Lynn did."

"Nobody cares about that, Lonnie. You and Jeff could go have a burger at the Dairy Queen tonight, and nobody would notice."

Lonnie didn't seem convinced, and Rhodes gave up. "Just tell me about Lynn. Secrets don't matter anymore, and some things aren't as secret as we think they are. Sometimes lots of people know already."

"Obviously," Lonnie said. "That doesn't make it any more palatable."

"But there it is," Rhodes said. "So tell me what you know."

Lonnie was reluctant at first, but after he got started, the stories came out. There was just one problem, and it was a big one.

Lonnie didn't know any names. Lynn had confided in him, all right, but she hadn't used the names of any of the men she'd told him about. Or any of the women. Lonnie suspected that he knew who some of those were, however, because they had their hair done at the Beauty Shack. Still, he wasn't sure.

"Now if you wanted me to tell you if Mrs. Weeks was a natural redhead or if Mrs. Tongate had any gray in her hair, I could do that," Lonnie said. "I can't tell you for certain who was jealous of Lynn or who she was having affairs with, though. I could guess, but I just refuse to do that. I don't want to cast suspicion on somebody who's innocent."

"Just tell me about the ones who might want to kill her," Rhodes said.

"Oh, nobody would want to do that." Lonnie had forgotten his grief for the moment, and the tissues stayed unused in their box. He must have forgotten his sudden outburst, too. "The men all loved her and wanted to marry her. They didn't want to kill her. She just toyed with them, you know? She led them on and had a good time, but she never intended to settle down."

"Some of them must have been married already," Rhodes said.

"Well, yes, they were, and their wives came to the shop, and a lot of them went to Lynn. She might have played the field, but she could cut hair better than anybody in town. Even me." Lonnie looked thoughtful. "There were an awful lot of men, now that I think about it. I didn't really think of Lynn as being . . . promiscuous, but she was. I didn't think of her as being a user, either, but she was that, too."

He got that thoughtful look again but seemed to have nothing more to say.

"Not a very nice person, then," Rhodes said.

"I guess not," Lonnie said, "but we all liked her anyway. She was pretty and funny. She could get away with a lot."

"Somebody didn't like her," Rhodes said. He was sure there was something Lonnie wasn't telling him. "Somebody killed her. I really need something specific, Lonnie. Anything you can remember might help."

"Well, I hate to say it."

"Go ahead. Nobody will know where I heard it."

"That's not it. I just feel bad about it. He couldn't be guilty."

"Maybe he could," Rhodes said. "You need to tell me who it is we're talking about."

"Oh, all right," Lonnie said. "I guess there's only one man in town who has a red Pontiac Solstice convertible. You know who I mean. He's a county commissioner."

"Mikey Burns," Rhodes said.

"He's the one," Lonnie said.

CHAPTER 7

One of Rhodes's problems was that when he was working on a case, he often forgot to eat lunch. Even so, he never seemed to lose any weight. It didn't seem fair, somehow.

This time, however, he was going to have to eat something. He didn't feel like facing a county commissioner and talking about murder, not on an empty stomach. So he went by the Dairy Queen drive-through and ordered a cheeseburger and a Dr Pepper. He figured that would have all the food groups covered.

He sat in the parking lot to eat, and while he savored the cheeseburger, he tried to imagine what might have happened in the Beauty Shack the previous afternoon.

The scissors on the floor might indicate that Lynn had tried to defend herself. Or she might even have been the aggressor. What if she'd snatched up the scissors and tried to attack someone, someone who then grabbed the hair dryer as a means of defense? It might not be murder at all.

It might have happened the other way, however. Lynn might have grabbed the scissors when someone came after her with the dryer.

It was better not to get too interested in reconstructing things, though, not at this stage of the case. Believing you knew what happened could lead to blind spots in your thinking.

Speaking of thinking, Rhodes wondered if Mikey Burns had been doing any of that when he had parked his little red car in front of Lynn Ashton's house.

Lonnie had gone to the housing addition one spring afternoon to visit a retired history teacher named Nora Fischer, who was very much a stay-at-home. She was eighty years old and lived in the first house that had been built in the addition. While she no longer drove, she was quite able to take care of herself and her small house. She also liked to have visitors, and Lonnie, who'd been in her class when he was in junior high, went by to see her now and then because he enjoyed hearing her stories.

"We talk about the old days," Lonnie had told Rhodes, "when Clearview was still alive. She says people used to fill the streets of downtown on Saturday nights. All the farmers came to town, and the stores stayed open late for them. It's kind of sad that there aren't any farmers around anymore."

Lonnie had stayed a little later than usual talking to Nora, and it was after dark when he'd left her house. That was when he'd seen Mikey Burns's car.

"It was right there by the curb." Lonnie pointed as if they were taking a tour instead of sitting in his living room. "I couldn't believe it. I didn't say anything to Lynn about it the next day because I didn't want her to think I was spying on her. Maybe I should have."

"Did she seem upset that day?" Rhodes wanted to know. "Distracted? Anything different about her?"

Lonnie couldn't remember anything, but it was enough to know that Burns had visited Lynn. It was a start.

Rhodes finished his cheeseburger and Dr Pepper, put the trash in a can, and drove to Mikey Burns's precinct office.

Burns's administrative assistant, Mrs. Wilkie, didn't smile when Rhodes came in, but then she seldom smiled at him these days. There had been a time when she had a crush on Rhodes, but that time had passed. She'd spiffed herself up, gotten a job at the commissioner's office, and changed her priorities. Rhodes had heard she and Burns had developed a relationship. He wondered how upset Mrs. Wilkie might be by what Lonnie had told him.

"Good morning," he said.

Mrs. Wilkie gave a slight nod in response. Her hair didn't move. Rhodes wondered if she had it done at the Beauty Shack. The color had certainly improved lately. It was no longer the unnatural orange that it had once been.

"Do you want to see Mr. Burns?" she asked.

"If he's available," Rhodes said.

"I'll let him know you're here." She punched a button on a console. "Mr. Burns, Sheriff Rhodes is here. He'd like to talk to you."

Rhodes heard a response, but he couldn't make out the words.

"You can go in," Mrs. Wilkie said, and Rhodes did.

Burns's office wasn't fancy, just an old desk, some folding chairs, and a couple of green filing cabinets that had seen some hard use. Rhodes thought that Burns didn't want the taxpayers to think he was wasting their money.

Burns was seated behind his desk. He didn't bother to get up and shake hands. He and Rhodes knew each other well enough to dispense with that formality, and Burns was hardly a formal person to begin with. He was known all over the county not just for his little red convertible but for his colorful aloha shirts. The one he wore today had a light blue background that was covered with brown and yellow seashells.

"What can I do for you, Sheriff?" he asked.

His shirt might have been colorful, but Burns was clearly not his usual jovial self.

Rhodes sat in one of the folding chairs. "From the way you look, I'd say you already know."

"Know what? We don't need to play games."

"All right. I'm here about Lynn Ashton."

Burns's face crumbled. He knew, all right. It didn't take long for word to get around a small town when something bad happened.

"Oh, lordy," Burns said.

"That's one way to put it," Rhodes said. "Anything you want to tell me?"

Burns straightened his face and sat up straight in his chair. "I don't want to tell you anything."

"But you're going to."

"Yes, I'm going to, but it's all confidential."

"There's no such thing as confidential in a murder case," Rhodes said. "Besides, I'm a sheriff, not a lawyer."

"Maybe I should call a lawyer."

"We're just talking here," Rhodes said. "You're not under arrest. You haven't even been accused of anything."

"I'm under suspicion, though," Burns said. "I'm . . . what do you sheriffs call it? A person of interest? Right. I'm a person of interest."

Rhodes looked out the single office window. There wasn't much to see other than a backhoe that was parked under a tree. Rhodes wondered what it was doing there. He looked back at Burns.

"I don't think I've ever called anybody a person of interest as long as I've been the sheriff."

"Well, that's what I am. You think I know something or you wouldn't be here."

Burns was doing a pretty good job of acting like a man who was guilty of something. That gave Rhodes an advantage.

"You might as well tell me where you were yesterday afternoon," Rhodes said. "You don't want to get in any deeper in this mess than you already are."

"I'm not deep in anything," Burns said. He crossed his arms in front of his aloha shirt. "I'm completely innocent of all charges."

Rhodes didn't bother to point out that there weren't any charges. Yet. He said, "Why don't we call Mrs. Wilkie in and see what she thinks you're guilty of."

"Oh, lordy," Burns said.

Rhodes applied the Hack Jensen method. He sat there and waited.

Burns took a couple of deep breaths. He uncrossed his arms and put his hands on the desk in front of him, one on top of the other.

"All right," he said. "I've been an old fool."

"A fool, maybe," Rhodes said. "You're not that old."

"Whatever. I'm a good bit older than Lynn Ashton."

Rhodes had to agree to that.

"I should never have had anything to do with her. She should've been just somebody who cut my hair. She was so flirty, though, and so cute. So . . . ."

"Young," Rhodes said.

"Yes. Young." Burns looked at the closed office door. "Maybe you know that Mrs. Wilkie and I have been going out now and then."

"So I'd heard."

"It's not that there's anything wrong with her," Burns said. "She's quite attractive in her own way."

He seemed to want some kind of affirmation, so Rhodes nodded.

"We get along just fine," Burns said. "She even likes my dogs. But she's not . . ."

"Young," Rhodes said.

"That's right." Burns took a deep breath and leaned back. "She's not old, not by any means, but she's not young. Did you ever know her husband?"

"Slightly," Rhodes said.

"Fine man. Terrible that he died so young. Heart attack, wasn't it?"

"It was. We're drifting a little here, aren't we?"

"I know. It's hard to talk about Lynn. What happened was this. One day I asked her if she'd like to go out for dinner." Burns paused. "Not here in town. We drove over to Colby."

Colby was a good twenty miles from Clearview, well into a neighboring county.

"Long way to go for dinner," Rhodes said.

"Well, that restaurant on the interstate's really good," Burns said.

"I've heard that," Rhodes said. "Never been there, though. What happened after

98

that first date?"

Burns flinched a little at the word "date," but he recovered quickly. "We saw each other a few more times. Then she told me she was getting serious with someone, and she couldn't see me again."

Rhodes hadn't known that Lynn was getting serious. Lonnie hadn't mentioned it. Maybe she didn't share as many secrets with him as he thought.

"That's likely to make a man jealous," Rhodes said.

"I know what you're thinking, but I didn't kill her. I swear to that."

"You were at her house, though."

Burns stared at him. "How did you know that?"

"I'm a trained professional. What were you doing there?"

"Talking to her. I wasn't jealous, though. I just thought maybe I could convince her to go out again. I couldn't. I should never have gone in the first place."

Rhodes didn't know if Burns regretted going because of what had happened or because he'd been seen. He said, "Who was she getting serious with?"

"She wouldn't tell me. That's another reason I went to her house. I wanted to know." He must have realized how that sounded, so he added, "I wasn't jealous. Just curious, and she'd quit answering my phone calls."

"That can upset a fella," Rhodes said.

"I never touched her, and anyway, that was weeks ago. I'd gotten over her."

Rhodes decided he'd reserve judgment on that. "Mrs. Wilkie know about any of this?"

"You saw her when you came in, didn't you?"

"I saw her."

"Then you know she knows."

"She'll get over it," Rhodes said. He didn't add *unless she thinks you killed Lynn.*

"There's one thing I know that might help you," Burns said, "and it's a little warning, too."

"A warning?"

"Not from me. It's about one other person I know who was seeing Lynn. Maybe even the one she was getting serious with."

That might be helpful, all right.

"Who might that be?"

"Clifford Clement."

"Mayor Clifford Clement?"

"The very same," Burns said. "He took her to Colby. I saw them there."

Rhodes thought about that. Then he said, "You never did tell me where you were yesterday afternoon. Say around six o'clock.

Maybe seven."

"I was right here. Working late."

"Anybody else here?"

"No. Mrs. Wilkie had gone home. I know what you're thinking. You're thinking I don't have an alibi."

"Well," Rhodes said, "you don't."

Burns held up his hands, palms out. "I'm innocent of all charges."

"We'll see," Rhodes said.

CHAPTER 8

As with just about every other serious crime Rhodes had worked on, the information came in in little bits and pieces. He never found out anything all at once, but if he kept on asking people questions, he managed to find out things that, while they might not mean much in themselves, sometimes fit together in a way that told him all he needed to know.

As Rhodes had told Ruth, however, sometimes people lied. Even to the sheriff. You'd think they'd have more respect than that for their hardworking local sheriff, but they didn't.

So now Rhodes had to decide about what Burns had told him about Mayor Clifford Clement. Was it the truth? Or was Burns just trying to divert suspicion from himself? It sounded true enough, but that was the way it was with lies. They almost always sounded true enough, or at least true enough to help the teller avoid the real truth for a while. That's why people told them.

Burns's story was that he'd taken Mrs. Wilkie to the restaurant on the interstate in an attempt to make things up to her.

"It's kind of a fancy place," Burns had said. "Fancier than anything here in Clearview, for sure."

Rhodes liked the restaurants in Clearview. He liked the Mexican food at the Jolly Tamale and the barbecue at Max's Place. He even liked the artery-clogging menu at the Round-Up ("Absolutely no chicken, fish, or vegetarian dishes can be found on our menu!"). Then again, he wasn't trying to avoid being seen by anyone.

"Anyway," Burns said, "we saw Lynn and Clement there. I was kind of glad. I thought maybe that would help smooth things over." He shook his head. "It didn't work."

Rhodes should have asked Mrs. Wilkie about Clement, but he didn't have the heart to do that to Burns, so when he left he smiled and told her to have a nice day. She didn't return the smile. Rhodes figured that Burns was in for another week or two of punishment before she relented.

After leaving Burns's office, Rhodes drove to the Clearview city hall. It was about the same age as the jail but in worse repair because there was no state agency that inspected city halls. It was a two-story building with a small auditorium on one side and the city offices on the other. It had been a fine place once, but now the roof leaked during heavy rains, the foundation was cracked, and the air-conditioning barely worked at all. The mayor's office was on the first floor, just down the hall from the water department offices. The door was open.

Being mayor of a town like Clearview wasn't a full-time job, and it paid only a token salary. Clifford Clement sold mutual funds and managed portfolios for a living. Although there weren't a great many to manage in Clearview, he seemed to do fairly well at it. He'd been voted into the office of mayor in the last election, after the former holder of the office had decided he'd had enough of not being paid for listening to people squabble and complain all the time, not that he'd put it that way. He'd used the old "spend more time with my family" line and gone into happy retirement from politics.

While the city wouldn't spring for a real salary for the mayor, it did supply an administrative assistant. Her name was Alice King, and like Sandra she'd been in school with Rhodes. She was a year younger, though, and he hadn't known her very well.

Alice was in a much better mood than Mrs. Wilkie had been, and she greeted Rhodes when he came in the office.

"Good afternoon, Sheriff. To what do we owe the pleasure?"

Alice had been a cheerleader in high school, and she had remained relentlessly perky ever since. She even had perky hair, and Rhodes wondered where she had it done. Her husband was a dour man named Wilbur, and Rhodes thought it must be hard on him to be faced with his wife's perkiness on a daily basis.

"I just dropped in to see the mayor," Rhodes said. "Is he here this afternoon?"

Rhodes figured he was. Clement did most of his business in the mornings, and he spent a couple of hours in the city hall nearly every afternoon.

"He sure is," Alice said. She bobbed her head, and her perky hair bounced. "You just go right on in."

Rhodes opened the door and saw that Clement was sitting at his desk, a newer one than Burns had, reading a book. He put the book down when he saw Rhodes.

"Come on in, Sheriff," he said. "It's good to see you." Unlike Burns, Clement got up, came around the desk, and shook Rhodes's hand. "Have a seat and tell me what's on your mind."

Clement had better chairs than Burns did, too, big leather ones, but they weren't new. The leather was scuffed and worn. Rhodes sat down and so did Clement. He was a short man with a gray buzz cut and a gray beard. He had blue eyes with deep crinkles at the corners. Like Burns, he was a good bit older than Lynn Ashton had been. If he knew about Lynn, he was a lot better at hiding his feelings than Burns.

"I need to ask you about Lynn Ashton," Rhodes said, closing the door and taking a seat.

The mayor assumed a solemn expression. "I just heard about that. A terrible thing. I expect you to wrap this one up quickly, Sheriff. It's a real black eye for the town."

"Not to mention an inconvenience for Ms. Ashton," Rhodes said.

"You don't have to take that tone with me," Clement said. "I wasn't being flippant. As mayor, I'm your boss, in a way, and I want this thing over and done with as quickly as possible."

Clement was Rhodes's boss in a way, all right, but that was all. Rhodes was paid by the county, but the city contracted with the county for its law enforcement.

"I do things the best way I know how," Rhodes said. "If you want to hire a police force for Clearview, and if I apply for chief and get the job, then you can push me a little harder. Might not do you any good, though."

"I didn't mean that the way you took it," Clement said.

He did, of course, but Rhodes didn't call him on it. He wasn't there to start a fight. Well, not about his job, at any rate.

"The real reason I'm here," he said, "is to ask you about your relationship with Lynn Ashton."

Clement gave him a puzzled look. "My relationship? What do you mean by that?"

He was good. Rhodes had to give him that.

"You were seen with her in a restaurant in Colby. That's the relationship I mean."

Clement didn't say anything for a couple of seconds. "Mikey Burns. I thought that was him. You can't miss those stupid shirts of his."

Burns had tried to be discreet. He'd told Rhodes that he didn't think Clement had seen him.

"I kind of like them," Rhodes said, "but we're not here to talk about the commissioner's taste in shirts."

Clement sighed. "All right. You got me. I

went to a restaurant with a young woman. What's wrong with that?"

"Not a thing," Rhodes said. "If your wife doesn't mind, why should I?"

"Fran and I are having . . . differences."

"About the company you keep?"

"Look," Clement said. "I was there. I admit it. Let's leave my family problems out of it."

"For now," Rhodes said. "Now, about that relationship."

"It was over," Clement said. "That's why we were there that night. She was telling me it was over. I took her word for it, and I haven't seen her since."

"So you didn't visit her yesterday afternoon to talk things over again?"

Clement sat up straight and puffed out his chest. "I resent the implication."

"What implication?" Rhodes asked.

"You know very well. You'd better watch your step, Sheriff. You're getting close to slander."

Bluster. Rhodes loved bluster. He especially liked to ignore it.

"Where were you yesterday afternoon late?" he asked.

"I was at home with my wife. You can ask her."

Rhodes thought that political wives always

backed their husbands, no matter what they'd done. It was certainly true at the national level, and it worked the same way in small towns.

"I might have to," he said. "Why was it over with Lynn?"

"You listen to me, Sheriff. I . . . what?"

"Why did Lynn say it was over? Did she give you a reason?"

Clement's chest deflated. "She said she'd found someone else." He tapped his desk with one finger. "And before you ask, she wouldn't tell me who it was."

"Not even a hint?"

"Not even a hint." Clement's chest swelled again. "I didn't go by yesterday to ask who it was, either."

Rhodes stood up. "Thanks for your co-operation. I might have a few more questions later on."

"Then you understand that I'm in the clear on this?"

"I understand that I might have a few more questions later on. That's about all I can say at this point."

"Well, you'd better find Lynn's killer, and you'd better do it soon. Remember that."

Rhodes could have responded in kind, but he was tired of Clement. Why not let him have a point?

"I'll remember," he said and left.

Rhodes had gotten distracted from his interview list, but that happened too often for him to worry about it. When he got a tip on a new direction, he was always willing to check it out, and sometimes it was worth it. He'd learned at least two things from Burns and Clement. One was that Lynn had told both of them that she was getting into a more serious relationship with someone else. The other was something unspoken that seemed to be at least part of a developing pattern. Lynn Ashton had liked older men. Not that there was anything wrong with that.

There was a third thing, too, one that Rhodes had been thinking about all along. Lynn was very good at keeping her affairs secret. Everyone seemed to know she was having them, and she did nothing to discourage the idea, but nobody so far knew much about the people she was having them with. Even Lonnie, the supposed confidant, didn't know. Rhodes found that a bit surprising, considering how hard it was to keep a secret in Clearview. Just something else for him to think about.

Rhodes's list had the names of two more people that he wanted to talk to more than

110

any others. One of them was Abby Tustin, Lynn's co-worker.

The other was one of Lynn's customers, the one he hadn't put on Ruth's list. Seepy Benton.

CHAPTER 9

When he left the city hall building, Rhodes stopped to look around before he got in his car. He was a block from what remained of the old downtown area. The Beauty Shack was only about three blocks to the south and east. In fact, there was hardly anything left between the two buildings. Clement could easily have walked there and back in a couple of minutes. Given the lack of traffic in town, he might even have been able to do it without being seen.

Just up the street a couple of blocks was the old hardware store where Lonnie's friend Jeff Tyler had his antiques, which put Tyler even closer to the beauty shop than Clement was.

Rhodes got in the county car and drove through the old central business district of Clearview. A little bit of life had returned to some of the few buildings that remained standing there. A thrift shop had opened on one corner. A couple of churches had set up in two other buildings, and Randy Lawless's law office took up most of a block. That building was new and white and clean, a stark contrast to some of the others nearby with their cracked plate-glass windows thick with dust and their spiderwebbed entrances.

Rhodes didn't linger.

Over on the highway things were livelier, and out on the community college campus a few students were still around even in the afternoon. Calling it a campus was something of an exaggeration, since it consisted of only one building, and it wasn't exactly a college. Instead it was a branch of a college in another county. That didn't matter, however. The people in Clearview were glad to have it in their town so that people could get some college hours or even a degree while living at home and saving money on gas, rent, and living expenses.

Rhodes had been to Seepy Benton's office a few times, and he had no trouble finding it on the second floor of the building. Benton was inside, sitting at his computer, as usual, looking at something mathematical that Rhodes couldn't possibly have understood even if Benton had explained it to him.

Benton's office looked like something on

a TV show about hoarding. Papers and books covered both desks so that there was barely any room for the computer. They also filled the chair that students would have sat in if they'd come in for appointments. Beside the computer desk a guitar stood in a stand. Rhodes hoped that Benton wouldn't pick up the guitar and strum a tune. He was prone to do that sort of thing without warning.

Rhodes tapped on the door frame with one knuckle, and Benton swiveled the chair around to see who was there.

"Hey, Sheriff," Benton said when he saw Rhodes. "Got a new case for me?"

Benton wore a battered black fedora and an aloha shirt that Mikey Burns might have envied. He had a closely clipped beard just as gray as Clifford Clement's. A year or so ago, Benton had enrolled in the Citizens' Sheriff's Academy, and now he thought he was practically a member of the sheriff's department.

"Not exactly," Rhodes said.

"Too bad. My deductive powers are amazing today. Well, they're amazing all the time, but especially today."

Rhodes nodded.

"Toss those papers on the floor and have a seat," Benton said. "I have something to show you."

Rhodes followed directions while Benton turned to the computer and fiddled with the mouse.

"What was that you were just looking at?" Rhodes asked.

"Oh, that." Benton didn't look away from the computer screen. "I was just spiffing up my posting on separable differential equations at doc-benton-dot-com. Want me to explain it to you?"

"No thanks."

"All right, then," Benton said, "but don't say I didn't offer. Here, take a look at this. It's easier to understand. I have a new math song loaded on my computer."

Rhodes forced himself to watch and listen as Benton's image on the computer sang about something called "simple groups." They didn't sound simple to Rhodes. The song was mercifully short.

"Where did you get the hat in the video?" Rhodes asked when the song ended.

"You like the hat?" Benton asked. "It's a little different from my usual."

It was a Western-style vented straw hat, and Rhodes had to admit he preferred it to the fedora.

"I can get you one," Benton said. "What size do you wear?"

"Never mind," Rhodes said. "How often do you get a haircut?"

Benton lifted the fedora. He was almost bald on top. "Not very often." He settled the hat back on his head. "I just need the sides and back trimmed, and a little shave on the back of the neck." He rubbed his chin. "What I need more often is a beard trim."

"Who does that for you?"

"Lynn, at the Beauty Shack. Are you thinking of changing haircutters?"

Benton probably hadn't been out of the building all day, and his students weren't likely to have reported Lynn's death to him. Some of the other faculty might know about it, but if Benton hadn't been hanging out in the lounge, he might not have heard.

"I have a different reason for asking," Rhodes said. "Somebody killed Lynn last night."

Rhodes had never seen Benton befuddled before. He just sat there, his mouth slightly open. Finally he said, "What?"

"Somebody killed her. Hit her in the head with a hair dryer."

"You're not joking."

"That's right. I'm not."

Benton shook his head and looked at the floor. "Who'd do something like that?"

116

"That's what I'm trying to find out."

Benton looked up. "You don't think I had anything to do with it, do you?"

"No, but I thought you might know something that would help me find the killer."

Benton perked up a little at the prospect of being of some help, but he didn't look hopeful. "How would I know anything?"

"Lynn must have talked about something when you got your beard trimmed."

"Not really. We didn't have much in common. It was hard to get her interested in differential equations."

Rhodes could understand why. As far as he knew, Benton was the only person in Blacklin County with a burning interest in that subject.

"What do you know about her reputation?" he asked.

"Oh," Benton said. "That stuff."

"Yeah. That stuff."

Benton removed his hat again and rubbed the top of his head. He put the hat on some papers beside the computer.

"I never believed a word of all that," he said. "Lynn wasn't the way people think. Maybe she didn't know anything about differential equations, but she could talk about other stuff."

"Such as?" Rhodes asked.

"Well, movies. She knew a lot about movies."

"For example?"

"The kind you like," Benton said.

Rhodes had talked about old movies with Benton once or twice. Rhodes had a fondness for bad movies, the kind that had once turned up on TV with some regularity but now had disappeared from the tube. They'd found new life on DVD, but somehow watching them that way didn't have much appeal to Rhodes.

"She knew about *Hercules in the Haunted World?*" he asked.

"Probably not," Benton said. "Who does? Besides you, that is. She knew about *Mega Python versus Gatoroid,* though."

"Ah," Rhodes said.

Recently the SyFy Channel had been showing a lot of movies like that one. Rhodes had even seen a few, including the one Benton mentioned. Again, it wasn't quite the same as seeing something older on a late-night show.

"So she never mentioned any men friends?"

"Not to me. I know some of the women who came in the shop supposedly didn't like her, but I never saw anybody have a problem with her. Let me help you with this case, Sheriff. I liked Lynn."

"Does Ruth know you liked her?"

Benton put on his hat again. "I didn't like her the way I like Ruth. Is she working on this?"

"We all are," Rhodes said. "You don't need to help out. Leave it to the professionals."

Benton looked hurt. "I'm a professional."

"A professional teacher, not a lawman."

"I've helped before."

Benton had inserted himself into a couple of Rhodes's cases, but he hadn't always been useful.

"I'll give it some thought," Rhodes said. "How's Bruce?"

Bruce was a dog. A large dog. Rhodes had sort of inherited him on a case, but having two dogs of his own, he hadn't been inclined to take on a third. Benton had been coerced into adopting Bruce.

"He's fine," Benton said. "He eats a lot, though. I hope I get a raise this year. Otherwise I'm not sure I can afford him." He stopped and looked at Rhodes. "You changed the subject, you know."

"And here I thought I was being smooth," Rhodes said.

"That'll be the day. Anyway, I have my own case to work on if you don't need my help with Lynn's murder."

That didn't sound good. "What case?"

"It's one that Ruth's been working on," Benton said. "Here at the college."

Rhodes knew the one. "The car batteries."

"That's it," Benton said.

Car battery thefts weren't a big problem in Blacklin County, but there had been several of them lately, all at night, and a couple of them had been at the college. Recyclers paid anywhere from two to twenty dollars for a battery, depending on the size.

Someone had stolen a few catalytic converters, too. That was a trickier proposition, but since the converters contained metals like palladium, rhodium, and platinum, they could be sold for around seventy-five dollars. Usually they were taken from SUVs because it was easier to get underneath them.

In fact, the battery and converter thefts had been the reason for one of Rhodes's previous visits to the reclamation center. He suspected that the stolen batteries ended up there or in some other recycling facility in a different county. There were plenty of other, similar, thefts, too. Copper was still a big-ticket item, and copper wire was best kept locked away. Aluminum continued to sell well, too.

Recycling centers were supposed to get full identification from anyone who sold those things. Some places even required a fingerprint. Rhodes suspected that the center in Clearview might be a little lax when it came to making the checks, but so far he hadn't been able to prove anything.

"Ruth doesn't need your help," Rhodes told Benton.

"I know that. I'm just asking around to find out if anybody remembers seeing someone lurking around after dark here. The batteries only go missing at night."

"Any results?"

"Not yet." Benton looked disappointed. "I guess if they'd seen anything, they'd have reported it."

Rhodes stood up. "If you hear something, you tell Ruth or call me. Don't do anything stupid."

"Me?" Benton said. "Stupid? I'm probably the brightest person in the whole town. The whole county."

"Right," Rhodes said, "but that doesn't mean you don't do stupid things now and then. Before you think, I mean. You'd never do anything stupid if you thought it over first."

Benton wasn't entirely mollified, but he

said, "I'm sorry I didn't have anything that would help you with Lynn's murder. I hope you find out who killed her."

"I will."

"Right," Benton said. "You always get your man."

"Or woman," Rhodes said, "as the case may be."

Rhodes sat in the county car and looked at the parking lot. Only a few other cars were there at this time of the afternoon, though when the evening classes began, the lot would fill up again. Some of the cars would be parked in places where the lighting wasn't so good, and those cars would be most vulnerable to battery thieves. If people locked their cars, they could make the thefts difficult, but in Blacklin County a lot of people didn't bother with locking.

Rhodes thought about the two men he'd chased that morning. They weren't living well, but they had enough money to buy a few things while they looked for jobs. A couple of batteries or a few pounds of copper would help out with expenses. It might be a good idea to watch the Environmental Reclamation Center for a few days to see what developed.

There were a couple of problems with that

idea. One was that Rhodes didn't have enough deputies to do stakeouts. He could have Buddy or Ruth drive by the place, as he was having Duke do with the old hotel, but they had other places to be, too. They had a big county to cover, and they couldn't devote a day or an evening to one place.

Another problem was that the two men didn't seem to have any means of transportation other than their feet. It would be hard to get the heavy batteries from one place to another without a car or truck, but maybe they had a friend with a vehicle.

Rhodes started his car. He still hadn't talked to Abby Tustin or Jeff Tyler, and he wanted to see both of them before he looked over Lynn Ashton's house and went home for the day.

The downtown was as quiet in the late afternoon as it had been in the early morning. Jeff Tyler's building was a block off the main street, but he often stayed open until well after six o'clock, maybe hoping he'd get a customer or two on the way home from work.

Rhodes doubted that Tyler ever got a sale by staying open, but he didn't have far to go to get home. He'd remodeled the back of the store and lived there. What had once been storage for pipes and fittings was now a two-bedroom apartment.

Rhodes parked in front and got out of the car. His was the only car in sight. The vacant building next to the old hardware store had once held an auto-parts dealership. The windows still showed part of the painted signs that had announced its name. Next door to it had been a bank that was now the office of the Clearview Chamber of Commerce. It wasn't open.

A block to Rhodes's left was the Beauty Shack, its parking lot vacant. Rhodes could see the crime-scene tape that wrapped the building.

Outside Tyler's antique store was an old metal lawn chair. The red paint on the metal had faded and in some places was entirely gone. Tyler sometimes sat there in the afternoons and drank lemonade.

Rhodes went into the store through the open double doors, the same ones that had been there from the building's beginnings. The old floor was made of wooden beams, solid and strong enough to hold up just about anything. The pressed tin ceiling was the original, but everything else was changed.

Once the store had held just about everything a person could need in the hardware line, and way beyond it. Tools, pipes, fishing equipment, pocketknives, camping gear, guns, cooking utensils, appliances, nails, nuts, bolts, and even a kitchen sink or two. The thing Rhodes recalled best, however, was the saddlery in the back of the store near where the apartment was now located. He could remember the smell of the leather, and the time his father had picked him up and seated him on one of the saddles before he was old enough to climb up himself.

All that was gone now, of course. Tyler's antiques didn't smell of leather at all. The store was divided into sections of booths that held the consignment goods, with Tyler's own things in front. There were booths with glassware, clothes, records (though Rhodes didn't see any record players), VHS tapes, old magazines and books, furniture, jewelry, and just about anything else a person could want. Or not want.

A big old overstuffed chair sat near the center of the profusion of things. A reading lamp and an end table stood beside it. Jeff Tyler could sometimes be found in the chair, reading or listening to the old radio that sat on the end table. The lamp was on, the radio wasn't, and Tyler wasn't there.

Rhodes figured Tyler was in his apartment, maybe starting to cook supper, so he looked around for a couple of minutes, waiting for him to return. Tyler didn't show up, so Rhodes went on back to the apartment, wending his way through shelves holding bottle collections and CDs and old metal signs.

The side door of the building was open and looked out on a building that had once been the local Ford dealership. Now it was a church of some kind.

The door to the apartment was open. Rhodes tapped on the frame. He could see that no one was in the living room, and when he didn't get a response to his knock, he called Tyler's name. Not getting an answer, he went inside. The kitchen/dining area was behind the living room, and that door was open, too. Rhodes went through it.

He found Tyler immediately, lying in front of the stove. There wasn't much blood on the floor around him, but there was more than enough. Rhodes saw a bullet hole in Tyler's head, and the front of Tyler's shirt was bloody where another bullet had hit him.

Rhodes's stomach felt suddenly hollowed out. He squatted down and felt for a pulse in Tyler's neck. He felt only the still-warm skin, not that he'd had much hope of anything else. Tyler was dead.

Rhodes stood up and went outside to get on the radio and have Hack make the calls that had to be made.

CHAPTER 10

After the body was gone, Rhodes and Ruth Grady were alone in the building. The only evidence that anything had happened there was the blood on the floor of the kitchen.

"What do you think?" Ruth asked.

During the time the body was being removed and put into the ambulance, Rhodes had considered what might have happened. He had a theory, but he wasn't too happy with it.

"I think somebody drove here and parked in the alley in back," he said. "Or maybe somebody just walked here. Then whoever it was came in through the side door. Tyler was in the kitchen, and the killer went in there. Tyler knew him, probably. Or her. No sign of any struggle. Then Tyler got shot."

"Nobody heard the shot?"

"There's nobody within a quarter mile of here, and the shots were inside the building."

"He hadn't been dead long before you found him."

"No. I wish I'd come by sooner, but I went to talk to . . . someone else first."

"You didn't know." Ruth looked around the kitchen. "This one's different, isn't it."

"Premeditated," Rhodes said. "I think Lynn was killed in a robbery or an argument, but whoever killed Tyler came here with intent and a gun."

"I'll work the scene," Ruth said, "but it doesn't look promising."

"I have to tell Lonnie," Rhodes said.

"I'm glad I have to work the scene," Ruth said.

"Be sure to check the alley in back."

"I will," Ruth said.

"See if there's a record of the consignors. You'll need to talk to them."

"Right."

"If you can find a record of the sales he's made today, that might help, too. Especially the last one of the day."

"I'll look for all that," Ruth said.

Rhodes looked around. The place seemed empty, even though it was full of things. Somehow the death and absence of Tyler had sucked the life out of the building.

"I'll go tell Lonnie," he said.

Rhodes and Lonnie sat in the same places they'd occupied that morning. Rhodes had expected Lonnie to take the news hard, but Lonnie surprised him. Oh, he teared up and sniffled a little, but he seemed in much better control of himself than he'd been when Rhodes had seen him earlier that day.

"I have to ask you some questions," Rhodes said after he'd delivered the news.

"That's all right. I understand."

"Did you talk to Jeff today?"

"Yes. I called him and told him about Lynn."

"Did it upset him?"

"Of course," Lonnie said, as if surprised that Rhodes would even bother to ask such a thing.

"I mean," Rhodes said, "did he seem to know anything about it? Did he say anything that might have implied that he did?"

"He didn't know anything about it," Lonnie said, but there was something in his voice that got Rhodes's attention.

"Was Jeff worried about anything? Did he have enemies?"

"Jeff? Why would he have any enemies? He hardly knew anybody besides me."

"Somebody killed him," Rhodes pointed out.

Lonnie sniffled. "I know. I know. I just can't understand it."

"What about the people who had things on consignment with him?"

"He hardly ever saw them. He just collected the money and gave it to them when they came in. There was never any problem with any of them." Lonnie looked around. "Do you think it was a hate crime?"

Rhodes hadn't considered that, but he didn't think it was likely.

"You told me he didn't have any enemies," Rhodes said.

"Well, he didn't. You can ask anybody."

Again there was something a little off in Lonnie's tone. Rhodes couldn't quite figure out what it was.

"Someone will have to tell his mother," Lonnie said. "She lives in Odessa. His father's dead."

"Do you know how to reach her?" Rhodes asked.

Lonnie did, and he got up to find the number. When he did, he wrote it down and gave it to Rhodes.

"She didn't know he was gay," Lonnie said. "You won't tell her?"

"That's not my job."

"She'll want him to be buried there."

Rhodes didn't know what to say to that.

"I have to go," Lonnie said. "I have to be there."

Rhodes didn't know what to say to that, either. He didn't want to tell Lonnie not to leave town because he was a suspect in a murder case, but Lonnie might get the idea to just keep on going when he got to Odessa. He might not stop until he got to California, and it would be hard to find him there if he didn't want to be found.

"I'll come back," Lonnie said. "I promise."

"It's not as if you're under arrest," Rhodes told him.

"I know you must suspect me. First Lynn, now Jeff, the two people in town I cared about more than anybody else. When someone's murdered, you always look for the close relatives or the . . . the lovers."

Rhodes thought Lonnie might break down then, but he pulled himself together.

"Isn't that true?" Lonnie asked, his voice shaky. "I know it's that way on TV."

"It's that way because it's true," Rhodes said. "Most people are killed by someone they know."

"I didn't do it," Lonnie said. "I'd never kill Jeff. Or Lynn."

Rhodes wasn't too sure about that. He

couldn't get over the sense that something wasn't quite right. He didn't have any evidence other than his feeling, but he asked Lonnie something else.

"I've heard that Lynn had somebody special and that she was going to give up everybody else," he said. "Do you know who that might have been?"

Lonnie said, "I told you I didn't know any names."

"Right, but wouldn't Lynn have mentioned a special someone?"

Lonnie was silent for a while. Finally he said, "I think so, but she never did."

Again Rhodes had the feeling that Lonnie was holding back, but he didn't know what to ask. That was all right. He could wait.

"You're going to get whoever killed Jeff, aren't you?" Lonnie asked.

"The funeral won't be for a few days," Rhodes said. "By then I'll have this all cleared up."

Lonnie looked away. "Really?"

"If you help me," Rhodes said.

"I've told you everything I know."

Rhodes wanted to believe him, but he didn't. "You're sure?" he asked.

"I'm sure. You find him, Sheriff. Please."

"I'll find him," Rhodes said.

■ ■ ■ ■

Before he went to see Abby Tustin, Rhodes
went back to the jail to call Tyler's mother.
It was a part of the job that was almost as
upsetting as finding a murder victim, but it
had to be done. Even Hack was serious
while Rhodes went about making the call.

When it was done, Hack said, "Been a
long day, ain't it."

"It's not over yet," Rhodes said. "How'd
the business with the wild hogs turn out?"

"Alton went out there and set a couple of
traps."

"Did that satisfy Bradley?"

"Not much. He wasn't hurt any, though,
so he's got no room for complainin'. Those
hogs are tearin' up this whole county. The
next thing you know, they'll be rootin' up
Main Street."

"Nobody will notice," Rhodes said.

Hack gave a rueful laugh. "You got that
right. I can remember Saturday nights when
people on the sidewalks downtown were
thicker than the hairs on a dog's back.
Stores were crowded. There was even a
picture show."

"Been a while," Rhodes said.

"*The Golden Child*," Hack said.

134

"What?"

"*The Golden Child.* That was the name of the last picture show we had in this town. I didn't go see it, but I remember that name."

"You should've gone," Rhodes said.

"Kinda wish I had. Too late now, though."

"Not as late as it is for Jeff Tyler."

"Nope. Or Lynn Ashton. You got any suspects?"

"Too many," Rhodes said.

"Well, you'll get it all sorted out."

"I'd better," Rhodes said.

Abby Tustin lived with her husband and son, age about five, Rhodes thought, on a county road south of town. When Rhodes got out of his car, a couple of barking dogs charged around from the back of the house and jumped around him as if hoping he might pat them on the head or give them a doggy treat.

Eric Tustin came out the front door and stood on the porch. He apologized for the dogs, but Rhodes said he didn't mind. He had dogs of his own.

"Supposed to be watchdogs," Eric said, "but they're about as much use as a sidesaddle on a sow."

He was a big man with dirty blond hair, a big nose, and big ears that stuck out from

135

his head. He had a great haircut.

"Come on in," he said. "I guess you're here about Lynn."

"That's right," Rhodes said. "I need to talk to Abby."

"She's fixin' supper." Eric held the door for Rhodes, who went inside. He could smell bacon frying.

"Black-eyed peas, cornbread, and bacon," Eric said. "A real country supper. You're welcome to stay. Abby'll set a plate for you."

Rhodes would have loved to, but he didn't have time. He just wanted to talk to Abby.

A little towheaded boy peeked around the kitchen door at Rhodes.

"That's Jeremy," Eric said by way of introduction. "He's never seen a sheriff before."

"Hey, Jeremy," Rhodes said, and the boy disappeared.

"He's a little shy," Eric said. "You take a seat, and I'll get Abby."

The living room was furnished with a big flat-screen TV, a couple of recliners, and a couch. Rhodes sat in one of the recliners, but he resisted the urge to recline.

In a minute or so, Abby came in. She was much smaller than her husband, with a round, pretty face. Eric and Jeremy stayed in the kitchen.

"I'm sorry to interrupt your supper," Rhodes said, standing up. "I'll try not to take long."

"You take as long as you want," Abby said. "Let's sit down. The peas and bacon will keep, and the cornbread will stay warm in the oven. I want to help you if I can."

Rhodes asked the standard questions and got the standard answers. Everybody loved Lynn, well, not everybody, but most everybody. She wasn't as bad as people said, and she sure could cut hair. Was she having affairs? That's what people said, but Abby didn't know for sure. Lynn never talked about things like that.

"Except maybe to Lonnie," Abby said. "They were good friends. Lonnie . . . he's . . . you know."

"I know," Rhodes said.

Abby smiled. "He thinks nobody knows. I don't know why he's so worried about it. It bothered Eric a little at first, but he's okay with it now."

"Did Eric know Lynn?"

Abby tensed and her mouth twisted. "That's not a very nice question, Sheriff."

"I didn't mean anything by it," Rhodes said, though it wasn't strictly true.

"I guess a sheriff has to ask things like that," Abby said, relaxing a bit. "Anyway,

137

Eric didn't know Lynn much. He gets his hair cut at the shop, but I'm the one who cuts it, not Lynn."

"It's a great haircut," Rhodes said.

"You could come by the shop," Abby said, smiling. "I'd cut yours just like it." She looked at him critically. "Except yours is a little thin. I might have to try something different."

"I appreciate the offer," Rhodes said.

"Lynn was even better than I am. Sandra was sure lucky she didn't go off and open her own shop in Waco or somewhere."

"Wasn't she happy here?"

"She would've been if she were making more money," Abby said. "We all need more, I guess. I'm just lucky Eric has a good job. The way things are these days, it takes two incomes just to get by."

"Lynn had . . . friends," Rhodes said.

"I don't think she ever took money from them," Abby said. "Besides, I'm not so sure she had as many friends as people seemed to think. She never talked to me about any of them."

Rhodes thought about that. Lonnie hadn't been able to give him any names, either, and Lonnie was supposed to be Lynn's best friend.

Rhodes talked to Abby a while longer, but

she didn't have anything useful to offer. Rhodes finally told her to call him if she thought of anything that might help.

"I sure will, Sheriff." She walked him to the door. "You sure you can't stay for supper?"

"I'm sure," Rhodes said, "much as I'd like to."

Before he got out the door, Jeremy came scuttling back into the room. He hid behind his mother and looked around her at Rhodes.

" 'Bye, Jeremy," Rhodes said.

Jeremy didn't say a word.

It was getting dark, but Rhodes had one more stop to make. He wanted to look at Lynn's house and see if there was anything there that might give him a clue to what had happened. He couldn't do a thorough search, but he could at least check the most obvious things. He'd have Ruth do a complete job the next day.

Before he went to Lynn's house, however, he stopped at Nora Fischer's. She'd lived in Clearview all her life, and Rhodes had been in her American history class long ago. In fact, that was one of the classes in which he'd sat next to Sandra.

Nora came to the door, but before she

opened it, she said, "Who's there?"

"Sheriff Rhodes, Ms. Fischer."

"That sounds like you, all right, Danny," she said, and Rhodes felt almost as if he were back in the tenth grade again.

The door opened. Nora Fischer was a small woman, not over five four, but she had seemed formidable to Rhodes when he was in her class. He wondered if she'd shrunk. She still wore her gray hair in a bun on top of her head, and she peered at Rhodes through thick glasses.

"You've put on a little weight, Danny," she said.

"Yes, ma'am, I expect I have," Rhodes said.

"That's good. You needed it. You were such a skinny young man."

Rhodes didn't know what to say to that, so he said nothing.

"You must be here about my neighbor," Nora said.

"That's right."

"You come on in, then. I don't know that I can help you, but I'll be glad to try."

Rhodes followed her into a living room that was furnished a bit like Lonnie's, the difference being that in Nora's case the furniture hadn't come from thrift shops. It had all been there for fifty years. It was worn

140

but not badly, and unlike Lonnie, Nora had a rocking chair. She went over to it and sat down.

Rhodes sat on the couch. He was afraid she might ask him to explain the Articles of Confederation or the Missouri Compromise or something along those lines, but she said, "Lynn was a good neighbor to me. She checked up on me now and then, and she didn't make noise or have any barking dogs like some I could name."

Rhodes was about to say he couldn't do anything about barking dogs, but she didn't give him a chance. She said, "She didn't visit much, though. I like having a little company now and then."

She gave Rhodes an accusing look.

"I'm sorry not to drop by more often," he said, not that he'd ever dropped by. "I know Lonnie Wallace came by now and then."

"He's a sweet boy," Nora said. "He and Lynn were good friends."

"Yes," Rhodes said. "They were. I was wondering about her other friends."

"You don't think that I pay any attention to the people who come and go in this neighborhood, do you?"

"Ms. Fischer, I remember how you were in history class. There wasn't anything that went on that you didn't see. You remember that time in history class when I tried to pass a note to Jennifer Stubbs?"

"I remember a lot of things, Danny, but I don't remember that."

"I was sitting in about the middle of the back row," Rhodes said. "You were writing something on the blackboard, so your back was turned to the class. I didn't think you could possibly see me. So I passed the note, and you said, 'Danny Rhodes, do you want me to read that to the whole class?' I thought you had eyes in the back of your head."

Nora laughed a dry little laugh. "I don't know how I did it, either. Maybe I just knew your character and took a wild guess that something was going on."

Rhodes grinned. "Maybe."

"Did I read the note to the class?"

"No, ma'am. You took it up and put it in the middle drawer of your desk. I appreciated that."

"So you owe me a favor."

"Maybe so, but I'm hoping you'll do me one. Do you want to take any wild guesses about Lynn Ashton's character?"

"That's a different kind of thing from knowing you were passing a note."

Nora rocked a little, and a calico cat wandered into the room. It looked at

Rhodes with disdain and walked over to Nora, who stopped rocking. The cat jumped into her lap, settled down, and started to purr.

Rhodes sneezed. Ivy had told him many times that he wasn't really allergic to cats, that he just thought he was. It didn't really matter. They made him sneeze either way.

"This is Clementine," Nora said, rubbing the cat.

"Hi, Clementine," Rhodes said, but the cat didn't bother to look at him again. The purring continued.

"Are you allergic to cats?" Nora asked.

"Maybe," Rhodes said. "I've never been to a doctor to find out for sure."

"I'm not," Nora said. "Clementine keeps me company when I don't have visitors." She glanced at Rhodes. "And even when I do."

"What about those wild guesses?" Rhodes asked, trying to get back to the topic at hand.

"You always were impatient, Danny," Nora said. She rubbed the cat and changed the subject again. "Do you remember what this town used to be like?"

"When?"

"When you were young and could walk downtown at night without anybody worrying about what might happen to you. When there *was* a downtown. When people didn't have to lock their doors, even at night. When you could accidentally leave your purse on a store counter and before long you'd get a call from the clerk to let you know where the purse was and that it was just fine. That's when."

"Times have changed, I guess," Rhodes said.

"Not for the better if you ask me," Nora said, "but nobody ever asks me. They don't ask me because I'm old, and all old people feel that way about the changing of the world. I'm sure my parents did, and theirs before them."

"I wouldn't be surprised," Rhodes said, stifling another sneeze.

"You didn't come here to listen to me rattle on, though, did you."

"I wouldn't call it rattling on."

"Well, it is," Nora said. "As for those wild guesses, I can't make any. I do know that Lynn had a few men visitors, but I didn't see anything wrong with that. I have one or two myself. Hers were older than mine." She looked at Rhodes. "Mostly."

"Did you know any of them?"

"One of them was a county commissioner, the one who has that flashy little car and wears those awful shirts."

"Mikey Burns," Rhodes said, smiling a little at her opinion of Burns's wardrobe.

"That's the one," Nora said. "He was only there once or twice. I don't really remember any of the others. They were better dressed than Mr. Burns, I can tell you that."

"Were there many of them?"

"Hardly any. She wasn't home a lot in the evenings. When I said a few visitors, that's what I meant. A few. At least, that I saw. I'm not one of those nosy old ladies who sit on the porch and watch the neighborhood comings and goings."

"I never thought you were," Rhodes said.

He was beginning to believe that Lynn's reputation had been exaggerated and that for reasons of her own she might have encouraged that. Maybe she liked having people talk about her. Some people were like that.

Rhodes stood up. "Thanks for your help, Ms. Fischer. I appreciate it. If you think of anything else, call the department."

"Does that Hack Jensen still work there?" she asked.

"He does."

"You tell him I said hello."

"I'll do that," Rhodes said. "I'll let myself out. Don't get up and disturb Clementine."

Nora rubbed the cat. "You were impatient, but you were thoughtful, too, Danny. I'm glad you haven't changed."

Rhodes wasn't sure whether he should thank her for that observation, but he did.

"I'll be next door having a look at Lynn's house," he said. "Don't call the department when you see the lights come on."

"I probably won't even notice," Nora said.

lay beside the one with the yellow roses. It
was the rock that Rhodes thought would be

CHAPTER 11

If this had been the old days that Nora
Fischer had talked about, Rhodes could
have gotten into Lynn Ashton's house easily
enough because the doors wouldn't have
been locked. Of course, that was then and
this was now, and as Rhodes had already
discovered earlier that day, he needed a key
to get inside. He hoped that Lynn had been
the kind of person who hid a key outside in
case she locked herself out and that if she
was that kind of person she had hidden the
key in a place that would be easy for him to
find.

He tried the garage first, but like the
house, it was closed and locked. A key hidden inside it would do him no good. Rhodes
looked around. The house had a small
concrete entranceway with a flower bed on
each side. There were no flowers, but there
were a couple of rosebushes, one with red
roses and one with yellow ones. A big rock

lay beside the one with the yellow roses. It was the rock that Rhodes thought was his best bet.

It was easy to see that it was a real rock, not some hollowed-out fake. Rhodes picked it up and saw nothing under it but sandy dirt. He set the rock aside and pushed his fingers into the dirt. They encountered something hard, and he dug around until he'd uncovered a brown plastic box. He opened the box and found a key. He tried it in the front door. It fit, and so he opened the door, flipped a light switch on the wall just inside it, and went in.

The floor plan wasn't much different from Nora's, a small living room, a kitchen/den/ eating area, two bedrooms, a bath and a half.

Rhodes figured that anything interesting would be in Lynn's bedroom, so he went there first. He always felt like an intruder when he searched a room, and even more like one when he searched someone's bedroom. It made no difference that the former occupant was dead and had no privacy left.

Rhodes didn't know what he expected to find, but it would've been nice if he'd run across a photo of Lynn with someone special. Or a diary, or a phone message from someone threatening to kill her.

He didn't find any of those things. The only photos he saw were of a younger Lynn and her parents. A book lay on a nightstand beside the bed, but it was a romance novel, not a diary. The drawers of the dresser held sweaters and underwear but nothing unusual. The jewelry box was full of costume jewelry. The closet held clothes, naturally enough, and shoes. Lots of shoes. Nothing unusual about that. The medicine cabinet of the adjoining bathroom was almost empty, and the strongest drug it held was aspirin.

Rhodes went into another bedroom, one that served as Lynn's computer room. He saw a desktop with a computer tower, monitor, scanner, and printer. The computer and monitor were turned off.

He could think of a few things that might be on the computer's hard drive, but that was something he'd get Ruth to check. It was clear that he wasn't going to find any obvious clues just lying around.

It was time for him to go home.

As soon as he stepped up onto his porch, Rhodes heard the scrabbling of doggie toenails on the floor as Yancey, the little Pomeranian, ran to greet him. Rhodes opened the door, and Yancey went into a veritable frenzy of joy.

"If everybody were as glad to see me as you are," Rhodes said, "life would be sweet."

He went on to the kitchen, with Yancey capering around his feet. Ivy stood at the stove, holding a lid in her hand and looking into a pot of something that smelled a little like chili.

Sam, the black cat, was in his favorite place in front of the refrigerator. He raised his head and gave Rhodes a slow once-over with his yellow eyes before settling back down to sleep. Rhodes resisted the urge to sneeze.

Ivy put the lid back on the pot, turned to Rhodes, and said, "Late again."

"Yancey's glad to see me, though," Rhodes said.

Ivy smiled. "So am I. Are you hungry?"

"Sure. What's cooking."

"Chili," Ivy said.

Rhodes knew that technically she was telling the truth, but only technically. He was pretty sure that whatever might be in the pot, it wasn't chili. It might look like chili, it might smell like chili, and it might even taste a little bit like chili, but it wasn't really chili. That was because Ivy was currently watching his diet and was on a vegetarian kick.

The alleged chili would have beans in it, three or four kinds, probably, and tomatoes and corn, but there wouldn't be any meat. The contents might include something that resembled meat, but it wouldn't be the real thing. It would be something that Ivy had once told him was called "textured vegetable protein," which to Rhodes meant soy. He was glad he'd had the cheeseburger for lunch, not that he was going to mention that to Ivy.

"Did we get any mail today?" Rhodes asked.

"You mean, did we get a book in the mail today?" Ivy asked back.

"You're reading my mind."

"I'm not reading your mind. I'm sure you've already seen a copy of *Terrorist Terror* at the jail. Am I right?"

"You're right."

"I get to read it first."

"That's fine," Rhodes said. "I can wait."

"Good," Ivy said. "Because I can't. I want to see what your alter ego is up to now."

"He's not my alter ego."

"So you say. You can go out and see Speedo if you want to. The chili will keep."

Rhodes went on outside. Yancey went with him. The heat of the day had drifted away with sundown, and it was almost pleasant.

Rhodes sat on the top step of the little porch while Yancey bounded on into the dark yard to harass Speedo, a border collie Rhodes had acquired on a case a few years ago.

Speedo was considerably bigger than Yancey, but the smaller dog either didn't know or didn't care. After barking at Speedo, Yancey grabbed up a chew toy and ran away with it. That was enough to rouse Speedo, who went after him. It always cheered Rhodes up to watch them, but he couldn't help thinking about the two murders.

Ivy came out and sat on the porch beside him, and he went through it with her. When he'd finished, she said, "So who do you think is the killer?"

"I wish I knew," Rhodes said. He watched as Speedo ran right over Yancey, who bounced back up without relinquishing his grip on the chew toy. "It could've been anybody I talked to, or somebody else entirely. What I need is a motive. That would be a big help."

"Mikey Burns and Clifford Clement have motives."

"I know, but I'm not sure how strong they are. Clement has an alibi. Mikey does, too, but not much of one."

"What about Lonnie?"

"I didn't even ask about his alibi, but considering that Jeff Tyler's dead now, I should have."

"You think Lonnie's capable of murder?"

"Just about anybody is," Rhodes said, "in the right circumstances."

"What about those two men you chased?" Ivy grinned when she said it. Rhodes thought she'd enjoyed that part of the story entirely too much.

"They could have done it, but if they did, why would they hang around? They could have been miles away before the body was discovered."

"Maybe they didn't think you'd look in that old building."

"Unlikely," Rhodes said.

"But possible," Ivy said.

"Jeff's the real problem," Rhodes said. "I don't see how his death ties in. The method was different, too."

"You'll figure it out," Ivy said.

"That's what I keep telling myself, and everybody else. I don't know that anybody believes it."

"I do," Ivy said.

The dogs came running up to Rhodes. The chew toy had disappeared. Rhodes patted Speedo, and Ivy said, "Be sure to wash your hands before we eat."

"When will that be?"

"Right now," Ivy said before going inside with Yancey close behind her.

Rhodes got up and looked at Speedo. "Do you think you need a bath or anything?"

Speedo thwacked his tail on the dry grass.

"That's what I thought," Rhodes said, and he went into the house to wash his hands and eat the supposed chili.

The chili wasn't bad, Rhodes had to admit. He was even enjoying it, along with some saltine crackers, when the telephone rang.

Ivy answered it. She stopped talking after she said hello, listened for a second, then handed the phone to Rhodes.

"I'm in hot pursuit," Benton said. "Battery thieves. Headed for the overpass in an old green Chevrolet pickup. No time to explain."

Benton hung up. Rhodes handed the phone to Ivy.

"Emergency?" she said.

"Of the Seepy Benton kind," Rhodes said, pushing back his chair. "Give Hack a call and let him know what's going on."

"I will," Ivy said. "Be careful."

"I always am," Rhodes said.

Ivy looked at him and laughed.

"Well, nearly always," he said, heading out

the door.

Rhodes turned on the siren and light bar as soon as he got out of his driveway. It was dark, and he didn't want to run into anybody or have anybody run into him, not that there'd be much traffic to worry about on the residential streets, or even downtown if they went there.

He was about as far from the overpass as Benton was, but maybe he could get there first. It depended on how fast the pickup was going, and that might depend on whether the driver knew that Seepy Benton was in hot pursuit.

Nowhere in Clearview was very far from anywhere else, and Rhodes arrived at the eastern foot of the overpass in about a minute, which was just in time to see the green pickup make a sharp, tire-squealing turn onto the street that led downtown and right on past the Beauty Shack. Benton's Saturn was right behind it, and it rocked on its shocks as it made the turn. Rhodes fell in line, light bar flashing, siren wailing.

They whipped past the deserted downtown, past Jeff Tyler's building, past the Beauty Shack.

Duke Pearson must have been nearby on his patrol, checking on the old hotel. Rhodes heard another siren and looked down the side street to his left to see Pearson's county car barreling toward him.

The pickup turned right and headed toward the reclamation center with a noisy parade following it, all the vehicles bouncing from side to side, from pothole to pothole.

The pickup sped up the incline to the railroad track and sailed for several yards before landing with a bounce. The bounce was so hard that a couple of tires blew out with sounds like gunshots. Or perhaps the tires had hit some metal detritus from the reclamation center. The result was the same. Pieces of rubber flew in all directions, and the truck spun around a couple of times before slamming into a Dumpster.

One of the pieces of rubber *thwanged* off the hood of Benton's car and wafted on over the top like some black night bird coasting on an air current.

The doors on the pickup sprang open, and three men jumped out and ran away. One of them looked a little like the one who'd hit Rhodes with the bucket, but Rhodes was too far away to be sure. They ran to the warehouse, but the doors were closed and chained. That didn't stop them. One of the men reached out, grabbed the edge of a piece of sheet metal, and pulled. The other two men helped, and they pulled the metal aside far enough for them to slip into the warehouse.

Seepy Benton had slowed down at the incline, as had Rhodes and Pearson, so they avoided a pileup. Benton went past the accident and stopped. Rhodes and Pearson stopped as well.

Benton got out of his Saturn. He stood in a pool of light from a mercury-vapor lamp high above the street. Red and blue flashes from the light bars strobed over him. He looked like some kind of lumpy distortion of John Travolta from the disco era as he pointed toward the cotton warehouse.

"They went thataway," he said as Rhodes and Pearson reached him.

Pearson looked at Rhodes. "Did he really say what I think he did?"

"Yes, he really did," Rhodes said. "Duke Pearson, meet Seepy Benton, master of the cliché."

The two men didn't shake hands because Pearson was already elsewhere, looking at the back of the pickup.

"No plates," he said. He walked around to look at the windshield. "No inspection sticker, either."

Rhodes thought the truck was a model

from sometime in the seventies, and it was barely roadworthy. It was probably used around a farm and not taken off the property often. Maybe only at night and seldom even then.

Benton hadn't finished confessing. "I said 'Stop where you are' earlier," he said. "They were trying to steal the battery out of my car."

Well, that explained the hot pursuit and maybe why the pickup was on the streets. Rhodes still had several questions he wanted to ask, but they could wait.

Pearson ignored Benton's comment. "Are the doors on the warehouse all chained shut?"

"I'm sure they are," Rhodes said. "It's full of valuable junk."

"So there's no other way out of there?"

"They can probably find a way," Rhodes said. "You can go on around to the side by the railroad tracks. Watch to see if they try to get out that way. I'll go inside. You don't try to get in. Just stay outside and watch. If you're not in there, we won't do anything stupid, like shoot each other."

"Got it," Pearson said.

"I'll go around to the south side," Benton said as Pearson walked away.

"You'll sit in your car until we get back,"

Rhodes said. "While you're there, give Hack a call at the jail and give him an update on what's going on."

"They might get away," Benton said. "I should guard the south side."

He had a point.

"All right," Rhodes said. "You can drive around there and watch the door. If those fellas come out of the warehouse, you don't do a thing. Just drive back here and wait for me to come out. Then you can tell me."

"I could go after them."

"I'm the sheriff," Rhodes said. "I've told you what to do. Don't get cocky."

Benton looked a little hurt by that last comment, but he got in his car and drove away.

Rhodes got his flashlight and took his pistol from the ankle holster. He didn't think the men were armed, but he was going into the warehouse to face something worse than battery thieves.

He was going in to face giant rats.

CHAPTER 12

Rhodes stood to one side of the opening the men had made, shielded by the outside wall, and shone the flashlight into the building. He saw stacks of junk pretty much like those he'd seen in the building across the street. He was beginning to wonder if any of the materials brought to the reclamation center ever got recycled or reclaimed.

He turned off his light since he didn't want to give the men anything to shoot at if they had guns. Then he squeezed himself inside. There were gaps in the sheet-metal roof, enough of them so that a little light from the full moon came through. Rhodes stood with his back to the wall and waited for his eyes to get adjusted to the darkness.

While he waited, he listened. He didn't hear anything at first, but after a while he thought he could hear stealthy noises from far back in the warehouse. Rats? Fugitives? Rhodes didn't know, and for that matter he might have imagined the sounds.

He waited some more.

After a couple of minutes had gone by, he still couldn't see much, but he thought he could at least walk through the aisles formed by the junk without stumbling over anything.

It wasn't a walk he wanted to take. What if the men were waiting to jump on him?

Even worse, at least from Buddy's point of view, what if the rats were waiting to jump on him?

The floor of the warehouse was built to hold stacked bales of cotton, each bale weighing hundreds of pounds. It was made of thick wooden beams, even thicker than the ones that floored the old hardware building where Jeff Tyler had been killed. They were shored up underneath by even thicker upright beams. With all the weight of the unreclaimed metal piled on them, they were held firm. They didn't make a creak or a crack when Rhodes planted his feet on them.

He started down the nearest aisle through the accumulated junk. Dark objects loomed above him on both sides. He tried to listen for anything that might give him a clue as to the men's whereabouts, assuming they hadn't run out the door on the opposite side already. He hoped that if they had, Benton had done what he was supposed to do, which was nothing. Benton was good at doing nothing. Otherwise, he might get into real trouble.

It seemed like an odd coincidence that Benton's car would have been the target of battery thieves, and Rhodes had a feeling there was a lot more to the story.

It wasn't so odd, however, that the thieves, if they were indeed thieves, had headed for the reclamation center. Rhodes was pretty sure that two of them were the same ones he'd chased earlier in the day, and they'd run to the same place. There was obviously a connection. Maybe that was why Al had seemed so wary.

The third man was a new part of the story. He had a pickup, and even though it was an old one, it ran. So the owner was the one who provided the wheels. He must have had better accommodations than the other two, as well, or at least different ones.

Rhodes stopped to listen. Not a sound. If the men were in the warehouse with him, they were quieter than they'd been that morning. Rhodes started to move forward, but he hadn't taken more than a couple of steps before he stopped. He'd heard something, but it wasn't coming from the warehouse.

The sound was the low, lonesome whistle of a train just coming to the first crossing after the overpass. That meant it was five blocks from the warehouse. In seconds it would be rumbling by, blowing its whistle for the next crossing and giving the men a perfect opportunity to make a break for it. Or to jump on Rhodes.

Rhodes didn't move. As the train drew closer, the whistle got louder. Rhodes imagined that he could feel the vibrations coming from the rails through the ground, through the underpinnings of the warehouse, right into the soles of his shoes and up through his legs.

The whole warehouse seemed to shake as the train thundered past, and as it moved on down the track, the vibrations stopped.

The noise, however, did not, but it wasn't coming from outside. Rhodes looked left, right, then up, and saw a gutted room air conditioner about to fall.

He moved quickly out of the way. The air conditioner toppled forward, fell, bounced off the pile of junk across the aisle, and dropped to the floor. Rhodes was already well away from it by the time it hit, but he wasn't ready for what happened next.

Disturbed by the fall or the jostling, rats scurried out of the stacks, chittering and squeaking. They ran across Rhodes's feet and brushed against the bottoms of his pants.

There weren't as many as Buddy had said, not in this group, and they weren't as large as Buddy had indicated, but even seven or eight regular-sized rats were more than Rhodes wanted to feel on the tops of his feet. Not that he was afraid of rats, but if one of them ran up his pants leg, he wasn't going to be happy about it.

The rats didn't seem interested in him at all, however. They just wanted to get away. They dashed across the aisle and vanished into the opposite stacks.

It was probably their sudden appearance elsewhere that made the men hiding there get excited enough to do some talking. Very loud talking it was, too.

Rhodes looked for openings in the wall of junk but didn't see any. Then a man dropped down from the top of the stack only a few feet away. He saw Rhodes and lunged at him.

Rhodes didn't have time to threaten him with his pistol because the man piled into him, shoved him against something hard and rough, and grabbed him in a bear hug.

Rhodes stomped down, hoping to get the man's feet, but he missed. Another man dropped down and then another. While the first man hugged him, the other two hit him with their fists. They couldn't get in any solid blows because Rhodes kept the metal to his back. He twisted his head and writhed as much as he could in the first man's grip, trying to keep moving all the time.

The hitting went on, and so did the squeezing. A man can take a good many punches in his arms and sides if he keeps moving and lets them glance off and avoids getting hit solidly in the face. Rhodes hoped they'd soon get tired of hitting him, or make a mistake.

They had considerable endurance and didn't make any mistakes, however, so Rhodes went to plan B. He'd managed to hold on to his pistol, which he now fired into the floor.

The man who had Rhodes in the hug had kept his head buried against Rhodes's shoulder, but at the sound of the shot he drew back in surprise.

Rhodes was ready for that. He pulled back his own head and then smashed his forehead into the man's nose. Rhodes heard and felt the crunch, and when the man's arms loosened, Rhodes shook him off and raised his pistol.

The other two men ran in opposite directions down the aisle. One of them jumped the air conditioner, stumbled, and kept on going. The other had a clear path and never slowed down.

The man in front of Rhodes was still stunned, but Rhodes raised his foot and kicked him in the stomach just to be sure he didn't go anywhere. The man reeled back against the stack of metal and slid down to the floor.

By then it was too late for Rhodes to catch the other two. Both had already disappeared, and Rhodes had a feeling they wouldn't be sticking around this time.

Rhodes rubbed his forehead. He didn't think he'd have a bump, but he might. If he did, it wouldn't be a big one. He checked the man on the floor. He was the one who'd hit Rhodes with the bucket that morning, so Rhodes didn't feel too sorry for him.

The man was breathing through his mouth, so he'd be all right. Rhodes put plastic cuffs on him and went to look for Pearson and Benton.

When he was almost to the opening, he heard the sound of an engine that wouldn't quite turn over.

Rhodes broke into a run, pushed his way

out of the warehouse, and went across the street. One of the men was in the cab of the old pickup, trying to start it.

He wasn't having any luck, and when he looked up and saw Rhodes, he got out of the pickup and started to run.

Well, at least he didn't steal one of the county cars. That would have put Rhodes in a really bad mood. He wasn't too thrilled about the idea of having to chase anybody, but it looked as if that was what he'd have to do.

The man ran to the railroad track and turned left and dodged among the tumbled metal tanks that lay in the moonlight like some kind of alien space pods.

Rhodes hoped there weren't any snakes lurking in there. Or if there were that they'd bite the man he was chasing instead of him.

The man threaded through the confusion of tanks, clanging into one occasionally and making it easy for Rhodes to keep up with his location. Then the noise stopped. So did Rhodes. He knew there could be only one reason for the quiet. The man was lurking somewhere ahead, waiting for him.

All Rhodes saw was the metal tanks, but one of them got his attention. It was turned so that the man could be hidden on one side, hoping Rhodes would pass him by.

Near the railroad track Rhodes found a rock about the size of a baseball. He walked close to the tank and heaved the rock at the side as hard as he could.

The rock struck with a resounding *clang*, and the man ran out from behind it. He caught sight of Rhodes and went straight for the railroad track. His feet slipped in the ballast, and Rhodes thought he might fall, but he regained his balance, hopped the rail, and began to run along the ties.

Rhodes went after him. It wasn't easy, what with the distance between the ties not being ideal for his stride, and the ballast rocks being there to slide under his feet if he missed the ties.

The man must have felt the same way. He left the tracks and ran down the little hill into an open area that had once been the parking lot for an oil-well equipment company. The company had been out of business for a long time, like a lot of businesses in that part of town. The building was still there, though in sad condition.

Rhodes decided he wasn't going to follow anybody into another old building. He'd had enough of that for one day. He was still holding his pistol, so he came to a halt and said, "Stop or I'll shoot." He was glad Seepy Benton wasn't there to hear him.

The man didn't stop. Rhodes fired a shot well over his head. The bullet *spanged* into the metal side of the building near the roof.

The man froze in his tracks. Rhodes went up to him and told him to put his hands behind him. The man complied, and Rhodes slipped his pistol in his pocket before putting on another set of plastic cuffs.

When that was done, Rhodes put his hand on the man's shoulder, turned him around, and said, "Let's go back now."

The man didn't say anything, but he started walking. Rhodes stayed behind him until they got back to the reclamation center, where Duke Pearson was standing by the county cars.

"Where've you been?" Pearson asked when Rhodes and his prisoner came along.

"Chasing this fella," Rhodes said, putting him into the backseat of Pearson's county car.

"I heard a shot," Pearson said.

"Warning shot," Rhodes said.

"I meant the one in the warehouse."

"Yeah, that was sort of a warning, too. I have another prisoner in there. You watch this one, and I'll go get him. Call for an ambulance, too."

"Is he wounded?"

"No," Rhodes said, "not unless you count

a broken nose."

"I'd count that if it was my nose," Pearson said.

When he went back into the warehouse, Rhodes took a look around before he went to check on his prisoner. Down at the end of one aisle, he found a solidly built room. It looked almost new, and it was large enough to hold quite a lot of junk, or a lot of something else. It had a metal door, and the door was secured with a dead-bolt lock. Rhodes didn't bother to try to open it. Maybe he'd have a look later on.

The prisoner was right where Rhodes had left him, sitting with his back against some junked air conditioners that had been stripped of their copper. Rhodes shone the flashlight in his face. The man blinked, and Rhodes saw the misshapen nose and a little blood. Rhodes helped the man to his feet and told him to go on outside. The man started on his way, with Rhodes following.

Once outside, they went over to the county cars. Pearson had the other man stowed safely in the backseat with his friend.

"You wait here with these two until the ambulance comes," Rhodes said. "Read them their rights. I'll go find Benton."

Pearson nodded, and Rhodes got in his

car. He drove down the block, turned left, and looked around. He saw Benton's car parked by the side of the street so that Benton could watch the south door of the warehouse.

Rhodes pulled up beside the Saturn.

"It's over," he said.

"You got them?"

"All but one."

"I saw that one," Benton said. "He came out the door and ran off down the street. He turned right down there somewhere. I would've followed him, but he was cutting across lawns. I couldn't go after him in my car."

"You did the right thing by waiting here," Rhodes said, "like I told you to. Now come on back with me. You have some questions to answer."

"I have a question for you, too," Benton said.

"What's that?"

Benton got out of his car. "Let me show you something."

Rhodes got out of his own car and went to the front of the Saturn where Benton was standing.

"See this dent?" Benton said, putting his hand on the hood. "A piece of that tire hit my car."

"I see the dent," Rhodes said. "Was that what you wanted to ask me?"

"No," Benton said. "I wanted to know if the county would pay to have it fixed."

Rhodes laughed. "Call your insurance company," he said.

CHAPTER 13

Rhodes and Benton drove back to where Pearson was waiting. The ambulance had arrived, and Pearson was talking to the EMTs. Rhodes went over and asked if Pearson had read the prisoners their rights.

"I did, but they claimed they didn't understand. So I flipped the card over and read them in Spanish. They didn't say so, but I don't think they had a very high opinion of my accent."

"It's the thought that counts," Rhodes said.

The man with the broken nose was in the ambulance, which was about ready to leave. Rhodes told the driver to wait while he asked the man a few questions.

He stepped into the ambulance where the man lay on a gurney. He didn't look happy to see Rhodes again. A med tech stood beside him. He moved aside to make room for Rhodes.

173

"Sorry about your nose," Rhodes said to the man on the gurney. "No hard feelings."

"No hablo inglés."

"I was afraid you'd say that. I'm not sure I believe it, though."

The man gave him a blank stare.

Rhodes knew the tech, Mac Simpson, and whispered, "To hell with him. Nobody will ever miss him, and we can't afford to put him up in the jail. You can give him the poison at the hospital. We'll pick up the body in the morning."

Mac grinned. "You want me to use the horse needle?"

"Sure. He's going to die anyway."

"You can't do that!" the man on the gurney said.

Rhodes turned to him. "I thought you didn't speak English."

"I speak it a little."

"Maybe we won't have to kill you, then. What did you say your name is?"

"I didn't say, but it's Guillermo. William. William Castillo."

"So, William. You have any identification?"

"No, I do not."

"No driver's license?"

"No. No license."

"Green card?"

Guillermo looked away. "No."

174

"All right, then. The county will pay to have you checked over and get your nose fixed. I'll have my deputy go along with you to be sure everything's done right and that you get safely to the jail when it's over."

Guillermo didn't thank him, but Rhodes was sure he was grateful. At least he wasn't going to be poisoned.

"Take good care of him," Rhodes told Mac and stepped down from the ambulance.

Pearson and Benton were looking at the dent in the hood of Benton's Saturn. Rhodes walked over to them.

"Duke, you follow the ambulance and bring Guillermo and his friend to the jail when they've fixed him up."

"Sure thing," Pearson said.

Pearson went to his car, and Rhodes said to Benton, "Now, then. Why don't you tell me all about how you foiled the battery theft and got into hot pursuit."

"Can't we go somewhere more comfortable?"

Rhodes had to admit that it was a little hot and humid. "We can go to the jail, in case I have to book you."

"I didn't do anything wrong."

"We'll see about that," Rhodes said, "but first let's do a little repair work."

175

"Repair work?"

"I need to fix that place where the metal's pulled away. I wouldn't want anybody else to get in there tonight."

"What about on the other side, where I was? That man got out some way or another."

"It's out of sight of the street," Rhodes said. "We won't worry about it."

"You're the sheriff."

"Right," Rhodes said, "and don't you forget it."

"As if I could," Benton said.

When Rhodes and Benton arrived at the jail after Rhodes had nailed down the metal on the warehouse wall, Pearson had already booked the prisoners and was getting them settled in.

"That didn't take long," Rhodes said.

"Broken nose," Hack said. "No big deal. The one without a broken nose says his name's Jorge Moreno. Jorge didn't have any more identification than Guillermo."

"Not that we expected it," Rhodes said.

Lawton came in from the cellblock with an expectant look on his face. Rhodes had a feeling he was about to get tag-teamed with something or other.

"I need to question this fella here," Rhodes

176

said, hoping to avoid the situation. "Seepy Benton. You know him."

"Sure do," Hack said. "How you doin', Dr. Benton?"

"Never better," Benton said. "How about you?"

"Fine as frog hair," Hack said. "You go ahead and answer the sheriff's questions. I guess he don't need to hear about the things that're goin' on in the county. He's got better things to do."

Rhodes sighed, sat at his desk, and gestured for Benton to take the chair nearby. Rhodes swiveled his chair so that he faced Hack.

"What important things?" he asked.

"Don't let me interrupt you," Hack said. "You got questions to ask. Go on and ask 'em."

"I'll ask them, but you tell me your news first."

"You sure you want to hear it?" Lawton asked. "Maybe you're too busy right now."

"I want to hear it," Rhodes said. He didn't look at Benton, who was grinning, Rhodes was sure.

"Well, then," Lawton said. "What happened was —"

"I'll tell him," Hack said. "I'm the one took the call."

Pearson had come in from the cellblock just behind Lawton. He stood by the door to listen. Like Benton, he was grinning.

"It was a lady in distress," Lawton said.

Hack turned and glared at him. Lawton glared back. After a couple of seconds, Hack turned back to Rhodes.

"See," he said, "this woman called and said she had a flat tire."

The flat tire reminded Rhodes of the pickup at the reclamation center. He hadn't told Hack about that, so he held up a hand. Hack waited.

"Call the wrecker," Rhodes said, "and have him bring in a pickup from the reclamation center. He can put it in the impound lot."

"Want me to do it now or after you hear what happened?"

"You can do it later, but don't let it go till morning. Those folks at the center might strip it for parts. Duke, you check it out and see if there are any batteries in it."

Pearson nodded, and Hack said, "I'll call soon's we're done here. Now where was I?"

"You mean you forgot?" Lawton asked.

There was another short glaring contest. Rhodes was never sure who won them.

"Lady in distress," Rhodes said.

"Oh, yeah," Hack said. "She called up and

said she had a flat tire."

"You said that already," Lawton said, but this time Hack ignored him.

"She said she needed us to come out and change the tire for her," Hack said.

"Not *us*," Lawton said. "She wanted the sheriff or somebody like that."

"He knows she didn't mean *us*," Hack said. "Who's tellin' this story?"

"You are," Lawton said, looking as innocent as he could.

"You bet I am. Anyhow, she said she wanted *the law* to come change the tire for her because she didn't have the money to pay anybody and she couldn't do it herself."

"Too bad we were busy chasing battery thieves," Rhodes said.

"Yeah, that's what I thought, but I was a little suspicious of her, anyway, 'cause I kept hearin' somebody talkin' to her."

"It was a man," Lawton said, and Hack whirled around.

Lawton held up both hands, palms out. "That's all I have to say. I'll keep quiet."

"You better," Hack said and picked up his story again. "It was a man talkin' to her, tellin' her what to say. I asked her why she didn't just let him change the tire, and she said she didn't know who I was talkin' about. Like she thought I couldn't hear him."

"Alcohol was involved," Lawton said. Before Hack could round on him, he added, "I'm bein' quiet now. Nothin' more to say."

Hack sulked for a second or two, then said, "I could tell the woman'd been drinkin' from the way she slurred her words. She finally said that the man she was with was too drunk to change the tire. I asked her what they were doing out on the highway in the first place, and she said they weren't out on the highway. They were at his place, and they wanted to *get* out on the highway 'cause they'd run out of booze at home. They couldn't go, though, 'cause of the flat tire."

"So in this case a flat tire was a good thing," Rhodes said.

"Sure was," Hack said. "I told her they'd better stay put and that we'd send somebody over in the mornin' to change that tire for her."

"She won't remember that, though," Lawton said, "not drunk as she was."

"Which is just as well," Rhodes said, "unless one of you two was planning to go change it for her."

"Not in my job description," Hack said.

"Mine, either," Lawton said.

"Or mine," Pearson said. "And speaking of that, I'd better get back on patrol so the citizens of our good county can continue their peaceful rest."

He headed for the door, and Rhodes said to Hack, "Did you get that woman's address when she called?"

"Sure did."

"Hold up, Duke. You better drive by and check to be sure the car's still in the driveway. We don't want that pair driving around in their condition."

Pearson got the address from Hack and left. Now Rhodes was finally ready to question Benton.

"If we don't get this done," he said, "I'll never get any rest tonight."

"I could use some, too," Benton said.

"Then tell me how you happened to be chasing some alleged battery thieves."

"Well, it was like this," Benton said, and then he started to talk.

Before he was finished, Rhodes said, "Okay, let me be sure I have this straight. You just happened to stay at the college late tonight because you had papers to grade, right?"

"That's right," Benton said. "Lots of grading, and some reports to write, all that kind of thing. Being a math teacher's not all fun

181

and games, you know. We can't just sit around and differentiate using the product rule all day, as much as we'd like to."

"Right," Rhodes said. "So you stayed late, and you just happened to have parked your car in one of the darkest spots on the lot."

"It wasn't dark when I parked," Benton said. "It was broad daylight."

"Don't start with me," Rhodes said. "Hack and Lawton have about finished me off."

Benton smiled and looked around. Hack was bent over his computer keyboard, and Lawton had disappeared back into the cellblock.

"Go on with your story," Rhodes said.

"All right. I just happened to park where I did. I had no idea I'd be staying late or that I might be parked where the car would attract thieves if they happened to come by."

"Sure, and you just happened to come outside and see those men trying to take the battery out of your car, too, I guess."

"How else could it have happened?"

"You could have been watching from somewhere, hoping to catch somebody doing that or maybe breaking into a nearby car."

Benton looked shocked. "Do you really think I'd do something like that?"

182

"Yes," Rhodes said.

"That really hurts," Benton said.

"I'll bet it does. Tell me the rest."

"As you know," Benton said, "I'm a graduate of the Citizens' Sheriff's Academy."

"I know," Rhodes said. "It seemed like a good idea at the time."

"It was a great idea. When are we going to have some refresher classes?"

"I'll think about it," Rhodes said. "Get on with it."

"You're sure impatient," Benton said.

Rhodes thought about what Nora Fischer had said. "So I've been told. Let's get on with it."

"It's just like I said. I saw two men trying to open the car hood. I yelled at them."

" 'Stop where you are,' " Rhodes said.

"That's right. They didn't stop. They ran to that old pickup and jumped in. The pickup took off, and I got in my car and went after them. That's it."

"All right, I'll go along with you. Do you know if they'd taken any batteries before they went after yours?"

"If they did, I didn't see them."

Rhodes thought it over. He didn't believe Benton hadn't been watching and waiting in hopes of something pretty much like what had happened, but there was no law against it, and Benton would never admit it.

"That's all I need," he said. "We can go home and get some sleep now."

"You're sure you don't need me to help investigate?" Benton said.

"I'm sure."

Benton left, and Rhodes was about to follow him when Hack got a call on the radio from Duke Pearson. Rhodes knew it must be important, and Hack didn't even try to drag out the message. Pearson had found a purse in the pickup.

Lynn Ashton's purse.

CHAPTER 14

Rhodes called Ivy to say he'd be home even later than he'd thought.

"You're all right?" she asked. "Not calling from the hospital?"

He said he was fine and told her about the purse. "I'll have to question a couple of prisoners about it. That might take a while."

"I'll wait up for you."

"You don't have to do that."

"I know, but maybe you'll want to talk about it. Or something."

Rhodes grinned. "We'll see."

"See what?" Hack asked when Rhodes hung up.

"You wouldn't understand," Rhodes said.

"Ha. That's where you're wrong. I might be old, but . . ."

"I don't want to hear it," Rhodes said. "I'm going to question our new guests. I'll be in the interview room. Have Lawton bring in Guillermo."

185

"That the one with the broken nose?"

"That's the one."

"They patched him up nice," Hack said.

"Good." Rhodes headed for the interview room. "Go tell Lawton."

"You know what that Benton fella said about you bein' impatient?"

Rhodes didn't answer.

"Well," Hack said, "he sure knew what he was talking about."

The interview room was bare except for a table, a digital recorder, and a couple of folding chairs. When Guillermo came in and took a seat, Rhodes pointed out the recorder and asked if Guillermo would waive his right to have an attorney present.

Guillermo shrugged. He was young, probably not yet thirty, with black hair and black eyes. He needed a haircut, and his nose was stuffed with cotton and covered by a bandage.

"Sure," he said in a nasal voice that made him sound as if he had a cold. "Why not? I don't need no lawyer. I didn't do nothing."

"You hit me in the head with a bucket," Rhodes said.

Guillermo tried not to smile, but he didn't quite succeed.

"Well," he said, "it was just a plastic one.

186

Not heavy or nothing." He put up a finger, almost touching his nose. "Look what you did to me. Now I'm not so pretty."

"It'll give you a lot of romantic appeal after it heals," Rhodes said.

"Yeah, I bet it will. Plenty of romance in my future."

"Let's forget that for a while," Rhodes said. "A broken nose isn't the bad part."

Guillermo leaned forward and put his arms on the table. "The bad part?"

"The purse we found in your pickup," Rhodes said.

"That's not my ride," Guillermo said. He leaned back and crossed his arms over his chest. "That belongs to Frankie."

"Frankie?"

"Francisco. He's our friend. He takes us to the Dairy Queen now and then."

"Does Frankie have a last name?"

"Rey. Means 'king.' He works for a man named Womack. It's really Womack's truck. Frankie, he just borrows it sometimes."

Rhodes knew Wallace Womack. He had a little place just outside of the little town of Obert where he raised a few cattle and had a sizable vegetable garden every year.

"Does Mr. Womack know Frankie borrows his truck?"

Guillermo shrugged again. "I don't know.

187

I never asked him. Not any of my business, you know?"

"Right. Now about that purse."

"I don't know nothing about a purse. I never saw no purse."

Rhodes wished he could believe Guillermo, but the way the young man's eyes kept looking away from Rhodes and the way he held himself with his arms crossed made Rhodes think that he was lying.

"We'll check the purse for fingerprints," Rhodes said. "I think yours might be on it."

Guillermo looked over Rhodes's head at the opposite wall. "Maybe I moved it around or something."

"Maybe you just told me you never saw it."

"I might've moved it without thinking about it, you know? Just shoved it out of the way."

"Sure. What about Lynn Ashton? How well did you know her?"

Guillermo looked genuinely puzzled. "Who?"

"Lynn Ashton. It's her purse. She worked across the street from where you and your friend Jorge were crashing. Very pretty young woman. You must have noticed her."

"Maybe. We didn't look around much."

"She's dead," Rhodes said. "Somebody

killed her. Somebody took her purse. You have it. I'd say that doesn't look good."

Guillermo sat up, and for the first time he looked a bit scared. "I don't know nothing about that. I don't know what you're even saying."

Rhodes almost believed him. "All right. I'll take you back to your cell."

"That's it?" Guillermo asked.

"That's it," Rhodes told him. "Let's go."

Guillermo stood up, blinking as if he still couldn't believe the questioning was over. Rhodes took him back to his cell, along with Lawton, who opened the door and let Guillermo back inside.

When the door was locked, Rhodes said to Lawton, "Let's get Jorge."

"Aw, man," Guillermo said from his cell, "you can't believe nothing Jorge tells you. Everybody knows he's a liar."

"We'll see," Rhodes said.

Rhodes stopped at Hack's desk while Lawton took Jorge on to the interview room.

"Get Pearson on the radio and tell him to check out Wallace Womack's place. That's where the driver of the truck is staying. Name's Francisco Rey."

"Sure thing," Hack said, and Rhodes went on to talk to Jorge.

Jorge was about Guillermo's age. Like Guillermo, he needed a haircut, but his nose was in better condition. He was considerably more nervous than Guillermo, and he sat rigidly in the chair, twisting his hands while Rhodes watched him. He had a slight tic under his left eye.

Rhodes let him twitch for a while and then said, "Guillermo told me that you were the one who took the purse."

Jorge's voice was shaky. "Then he is a liar. I don't know about a purse."

"We found one in Mr. Womack's pickup. The pickup you stole."

"I didn't steal it! Frankie borrows the truck all the time. Mr. Womack, he don't care."

"You use the truck when you're out stealing batteries?"

"Stealing? We weren't stealing."

"The man who chased you will testify that you were trying to steal his car battery. If you didn't steal the purse, who did? Did Frankie kill Lynn Ashton?"

The tic under Jorge's eye had gotten worse, and Rhodes thought the young man might twist all his fingers off if he kept at it much longer.

"I don't know what you're saying. Who is this Lynn? We didn't kill nobody. We were just out for a ride."

"Lynn Ashton worked in the Beauty Shack across the street from where you were staying. She was pretty, and now she's dead. Her purse was in your pickup."

Jorge looked as if he might cry. "I told you, man. We were just out for a ride. We didn't kill nobody. We didn't steal any purse."

"Where'd you get it, then?"

"We found it, that's where. Just found it. That's all."

Rhodes wondered how many times he'd heard the old "we found it" story. Probably hundreds by now.

"Have you already used the credit cards and spent the money?"

"If you got the purse, you know better. We didn't have it long enough to spend the money or use the cards."

Another likely story. "You sure about that?"

Jorge looked away. "Maybe we bought a couple beers and some sandwiches."

"Did you hit her with a baseball bat?"

"Hit? I told you, man, we found that purse."

"You didn't tell me where."

"In the alley."

"Lots of alleys in this town."

"The one behind that antique store, where the *maricón* stays."

"Now that's too bad," Rhodes said.

"Why is it too bad? We found it, like I said. In the trash right there."

"It's too bad that you used that word."

"It's a bad word, but it's the one I know."

"The man who owned the store was Jeff Tyler," Rhodes said.

"Okay, if you say so. Why is that so bad?"

"Because somebody killed him, too," Rhodes said.

CHAPTER 15

Jorge didn't break down and confess. He was too shocked. He didn't say much of anything until Rhodes pressed him to explain how they'd supposedly found the purse.

Jorge's story was that after Rhodes had chased him and Guillermo that morning, they'd gone out to the Womack place. Frankie lived in a little three-room house out there and did whatever needed doing, mowing the lawn, feeding the few cows, riding a tractor to run the weed shredder, but there wasn't much pay, so Frankie sometimes toured the alleys of Clearview and checked out the trash to see what people were throwing away. Sometimes he'd find something he could sell. After they'd helped him do some yard work and feed the cattle, they drove to town in the old pickup to see what they could find. Today they'd found the purse.

"I swear it," Jorge said. "We found it in the trash. We did take some of the money and buy some beers, but that was all. We didn't kill nobody. I swear it."

Rhodes took him back to the cell, and Lawton locked him in. When Rhodes returned to the outer office, Pearson was there with the purse.

"I went out by the Womack place," he said. "No sign of Francisco."

Rhodes hadn't thought there would be. Frankie was most likely long gone by now, halfway to Houston or San Antonio or Mexico. Especially if he'd killed Lynn Ashton and Jeff Tyler. Rhodes gave Pearson an abridged version of what he'd learned from Guillermo and Jorge.

"Womack see him today?"

"Sure. Him and his friends, but not since this afternoon."

No help there, Rhodes thought.

"What if they're telling the truth?" Pearson said.

Hack snorted. "Who tells the truth these days? Aside from me and Lawton, I mean."

Rhodes ignored him and told Pearson that he could get back to his regular patrol and Rhodes would take a look at the purse. Pearson said so long to Hack and left Rhodes to his purse inspection.

Rhodes was careful not to touch the outside of the purse. It was smooth gray leather, and he knew there would be fingerprints all over it. They'd mostly belong to Francisco and his pals, though.

Lynn's cell phone wasn't in the purse. Her wallet was, but it didn't hold anything of interest. Her credit cards were still inside it, which didn't mean that Frankie and his friends were honest, just that they hadn't had time to use them yet. The phone, however, had been irresistible.

Rhodes sighed, put the purse in the evidence room, and went to see Guillermo, who was lying on his bunk.

"It's uncomfortable in here," Guillermo said by way of greeting. "It's too hot, and there's no TV."

"It's a jail," Rhodes said.

"Yeah, but even us prisoners have some rights."

"You do, and one of them is not to talk to me if you don't want to."

"I don't mind talking, man, but I could use a better mattress."

"What about a cell phone?" Rhodes asked.

"Yeah, that, too. Would be nice to talk to somebody. Besides you, I mean. No offense."

"None taken," Rhodes said. "You didn't

195

have a phone when you were booked."

"Can't afford one. Frankie, he has one."

"I think he has two," Rhodes said.

"My nose hurts," Guillermo said. "It's hard to breathe when it's so hot in here."

"We're talking about Frankie's cell phones, not your nose. Two cell phones."

"I don't think there's two." Guillermo squirmed on the bunk. "Just the one he bought at Walmart."

"You're forgetting the one in the purse," Rhodes said.

Guillermo turned his head away. "I don't know about that one."

"It'll be easy to trace. Those things all have a built-in GPS." That wasn't true, but Rhodes thought Guillermo might not know it. "We'll track it down tomorrow. You might as well tell me."

Guillermo turned back to face Rhodes. "Okay, if there was a phone in the purse, Frankie's the one that took it. Jorge and me, we don't have it."

"How many calls did he make?"

"I didn't say he made no calls."

"Free calls," Rhodes said. "How could he not make calls?"

"He might have called his mother. She lives in Matamoros."

Rhodes had been almost certain that

Frankie had the phone. Now he knew for sure. He also knew he was unlikely to see Frankie again.

"His mother's a nice lady," Guillermo said. He glanced at Rhodes's belt line. "She's a really good cook, man. You'd like her."

"I'm sure I would," Rhodes said. "Good night, Guillermo."

Rhodes drove home and thought over all that had happened that day. It had been a long one, and two people wouldn't be seeing the next one come along. Lynn Ashton and Jeff Tyler. The two deaths had to be connected, but Rhodes couldn't see how. Rhodes wondered about Lonnie, who Rhodes thought wasn't telling everything he knew. Why would he hold back if he didn't have anything to do with Tyler's death, or Lynn's? He should be the first to want the murders solved.

Lynn's purse worried Rhodes, too. Maybe it had been in the trash, maybe not. What if Guillermo and his friends had found it inside Tyler's store and killed him for it? As unlikely as that seemed, it could've happened. Tyler, jealous of Lynn's relationship with Lonnie, might have killed her and taken the purse. The possibilities multiplied

197

when Rhodes thought of things that way. Lonnie might have found out what Tyler had done and killed him, then thrown the purse away. Or . . . Rhodes was too tired to go on with that train of thought. It was time he went home and got some rest.

Yancey greeted Rhodes at the door, but he wasn't as enthusiastic as usual. The late hour might have had something to do with it. Rhodes took a quick bath and went into the bedroom, where Ivy was reading *Terrorist Terror*.

She put someone's business card in the book to mark her place, closed the book, and put it on the nightstand by the bed.

"What you need is a sidekick," she said. "Somebody who knows martial arts. Like Wade Winslow."

"Who?"

"In the book," Ivy said. "Wade Winslow. He's Sage Barton's new sidekick. He knows something called Chen Shuan. He studied with somebody named Professor Lansdale in East Texas."

"A sidekick like that would come in handy, all right," Rhodes said, thinking about his recent encounter at the Environmental Reclamation Center. "This morning, somebody told me what I needed was more angst. Some kind of secret sorrow, like a dead sweetheart."

"You have a live sweetheart," Ivy said. "Want me to prove it?"

Rhodes realized he wasn't so tired, after all.

"Is 'turkey bacon' an oxymoron?" Rhodes asked Ivy the next morning while he was eating breakfast.

Ivy was putting food in Sam's bowl while the cat pretended not to be interested. She looked up and said, "You mean like 'artificial grass'?"

"That's it," Rhodes said. He held up the piece of bacon he'd been eating. "What do you think?"

Ivy walked over to the table, and Sam waited until she was well away from him before he'd deign to eat.

"You think the bacon tastes funny?" Ivy asked.

Rhodes shook his head. "No. I just wondered if you could call something 'bacon' if it wasn't associated with a pig."

"Considering your adventures with pigs," Ivy said, "I'd think you'd be glad this bacon came from a turkey."

Rhodes grinned. He'd had more than his share of adventures with pigs, all right, though they weren't really pigs, not exactly.

"They were wild hogs," he said, "and they're overrunning the county. Before long they'll be taking over the town. You just wait."

"Maybe we should go into business for ourselves," Ivy said. "We could sell wild hog bacon. It might be a big hit."

"Anything to get rid of the feral hogs," Rhodes said, and that ended the discussion, though Rhodes still thought he was right about the oxymoron.

After breakfast, Rhodes skipped his usual visit with Speedo, but he got Ivy's assurance that she'd see to Speedo's needs and let Yancey out for a romp. Sam didn't care one way or another what Rhodes did.

As soon as he left the house, Rhodes went to Ballinger's Funeral Home. The building had once been a mansion owned by one of the richest families in town, and Clyde Ballinger lived in back in a much smaller building that had been the servants' quarters. He was an early riser, and Rhodes knew he'd be up and about.

Ballinger answered Rhodes's knock and told him to come in. Rhodes entered what once had been a small living room but was now Ballinger's unofficial office. There was something different about it, and it took Rhodes a second or two to realize what it was. The desk, usually covered with old paperback books with trashy covers, was almost bare.

"You quit reading?" Rhodes asked.

Ballinger grinned. He might have been a mortician, but he was always cheerful. "Nope. Got me this." He picked up a rectangular leather-covered object that looked like a notebook of some kind and flipped it open. "It's an e-reader."

"A what?"

"An e-reader," Ballinger said. "It's kind of like a computer, but for reading. You can put thousands of books on this one reader."

Rhodes had heard of e-readers, but he'd never seen one. It didn't seem much like a book to him.

"Let me show you," Ballinger said. He switched the machine on and handed it to Rhodes. "Take a look."

Rhodes looked. The screen showed what appeared to be a table of contents.

"Those are the books on the reader," Ballinger said. "I have about ten so far, but I'll have more."

Rhodes looked at some of the titles. *The Desperado, Renegade Cop, The Cheaters, To Kiss or Kill, Dig My Grave Deep.* They sounded like Ballinger's kind of material, all right.

Except for one of them.

"*Terrorist Terror?*" Rhodes asked.

Ballinger gave him a grin. "You know me. I can't resist a story about a crime-busting sheriff who just happens to be based on a person I know. Just got it downloaded today."

"I'm nothing at all like Sage Barton."

"If you say so."

"I do say so."

"It even has pictures of the covers," Ballinger said, changing the subject.

"I thought you liked finding things at garage sales," Rhodes said.

"Can't do that much anymore, what with the Internet. People snap up anything they think they can sell on eBay, and that doesn't leave a lot for me. Sad thing is, I've read most of those on the reader before. I just thought it'd be fun to have them."

"Anything by your favorite writer?"

"Who do you mean?"

"You know. The one who writes about the Eighty-seventh Precinct."

"Ed McBain," Ballinger said. "Nothing on there by him yet. He's dead, you know. No more books about Carella and Hawes and Meyer Meyer. It's a shame."

Rhodes handed the reader back to Ballinger, who shut it off and set it on the desk.

"Speaking of a shame," Rhodes said, "what about the autopsy reports on Lynn Ashton and Jeff Tyler?"

"Dr. White left those for you," Ballinger said. He opened a drawer, took out a couple of folders, and passed them to Rhodes. "Have a seat and look them over."

Rhodes did. He didn't find anything he hadn't already known or suspected. Lynn Ashton had been killed by a blow to the head that had driven splinters of her skull into her brain. Tyler had been shot with two .38 caliber bullets. It was the bullet in the head that had killed him.

"Carella and the gang at the eight-seven would have this one wrapped up by now," Ballinger said when Rhodes closed the second folder.

"It's only been twenty-four hours," Rhodes said.

"Well, maybe they wouldn't have," Ballinger said. "They'd have some suspects, though."

"I have suspects," Rhodes said.

"Randy Lawless, right?"

Rhodes's face must have shown his surprise.

"You didn't know?" Ballinger asked.

"No," Rhodes said. "I didn't."

"I thought everybody in town knew about those two."

"Nobody's mentioned them to me."

"Then let me be the first."

Randy Lawless was an attorney, the best at criminal defense in the county if reputation meant anything. He and Rhodes had a more or less friendly relationship, though they were occasional adversaries in court. He was also a married man, like most of the others that Lynn Ashton had been seeing, at least the ones Rhodes knew about.

"Details?" Rhodes asked.

Ballinger shook his head. "Not a one. I heard it from somebody a few weeks ago. I'm usually the last one in town to hear things like that, so I figured it wasn't much of a secret."

"Maybe it wasn't a secret," Rhodes said, "but I didn't know about it."

"Well, now you do."

"Yes," Rhodes said. "Now I do."

Rhodes left Ballinger's office, and before he could start the county car, Hack called him on the radio.

"That reporter's here," Hack said. "She wants to know all about Jeff Tyler."

"I'm officially promoting you to the office

of spokesperson for the Blacklin County Sheriff's Department," Rhodes said. "Tell her what she wants to know."

"I don't know anything," Hack said.

"Tell her that."

"She's not gonna like it. She wants to talk to you."

"She'll have to find me first," Rhodes said.

CHAPTER 16

Rhodes had intended to go to see Randy Lawless next, but Lawless didn't open his office until nine, and it was still only eight thirty. That was all right. Rhodes had another idea he wanted to try out first, so he drove out to Seepy Benton's house.

Benton wasn't a morning person, but lately he'd started to get up early enough to go out for a walk before going to the college to teach. He lived out on one of the county roads not far from the school, and Rhodes thought he could get there in plenty of time to have a chat with him.

Sure enough, just as Rhodes drove up, Benton and Bruce were starting on their constitutional. Bruce started barking as soon as Rhodes pulled into the driveway. He was a fierce-looking animal, a leopard dog, colored like a calico cat, descendant of mastiffs, and he could be as fierce as he looked if the mood was on him. It had been on him all too often when he was living in a pen at the trailer owned by the Eccles cousins. However, since he'd been living with Seepy Benton, he'd calmed down considerably. Benton had been good for him.

Rhodes got out of the car and said, "Hey, Bruce."

Bruce stopped barking and walked over to Rhodes, who held out his hand for the dog to sniff. Satisfied after a couple of quick whiffs, Bruce started to wag his tail.

"Good morning, Sheriff," Benton said as Bruce walked back over to him. "You must need my help or you wouldn't be out here so early in the day."

"Maybe I just wanted to see Bruce, your faithful animal companion."

"A look at Bruce is worth the trip, but I don't think that's why you came."

"You're right," Rhodes said. He might as well admit it. "I do need your help. That is, if you have time. When's your first class?"

"It's Friday," Benton said, "so no class until ten. I can spare an hour or so to engage in fighting crime for the county."

"Just as long as you don't start trying to engage in punishment."

"Crime . . . punishment," Benton said. "Is that a literary joke? If it is, you'll have to explain it to me. Remember, I'm a math teacher."

"Never mind," Rhodes said.

"I won't," Benton said. "Anyway, I'm a skilled martial artist. I can deal out punishment with the best of them. Want a demonstration?"

He struck what Rhodes assumed was a martial arts pose, maybe something from *The Karate Kid*. Bruce gave him a skeptical look. Rhodes thought that Bruce was a pretty smart dog.

"What I had in mind won't require martial arts," Rhodes said, "although Ivy did say last night that I needed a sidekick who was good at them."

Benton relaxed his pose. "I'm more the hero type than the sidekick type, but I might be able to adjust."

Rhodes looked at Bruce. Bruce remained skeptical.

"Right," Rhodes said. "Anyway, I'm not in the market for a sidekick or martial artist. What I need is somebody skilled in conducting a search."

"I can do that, too. We learned about it in the Citizens' Academy. Bruce didn't attend, but he can help." At the sound of his name, Bruce thumped his tail on the ground. "He can sniff things out even better than I can."

"You can take him along, then," Rhodes said.

"Good. Before we go searching, though, you might want to tell us what we're looking for."

"A cell phone," Rhodes said.

The idea had come to Rhodes when he woke up that morning. Frankie might believe the phone could be traced, and even if he didn't believe it, he might prefer getting rid of it to having it found on him if he was caught.

"You saw where the man ran from the building last night, didn't you?" Rhodes asked Benton.

"Sure. I would've followed him, but —"

"— he was cutting across lawns. I know. Did you see him throw anything away while he was running?"

"I couldn't tell. The moonlight wasn't bright enough for me to see details."

Rhodes wasn't too concerned that Benton hadn't seen anything. That didn't mean Frankie hadn't gotten rid of the phone. If he had, Rhodes hoped he'd done it soon after leaving the warehouse. The whole block next to the building was bare except for weeds and junk that people had dumped there. If the phone was there, Benton might get lucky and find it.

209

"What I'd like for you to do is find a cell phone that Frankie might have thrown away last night."

"Who's Frankie?"

Rhodes explained, and Benton said, "Why would he throw away a cell phone?"

Rhodes explained that, too.

"If it's there," Benton said, "Bruce and I can find it. Right, Bruce?"

Bruce thumped his tail on the ground.

"See?" Benton asked. "Bruce understands everything I say. He believes we can do it."

"I can tell," Rhodes said.

"What kind of phone is it?" Benton asked.

"I don't know," Rhodes said. "Does it matter?"

"I wouldn't want to bring in the wrong one."

Rhodes wondered how many cell phones Benton thought he was going to find. He said, "Bring in as many as you can."

"Right," Benton said. "You can count on us, Sheriff. Seepy Benton and Bruce are on the case. And if you need a martial arts sidekick anytime at all, just give me a call."

"Sure thing." Rhodes was sorry he'd mentioned the sidekick.

"Come on, Bruce," Benton said. "Let's get the Seepymobile on the road."

Rhodes watched them go. It occurred to

him that Benton already had a sidekick. Maybe Yancey would like a career in crime-busting. No. It would never work. Sam the cat would be jealous.

Rhodes got in his car and went to see Randy Lawless.

Lawless's offices were in a large white building that dominated Clearview's downtown, mainly because it was the only one in the area that wasn't about to collapse. Rhodes sometimes called the building the Lawj Mahal. In front of it was a wide asphalt parking lot. Only one car was parked there now, and that was Lawless's black Infiniti. Rhodes pulled in beside it and got out, feeling a little shabby driving the county's Dodge.

Rhodes entered the building, which was already cool, thanks to the air-conditioning that probably hadn't been turned off the previous night. Lawless could afford to let it run twenty-four hours a day if he wanted to, and apparently he did. Rhodes didn't blame him.

Rhodes looked around the outer office just to be sure that Lawless's administrative assistant hadn't arrived, but he didn't see anyone lurking around. He walked down a short hall to Lawless's private office and looked in.

Lawless sat behind a black desk that wasn't much smaller than a Ping-Pong table. The slick glass top was immaculate. If gambling hadn't been illegal, Rhodes would have bet a dollar that there wasn't even a fingerprint on it.

"Good morning, Sheriff," Lawless said, leaning back in a big leather chair that would have set Rhodes back a month's wages. Or maybe two. "How can I help out the head honcho of the county's law enforcement today?"

Rhodes decided he might as well get right to it. "You can tell me about you and Lynn Ashton."

Lawless didn't flinch. "Is Carol here yet?"

Carol was his administrative assistant.

"I didn't see her," Rhodes said, "and her car wasn't outside."

"Good. Would you mind closing the door before you have a seat?"

Rhodes closed the door and sat in a cushioned chair upholstered in red leather.

"What do you want to know?" Lawless asked.

"I've already told you," Rhodes said.

"What you said was a little vague. You need to be more specific."

"Did you kill her?"

Lawless didn't flinch that time, either.

"Sheriff," he said, "you know you shouldn't just come right out and ask me that. You haven't even read me my rights."

"You know them as well as I do," Rhodes said. "Maybe better. Anyway, you're not under arrest. We're just two friends talking here, except that one of us has been running around on his wife."

"You don't have any proof of that."

"You're right," Rhodes said. "Just unsubstantiated rumors."

"And you want me to substantiate them."

"Bingo. I'll bet you graduated at the top of your class."

"Close enough," Lawless said. "Thanks for being so perceptive."

"I'm also impatient," Rhodes said. "Or so people keep telling me."

"All right," Lawless said. He flicked imaginary dust off the lapel of his navy blue suit jacket. "I'll substantiate the rumors. I had a brief moment of the middle-age crazies." He paused. "You remember the song that Jerry Lee Lewis sang about the middle-age crazies?"

Rhodes looked for the gray in Lawless's hair. He didn't have any.

"I remember," Rhodes said.

Lawless gave him the once-over. "Did you

remember the lyrics?"

"Well enough," Rhodes said. "You thought a pretty young thing would understand what you were trying to prove."

"I wasn't trying to prove anything, much less that I still could. I want you to know that. It was just something that happened. It's been over for a while."

"Let me guess," Rhodes said. "She told you that she'd found someone else, that certain someone she'd always been looking for."

Lawless surprised him. "No. It wasn't that at all."

"It wasn't?"

"Nope. The little gold digger was going to blackmail me."

That was an entirely new wrinkle. Or maybe it wasn't, after all. Rhodes had suspected that Clifford Clement and Mikey Burns hadn't been entirely straight with him. It might well be that their story about Lynn's finding someone else was just a cover for the more embarrassing fact that she'd tried a little blackmail with them, too. Maybe they'd even paid her.

"Tell me about it," Rhodes said.

"I just told you."

"Remember what you said about being specific?"

"All right. Why not? I knew I was making a mistake, but like I said, it happened. I was discreet, or as discreet as you can be in a town this size. I don't think anybody knew we were going out, and that's the way I wanted to keep it. There was nothing serious about it. We were just friends."

Rhodes tried to keep a straight face, but a little of his doubt must've shown.

"You have a dirty mind, Sheriff," Lawless said.

Rhodes shrugged.

"I'm being honest about this," Lawless said. "Trust me."

At that comment, Rhodes thought of about a hundred lawyer jokes, but he refrained from telling any of them. He just said, "All right."

"Good," Lawless said. "Things between Lynn and me were going along fine. In a friendly way, of course. Then one night she said she was going to tell Sharon about us."

Sharon was Lawless's wife. She was a statuesque blonde with, so Rhodes had heard, a fiery temper. She'd be the kind to wreak a terrible revenge if the rumors were true. Not to mention taking Lawless to the cleaners in a divorce case. She'd get the bank account, the Infiniti, the house, and maybe even the Lawj Mahal. Lawless's own standing as an attorney wouldn't save him. Nothing would.

"She must not have told," Rhodes said. "Otherwise, you'd probably be standing out at the entrance to the Walmart parking lot, holding up a sign that said WILL GIVE LEGAL ADVICE FOR FOOD."

"You're funny as well as perceptive and impatient," Lawless said, but he wasn't laughing. He wasn't even smiling. "Maybe you could try going on the comedy club circuit."

"I don't have the patience," Rhodes said.

Lawless ignored him. "You're right about Lynn. She didn't tell Sharon. I made it clear to her that while she might damage my reputation and mess up my marriage, I'd see to it that she got some jail time. She must've believed me. After all, I'm a lawyer."

"Did you say 'trust me'?"

Lawless grinned, but it wasn't a pleasant sight. "I might have."

"You won't have to worry about her now."

"Neither will anybody else. I'm not a special case, Sheriff. She was pretty, she was bright, but she was rotten. I wasn't smart enough to see that at first."

"Sharon must have found out, eventually," Rhodes said. "If I know, a lot of others must know, too."

"She did find out, but the fling was over. Sharon now has a new car and some very expensive jewelry."

"Good for her. Who else was seeing Lynn, do you know?"

"I don't have any idea," Lawless said.

"Would you tell me if you did?"

"Probably not."

"That's what I thought," Rhodes said.

CHAPTER 17

Rhodes had a lot of things to do and not enough time to do them in, a condition that seemed to occur more and more often to him. The older he got, in fact, the less time he seemed to have. There was something unfair about that, but there wasn't anything he could do to change it.

He was on his way to the recycling center when Hack called on the radio.

"Seepy Benton says he's got the phone you sent him to find," Hack said.

Rhodes was surprised. He hadn't been at all optimistic about Benton's chances of finding the phone. Maybe Bruce had helped.

"Where was he when he called?"

"He was out by the Environmental Reclamation Center somewhere. He said you'd know. He said to tell you he hadn't touched the phone and he'd be waiting there for you. Unless it was after ten. He has a class at

218

ten, he said."

"Tell him I'll write him an excuse if he's absent," Rhodes said. "I'll be there in two minutes."

He got there in one. Seepy's car was parked on the shoulder of the road, and Rhodes parked behind it. Benton stood beside it, while his sidekick cavorted in the vacant lot.

"I remember about the chain of custody from the academy classes," Benton said. "So I left the phone right where it was. You're the officer, not me. I didn't touch it."

"What about Bruce?" Rhodes asked.

"He didn't touch it, either," Benton said.

They both looked across the big lot to where Bruce seemed to be trying to catch something or other that fluttered just above his head. When Bruce jumped for it, it would flutter away. Rhodes thought it might be a butterfly.

"His bark is worse than his bite," Benton said.

"Thanks for that information," Rhodes said. "What about the phone?"

"Over here," Benton said. "It's not far from the warehouse."

Rhodes got some polypropylene gloves and followed Benton across the lot. Looking down he saw a plastic bottle lying in the dead grass. A beer can was off to one side. The reclaimers should come over here and pick up a few things.

Benton stopped and pointed at the ground. "Here it is."

Rhodes put on the gloves. He didn't know one smart phone from another one. This one lay faceup, so Rhodes could see a screen and a tiny keyboard, but that didn't tell him much. He picked it up and saw the word SAMSUNG printed above the keyboard.

If the Blacklin County crime lab had been equipped like the labs on TV shows, Rhodes could have hooked the phone up to an extraction device and downloaded everything on it: pictures, phone numbers, e-mails, texts, and even every location where Lynn had been. However, Blacklin County didn't have one of the extraction devices, so Rhodes would have to take other measures.

"Do you know how to use these things?" he asked Benton.

Benton looked at him. "Doesn't everybody?"

"Just about," Rhodes said, "but I need an expert."

"You're looking at him."

"Good. Call the college and have the dean dismiss your class."

Benton was horrified. "I can't do that. It's

a calculus class. My students love calculus."

"I'm sure they do, but this is more important."

Benton's horror increased. "More important than calculus?"

"It's a murder case," Rhodes said. "I'd call that more important than calculus."

Benton didn't look convinced, but he got out his own cell and made the call. When he was finished, Rhodes said, "Let's go. I'll meet you at the jail."

"I'll have to take Bruce home first."

"That's fine. I have some things to take care of, too. Just get there as soon as you can."

"I have another class at noon."

"You might have to phone in about that one, too," Rhodes said.

Since Benton was going back home, Rhodes thought he had time to make a call on Al, or whoever was in charge at the Environmental Reclamation Center today. The gate was open, but Rhodes drove past it and parked on the side of the street. He went inside the center, and when he knocked on the office door, Al opened it. He seemed to be wearing the same shirt he'd worn the previous day, the one with his name stitched on it. Maybe he had two of them.

221

"Yeah?" Al asked.

Rhodes decided that since neither Al's manners nor his vocabulary had changed, the shirt was probably the same one, all right.

"Your warehouse across the street was broken into last night," Rhodes said. "I came by to let you know."

"Yeah?"

Al could profit by taking vocabulary lessons from Lonnie.

"Yeah," Rhodes said, just to see if Al would react. He didn't, so Rhodes said, "Don't you want to know what happened?"

"Yeah," Al said. "I guess so. Place looks okay to me."

"Let me show you where they broke in," Rhodes said.

He took Al across the street and pointed out the recent repair to the wall of the warehouse. Al didn't thank him for fixing it.

"You'd almost think they knew they could get in that way," Rhodes said.

"Yeah," Al said.

Rhodes suppressed a sigh. "The thing is, it was the same fellas I chased in your place across the street yesterday. They seem to like it here."

Al shrugged and opened up. "Can't blame 'em. It's a nice place."

"Palatial," Rhodes said.

"Huh?"

"Never mind. Let's go inside. I want to show you the damage."

"That's okay," Al said. "Not much they could do to hurt the stuff in there."

"There's a big room back there we should check," Rhodes said.

Al looked around as if he had no clue as to what Rhodes was talking about. "What big room?"

"The one with the dead bolt on the door."

"Oh, that one."

"Yeah," Rhodes said. "Let's make sure it's okay. Maybe they broke into it."

"You got a search warrant?"

Rhodes really wanted to say *Yeah*, but instead he told the truth. "No."

"Then no looking," Al said. "I'm gonna ask you to leave now. I got work to do."

"You have any records of buying batteries or catalytic converters from some fellas named Guillermo and Jorge?"

"Never heard of 'em. I asked you to leave."

"I'm leaving," Rhodes said, "but not before we both go back to your office so I can check your records."

"I don't know if I can let you do that."

"Sure you can. I'm the sheriff."

"Yeah," Al said.

■ ■ ■ ■

Rhodes had to admit that the books looked good, but then they would, wouldn't they. If they hadn't, Al would have brought up the search warrant again.

"You satisfied?" Al asked.

"Not really," Rhodes said. "I think you've done some transactions that haven't been recorded here. Maybe you have another set of books. I also think you've done some business with Guillermo and Jorge and haven't put down their names."

Al didn't say anything. He just smiled.

"I can't prove it," Rhodes said, "so from now on I'm going to have this place watched twenty-four hours a day. I'm going to check on everybody who comes in here, and if I find out you've been dealing in stolen goods, I'm going to shut you down."

"I just work here," Al said.

"You won't. Not after I shut you down. You won't be working anywhere, but I can promise you free room and board. The room might not be comfortable, but the board's not bad."

"Yeah," Al said, and that was when Frankie stuck his head in the door.

He saw Rhodes, and his mouth dropped

open. His head disappeared, and Rhodes turned to go after him.

Al stuck out a foot, and Rhodes tripped over it. He stumbled through the door and fell down the steps. As he tried to get up, Al appeared. He grabbed at Rhodes's arms and pulled.

"Didn't mean to get in the way," he said. "Let me help you up."

"Get away," Rhodes said, but Al kept tying him up every time he tried to move. Rhodes thought they must have looked as if they were trying to re-create a scene from a Three Stooges comedy.

Rhodes got partially untangled, bent over, and pulled up his pants leg. He pulled out his pistol. With Al hung over his back, Rhodes said, "I might not be able to kill you with this, but I think I can put a hole in your foot. Or shoot off your big toe. Want me to try."

Al slid off Rhodes's back and moved away from him, hands in the air. "I was just being helpful."

"Tell it to the judge," Rhodes said, and he took off after Frankie.

Frankie had a good head start, and Rhodes saw after only a couple of seconds that there was no hope of catching him. He didn't have any idea which way he might have gone. So Rhodes did the next best thing. He went back to the office and arrested Al.

After booking Al and charging him with everything he could think of except mopery, Rhodes tried to give Seepy Benton the cell phone.

"See if you can find Lynn's appointment schedule," Rhodes said.

Benton held his hands in the air just the way Al had. "I'll get my fingerprints on it if I touch it."

"It doesn't matter," Rhodes told him. "We know Frankie had it. Fingerprints on a phone will be the least of his worries if he shows up again."

Rhodes was surprised Frankie had showed up at all. He must have come into the center through a back way, or maybe he'd been there all along. That was something Rhodes wanted to take up with Al or Guillermo if he ever had a chance.

While Benton was looking at the phone, Rhodes read over the reports that Ruth Grady and Buddy had left for him earlier that morning. Neither of them had learned anything helpful from their interviews with the Beauty Shack customers. That was about what Rhodes had expected.

Ruth had checked the fingerprints on the

purse and the hair dryer. There were prints on the purse, all of them too smeared to make out. Rhodes thought the prints were probably from Frankie, Guillermo, and Jorge, who'd handled the purse to see what was inside it. Not much help there, though it would've been interesting if Jeff Tyler's prints had showed up. The prints on the dryer were smeared, too. Nothing but a couple of partials looked good. Not much help there, either.

"I'm going out for a while," Rhodes said to Hack. "You know where to reach me."

That was the code they used in front of others when Rhodes was going to his office in the courthouse. He hardly ever used that office unless he needed to get away for a while and think things over.

"Got it," Hack said.

"Don't you want the appointments?" Benton asked.

"You have it already?" Rhodes asked.

"Sure. They aren't even password protected."

"Does she have anybody down after five o'clock yesterday?"

"Yeah," Benton said.

Rhodes wondered if Benton might be related to Al. "Who was it?"

"Jeff Tyler," Benton said.

CHAPTER 18

Rhodes sat in his courthouse office drinking a Dr Pepper and thinking about all he knew and didn't know about the death of Lynn Ashton. He realized that he didn't know a lot more than he did.

He knew that Jeff Tyler had been Lynn's late appointment. He knew that her purse had been found in the trash behind Tyler's antique store, so there was a nice connection. Except that Rhodes found it hard to believe Tyler would be so stupid as to steal the purse and put it out where anybody could see it. Maybe Tyler had known Frankie and his friends and their visits to the alleys. If so, he might have put the purse out there so they'd take it. Although what was Tyler doing with it in the first place?

Rhodes wondered how much Lonnie knew about the purse and about Tyler's late appointment. Rhodes was sure Lonnie hadn't told him everything, but he wasn't sure what he hadn't been told.

Even if Lonnie knew about the appointment, that didn't explain who'd killed Tyler. That murder was different from Lynn's, which appeared to have been a spur-of-the-moment thing. Whoever had killed Tyler had planned it, at least to some extent. Someone had gone to Tyler's place with a gun and had been ready to use it.

How many men had Lynn blackmailed or tried to blackmail? She might have been successful with some of them, but certainly not all. Randy Lawless wasn't the only one who would have refused to go along with her. What about Mikey Burns and Clifford Clement? Had they really broken it off with Lynn because of another man, or had blackmail been the problem?

Rhodes would also have liked to know if there was any connection between the Environmental Reclamation Center and the deaths. It didn't seem likely that there was one, but he couldn't rule it out. There were plenty of odd things going on at that place.

While he was thinking about it, he used the phone on his desk to call the county judge to request a search warrant to take a look in the locked room. The judge granted it without any questions.

"I'm in the building," Rhodes said. "I'll

stop by and pick it up on my way out."

"Hiding out, are you?" the judge asked.

"Just taking a break."

"Right," the judge said. "Give me half an hour. My secretary, I mean administrative assistant, will have the warrant ready when you get here."

Rhodes thanked him and hung up. Before he executed the search warrant, he should probably talk to Sandra again. She might have thought of something helpful by now, and he should let her know that it wasn't at all likely that the men in the old hotel building had been the ones who'd killed Lynn.

The truth was that Rhodes wasn't much closer to finding the killer than he'd been at the start. He had plenty of suspects, but that wasn't helping.

Rhodes finished his Dr Pepper and got up to leave just as Jennifer Loam came in.

"Caught you," she said.

She'd located him in the courthouse before, so it hadn't taken much detection for her to run him down.

"I'd like to talk to you about the murders," she said. "If you can spare the time, that is."

"I can't," Rhodes said. He continued to stand, hoping she might leave.

"Maybe I can help you," she said, sitting in one of the big chairs across from the desk.

Rhodes sighed and sat back down. "I'll take all the help I can get."

"I can't really do much for you," Jennifer said. "It's just that getting a big story would mean a lot to me. Really, I'm the one who needs help."

"Why would that be?" Rhodes asked.

"It would be because my job with the *Herald* is just about over."

"That would be a big loss for the paper," Rhodes said. "For the town, too. You're very good at what you do."

"Thanks, but nobody really cares about that. It's all about money now, and newspapers are losing money all over the country. Little ones like the *Herald* are barely hanging on. Since the *Herald* went weekly, they don't need me anymore."

"Can't you get a job with a bigger paper?"

"They're laying people off," Jennifer said, "not hiring them."

Rhodes couldn't see where this was going. "So how would a big story help you?"

"I'm starting an Internet news site. I'm calling it *A Clear View of Blacklin County*."

Rhodes just looked at her.

She smiled. "Okay, I'll admit it's corny, but it's catchy enough to work. Mostly I'll have crime news, of which there seems to be plenty around here. Not just murders, but wrecks and burglaries and things like that. Smelly chicken farms. I'll have social notes, too. I'm going to line up advertising, or try to, and maybe I can earn enough to make a go of it."

"I hope it works," Rhodes said, trying to keep his skepticism out of his voice, "and I think we can help each other."

"Good. You help me first. Give me all you have on the murders."

"I would if I had anything, but I don't. What I do have is a different story, something you can investigate for your Web site. You can break the story there, and it'll get a lot of attention."

Jennifer leaned forward. "Tell me about it."

"I have a question first. Since you're working for the newspaper, would it be ethical for you to be working on a story for your Web site at the same time?"

"You know I said my job was just about over?"

Rhodes nodded.

"In this case, 'just about' means it's over today. This afternoon. I'll turn in my last stories for the Monday edition, and my illustrious career as a newspaper reporter will come to an end."

"How long have you known?"

"Awhile. I didn't want to mention it to anybody. So you don't have to worry about ethics, if that makes you feel any better."

"It does," Rhodes said. "I do have ethics, you know."

"I do know."

"Thanks. Now here's the story."

Rhodes told her what he knew and suspected about Al, whose last name had turned out to be Swanson, and about the Environmental Reclamation Center, which was now closed for business as far as Rhodes knew, since Al was in jail.

"I'm not even sure who owns the place," Rhodes said, "even though there've been some problems there before. Maybe you can find out who the owner is, and then maybe you can find out what Frankie and his friends have to do with the place. Enough people have had their copper wiring and their batteries stolen to guarantee you a good-sized readership for a story like that. It would get you off to a good start."

"If I hook them at first, they'll keep coming back," Jennifer said. "I'll start poking around. Thanks, Sheriff."

"No," Rhodes said, "thank *you*. I appreciate the help."

It was true. If the commissioners would hire a few more deputies, he wouldn't have to resort to using amateur assistance, but Jennifer was a professional at gathering information, and looking for it wouldn't put her in any danger. Benton loved helping out, and he could be useful as long as he didn't interfere with the investigation.

Jennifer left the courthouse, and so did Rhodes. He thought he'd better have a little talk with Sharon Lawless before Randy got home.

Sharon Lawless was an attractive blonde who didn't work anymore, though she'd once been a clerk in Billy Lee's drugstore. Rhodes found her at home, and she invited him into her computer room, which was small and neat. Her computer desk didn't have any dust on it, and there was nothing there except the computer and a few sheets of paper.

"I need the computer to keep up with things," she told him.

Although Sharon didn't have a job, she volunteered. She was president or vice-president of so many organizations that Rhodes couldn't keep up with them. She was on the historical commission and in the Garden Club, the Friends of the Library, the AAUW, the DAR, the Daughters of the Republic of Texas, and others.

She also had on the biggest diamond ring Rhodes had ever seen.

"This is why I didn't have any reason to worry about Lynn Ashton," she told Rhodes as she held out her slim hand for him to see the ring. "Randy was very contrite about straying. I accepted his apology, and we're very happy now that things have settled down."

Rhodes couldn't blame her for being happy. The ring would have choked a horse had the horse been so unfortunate as to swallow it.

"Weren't you angry before you got the ring?" Rhodes asked.

Sharon smiled. She had great teeth. "Of course. That's why I have the ring. Anyway, if you're thinking of me as a suspect in Lynn's death, I have an alibi. Lynn died yesterday afternoon, I believe. I was in a committee meeting with several people from four until nearly seven. I can give you a list of names."

Rhodes said that would be fine, and she wrote down the names on a sheet of paper from her desk. She handed him the paper and said, "I hope this will get me off the hook."

"I'm sure it will," Rhodes said, and he was sure it would. It was time for him to get back to the jail.

"Gone?" Rhodes asked when Hack told him that Al had bonded out. "Already?"

"Didn't take him long," Hack said. "Made his phone call and bonded out fifteen minutes later. Got some powerful friends, I guess."

So much for the little chat Rhodes had hoped to have with him. It didn't matter, however. Guillermo and Jorge might do just as well.

Jorge seemed to be the more cooperative of the two. Lawton was lounging by the door, so Rhodes told him to bring Jorge to the interview room.

"There's somethin' else you might want to hear first," Lawton said. "There's a problem. See —"

"I'll tell it," Hack said. "I'm the dispatcher here."

"Sure," Lawton said. "You go right ahead. I didn't mean to take over your job."

"Sure you didn't," Hack said.

"The problem?" Rhodes asked.

"Pregnant nanny," Hack said.

Rhodes didn't know of anybody in Blacklin County who had a nanny. He said, "A child-care problem?"

"Not that kind of nanny," Hack said.

"The goat kind," Lawton added.

Hack's head turned so fast that Rhodes wondered if it was on ball bearings. "What was that you said about not doin' my job?"

"Just thought I'd help you out a little," Lawton said.

"I don't need no help." Hack turned back to Rhodes. "It's not Mary Poppins. It's a goat."

"Would be a good name for a nanny goat," Lawton said. "Mary Poppins, I mean."

Hack ignored him and said to Rhodes, "You know Vernell Lindsey's goats?"

Vernell was a romance writer who'd had some moderate successes. She also kept goats, three of them, named Shirley, Goodness, and Mercy. Like a lot of goats, they didn't like to stay penned up, and they could get out of just about any kind of enclosure. Vernell tried to keep them on her property, but it wasn't always possible.

"I know them," Rhodes said.

"Turns out Shirley has strayed from the straight and narrow," Hack said.

"I can believe it," Rhodes said, "but goat morals aren't a problem for the sheriff's department."

"Vernell blames Otis King's Old Ben," Lawton said.

Old Ben got out now and then, too.

"I'm tellin' this," Hack said.

"Never mind that," Rhodes said before Lawton could chime in. "Alton's the animal control officer, and he does what he can. He's taken Old Ben back home more than once."

"Not soon enough," Hack said. "Accordin' to Vernell, that is."

"I still don't see what she expects us to do about it. Provide goat birth control?"

"That ain't the problem," Lawton said.

Hack ignored him again. "That ain't the problem. Seems like Shirley's escaped again, and pregnancy's not agreein' with her."

"Nannies gone wild," Lawton said.

Hack sat stone still. The silence grew until Rhodes said, "Just tell me what happened."

"Let Lawton tell it," Hack said. "Seems like he's the one knows all about it."

"It's your story," Lawton said. "You tell it."

Rhodes reached in his pocket, pulled out a quarter, flipped it, and caught it on the back of his wrist, covering it with his hand. "Heads, it's Hack. Tails, it's Lawton." He uncovered the coin. "Heads. Tell it, Hack."

Rhodes put the quarter back in his pocket. He hadn't looked at it, but he knew Hack would be mollified. He liked to win.

"What happened was this," Hack said. "Shirley got out. She does that a lot."

"I know," Rhodes said. "Get on with it."

"Impatient," Lawton said. "Always in a hurry."

"Sure is," Hack said. "You'd think he was a busy man."

Rhodes kept his mouth shut.

"Anyway," Hack continued, "the goat got out and ran down to the Walker house. You know where that is?"

"About a block from Vernell's," Rhodes said.

"Right. The two Walker kids was playin' in the yard."

"One of 'em's three," Lawton said. "Other one's four."

"Just the right age to be scared of a crazy nanny goat," Hack said. "They ran behind some pittosporum bushes in front of the house, and the goat trapped 'em there. Wouldn't let 'em out."

"Their mama is the one that called," Lawton said.

"I'm the one took the call," Hack said. "Thing of it was, Miz Walker's like her kids, scared of goats, 'specially crazy pregnant ones. So she called us."

It had taken a while, but now the whole thing was out. Or Rhodes hoped it was.

"So what did you do?" he asked.

"Called Alton Boyd. He's the animal control officer, ain't he?"

"Did he take care of it?"

"Guess so. Haven't heard back from him. Hope Shirley didn't gore him or somethin' like that."

"He's got the county insurance," Lawton said. "If he got gored, he'd be covered."

Rhodes had enjoyed about as much of the conversation as he could stand. It was time to get back to the business of being the sheriff.

"Lawton," he said, "would you please bring Jorge to the interview room?"

"Sure thing, Sheriff," Lawton said. "You know all you got to do is ask."

CHAPTER 19

Jorge was even twitchier than the other time he'd been in the interview room. He didn't relax even after Rhodes told him that he wasn't in any more trouble and that in fact Rhodes didn't even want to talk about Frankie or Guillermo.

"It's about the Environmental Reclamation Center," Rhodes said.

That topic didn't seem to appeal to Jorge any more than talking about his friends. He looked past Rhodes's shoulder at the wall as if he might see something interesting there.

"I saw Frankie there today," Rhodes said. "I thought he'd be long gone by now, maybe visiting his poor old mother down in Matamoros."

Jorge dropped his gaze to the table in front of him and thought that over.

"She's a good cook," he said.

"So I've heard, but he didn't go to Matamoros, did he."

"That's what you say."

"Just tell me why he showed up at the junkyard. That's all I want to know. What kind of deal do you have with Al?"

"We don't have no deal."

"Then why would Frankie show up there? Or was he there all along?"

Jorge shrugged.

"I think he was," Rhodes said. "He couldn't have gone back to Womack's place because Womack would've called me. So Frankie went where he knew he could hang out for a while."

"No way," Jorge said. "We got to stay away from there most of the time."

That was more like it. "Where could he go then?"

"Lots of places in town," Jorge said. "Old places."

"You mean empty buildings."

"Sure. Nobody bothers you in those places." He gave Rhodes an accusatory glance. "Mostly."

"You know, I've been wondering if you saw anybody there yesterday afternoon after closing time. You must look out the window now and then, especially after everybody's supposed to be gone home."

"We look out. We didn't notice anybody there."

"The parking lot was empty?"

"When I looked. I don't sit there and watch, you know?"

"Let's get back to Frankie and Al. What's the deal?"

"I told you we don't have no deal. Frankie must've needed money. Maybe he had something to sell."

Rhodes hadn't thought of that. If Lynn didn't carry much cash in her purse, Frankie might have been broke or close to it. He'd hidden out for the night and gone to see Al in the morning.

"Maybe he thought he could get a loan," Rhodes said. "You ever do that?"

"Sometimes. If we promise to bring something in. Just things we find, you know?"

"Right. Nothing that you steal."

"Now you got it. We don't steal."

Rhodes would let it ride for now. Jennifer would be looking into it, and he suspected she'd know plenty in a day or two. He'd gotten a search warrant, too, and he'd have a look around. He sent Jorge back to his cell and told Hack he was going to see Sandra Wiley.

"Buddy called in," Hack said. "He says he's been lookin' for that Frankie fella all mornin'. Hasn't see him, though."

"He'll turn up," Rhodes said, "unless he got some money. If he did, we won't see him again."

"Just as well," Hack said.

Sandra Wiley was wearing black and smoking. Her husband, Jimmy, was doing neither. He wore jeans and a clean white shirt, and he no longer looked like the football player he'd once been. He seemed to have shrunk, except for the head that wobbled on his now thin neck. The skin of his face sagged, and his eyes were sunk in his skull.

"How long do you think I should keep the shop closed?" Sandra asked. "I don't want to open too soon and look bad."

"Nobody's going to hold it against you if you open tomorrow," Rhodes said. "It's business."

They were all sitting in the Wileys' living room, in an old house that had once been much nicer than it was now. That was true of a lot of houses in Clearview. The furniture was shabby, and the TV set was an old one with a little box on top that allowed the Wileys to get reception by way of their antenna until they bought a new high-definition set. The room smelled of smoke, and Rhodes knew his clothes would, too, by the time he got out of there.

"That Lynn's always been trouble," Jimmy said, his voice almost a whisper. "Sandra would've let her go long ago if she hadn't brought in the customers."

"She must have lost a few, too," Rhodes said.

"Sure, but she was a good draw. You know how it is. People like to be around somebody like her, young and saucy."

It had been a long time since Rhodes had heard anybody described as saucy, if he ever had, but it seemed apt for Lynn.

"I didn't really come here to talk about Lynn," Rhodes said. "It's Jeff Tyler this time."

Sandra started coughing. She stubbed out her cigarette in an ashtray that was already overflowing, got out another one, and lit it.

"She's nervous about all this," Jimmy said. "She knows smoking's not good for her. Me either, for that matter, all that secondhand smoke coming in. What about Tyler?"

"He was Lynn's after-hours appointment yesterday," Rhodes said.

"She always cut his hair," Sandra said. "He wouldn't let Lonnie do it."

"You think Lonnie was jealous of Lynn?" Rhodes asked.

Sandra blew out a plume of smoke. "You

know about Lonnie?"

"Everybody knows," Rhodes said.

"Then you know he didn't have anything to be jealous of. Jeff didn't like women any more than Lonnie does."

"Seems to me that Lynn was better about keeping secrets, though," Rhodes said.

Jimmy wheezed what might have been a chuckle. "You can say that again."

Rhodes didn't say it again. Instead he asked Jimmy what he meant.

"I mean just what I said. You know about her and men. She sure kept that stuff secret."

Rhodes knew that, but it sounded as if Jimmy had something else in mind. Because of that whispery voice, it was hard to tell. Could Jimmy have been one of those men Lynn had kept secret? Not in his condition, surely.

"Life's not what it used to be," Jimmy said. "Used to, you could trust people. Remember how it was, Danny, back when we were playing for the Catamounts? Never had to lock a door in this town back then. People kept their word, and a handshake was as good as anything you might put on paper. Not anymore."

"Maybe we just remember it that way," Rhodes said.

"You think it's just because I've been sick and I'm getting old," Jimmy said. "That's not it. The world has changed, and not for the better if you ask me."

Rhodes believed that at least a few things were better now, but he hadn't come there to argue with Jimmy about that.

"One thing that's changed," Jimmy continued, "is that now we got illegals coming into town and living in old hotels and killing people. There wasn't any of that back then."

"I don't know that those men who stayed in the hotel were illegals," Rhodes said, "and I don't think they killed anybody."

"You didn't check out their status?"

"That's a job for the federal government," Rhodes said. "I'll find out later if they have their green cards, and if they don't, I'll notify ICE. The problem is that it might be a while before ICE gets around to doing anything, and they'll be bonded out. They might be bonded out already."

The truth of the matter was that Rhodes and his small department had their hands full just doing the things that the county expected of them, and enforcing the federal laws was an imposition on them. The state legislature was threatening to pass a law requiring local officers to ask about residence status, despite almost universal opposition from every law enforcement department there was. Rhodes would do what he was required to do, but until the law forced him, he was going to stay out of it as much as he could.

"You mean those killers might be out there walking the streets?" Jimmy asked. He was getting worked up, and his voice got even huskier. "I know they're the ones who killed Lynn. Bound to be. Nobody else could've done it."

"We're getting sidetracked," Rhodes said. "What I need to hear is what Jeff Tyler had to do with Lynn Ashton."

"Nothing except that she cut his hair," Sandra said. "Do you think the same person killed both of them?"

"If it was the same one," Jimmy said, "it was those illegals. I'll bet they were the ones. Have you tried to find any evidence that they did it, or are you in favor of letting them back out to terrorize the town?"

Sandra mashed out a cigarette and put a hand on Jimmy's arm. "You better calm down. You're going to have a stroke or something. You know what the doctor said."

Jimmy didn't calm down. "I thought we had good law in this town. I though Danny Rhodes was a good sheriff, but he can't see the truth when it's staring him in the face."

Rhodes could see he wasn't going to get any further here. He stood up and said, "If you can think of anything that would help, give me a call. I have everybody on the force working on this. We're doing the best we can."

Jimmy didn't say anything. Sandra reached for another cigarette. Rhodes found his own way out.

On his way to the reclamation center, Rhodes called Hack to check in.

"Guillermo and Jorge bonded out," Hack said. "I bet we never see 'em again."

"Maybe not," Rhodes said, thinking that Jimmy wouldn't be happy about that. "Who went their bail?"

"It was the AAA Bail Bonds guy. He didn't do much talkin'."

"All right. Anything else?"

"Mayor Clement's been callin' ever' five minutes. He's really in an uproar. You might wanna go by and see him. Jennifer Loam called, too. She said she had something already."

Rhodes thanked Hack and hooked the mic. He was near the Beauty Shack, so he pulled into the parking lot and stopped. He didn't see any movement behind the dusty windows, not that he thought it likely that

Jorge and Guillermo would be going back there. They hadn't had anything to go back for.

Rhodes dug his cell phone out of his pocket. He didn't have any affection for cell phones, but he'd started carrying one. Sometimes it came in handy, but he didn't give the number out to anybody other than Ivy, Hack, and the deputies.

He called Jennifer Loam first. Now she'd have his number, too. He shrugged off that thought and asked what she'd learned.

"I started doing some digging on the reclamation center," she said. "I found out who owns it."

"You work fast."

"So I've been told."

"And the owner is?"

"There are several, but the main one is the surprise."

"Surprise me, then," Rhodes said.

"Clifford Clement," Jennifer told him.

Instead of going to the reclamation center, Rhodes headed for the mayor's office. He realized on the way there that he'd missed lunch, as happened all too often, but it was too late to do anything about that now.

The inside of the city hall was cool, and the air smelled like the air in the courthouse. Rhodes didn't know what it was about old public buildings, but they all seemed to smell the same.

Alice King ushered Rhodes right into Clement's office and closed the door behind him. Clement sat behind his desk, and he looked both angry and depressed. He stared at Rhodes and didn't say anything, so Rhodes took a seat and stared back at him.

After a few seconds, Clement got tired of the staring game and said, "Have you found out who killed Lynn?"

"Not yet," Rhodes said. "I'm working on it."

"You'd better be. Things are getting serious."

"How serious would that be?"

"It turns out that my wife knew more than I thought she did about my private life."

Rhodes wasn't sure how much of a private life a married man was supposed to have, at least as far as his wife was concerned. Maybe Clement had different ideas about that sort of thing.

"You told me that you were having differences," Rhodes said.

"I thought the differences were about what she suspected," Clement said, "not what she knew." He scratched his beard. "She knew a lot more than I thought."

251

Rhodes figured this was the time to test one of his own theories. "You mean she knew about more than just Lynn. She knew about the blackmail."

Clement started, then recovered himself. "Who said anything about blackmail?"

"I did," Rhodes said. "Didn't you hear me?"

"I don't like your jokes, Sheriff."

"Hardly anybody does, but sometimes I can't help myself. Why don't you tell me about the blackmail."

"I thought you already knew."

"Not enough," Rhodes said. "You broke off with Lynn, but was it because she had someone else, or was it because she tried to get money from you?"

Clement thought about that. Rhodes waited, doing some thinking of his own, about Clement's wife and the possibility that she might get violent if she thought someone was trying to steal her husband.

"It was the money," Clement said after a while. "I have to tell you something about Lynn. She was fun to be with, she was pretty, she was young."

"We've gone over all of that," Rhodes said.

"There's more. She wasn't exactly blackmailing me. I suspected Fran knew something was up, but I didn't care. Like I said, we were having differences. So when Lynn started asking for money, I didn't really mind. She said she had bills to pay, car payments, that kind of thing. I was glad to help. Somehow Fran found out."

"I take it that Fran wasn't glad."

"No, she wasn't. Not at all. She hadn't said anything about it to me, though. She was holding it back. Then Lynn was killed."

Rhodes wondered if Fran had stopped holding it back and gone by to see Lynn. He needed to talk to Fran.

"She think you did it?" he asked Clement.

"She might have," Clement said. "I didn't, though. I told her that."

"Did she ask if you killed Lynn?"

"No," Clement said. "Naturally the murder came up when I got home yesterday, though. I didn't kill Lynn, so I told her that."

"Did she believe you?"

"I'm not sure. Do you believe me?"

"I'm not sure, either," Rhodes said.

"Damnation," Clement said. He leaned back in his chair. "What can I do to convince you?"

"Good question," Rhodes said. "Let's start with the Environmental Reclamation Center."

Clement sucked in a breath. "What do you mean?"

"You know what I mean. The junkyard with a fancy name that's a few blocks from here. The one that you're the part-owner of."

Clement didn't bother to deny it. "How did you find that out?"

"Good police work," Rhodes said with a straight face. "Now tell me all about it."

"I don't know anything about it. It's just something I have a monetary interest in. An investment. You know."

Rhodes didn't know. He didn't have a lot of investments.

"That's all it was," Clement went on. "A way to make a little money. I didn't look at it too closely."

"Somehow I doubt that. You're too smart to invest in something you don't know anything about."

Rhodes sat and listened to the air conditioner hum somewhere in the bowels of the building while Clement decided how much he was going to say.

"All right," Clement said after a while. "I do know something. I thought it was a good investment because it was good for the environment and because I thought I could make a little money."

Not exactly the kind of responsive answer Rhodes had hoped for. "Who are the other owners?"

"Some men from Houston. I met them when we did the deal. That's all I know about them."

"You know there's been some trouble there now and then," Rhodes said. "Don't you?"

"I don't have anything to do with the way the place is run," Clement said.

"You just take the money."

Clement frowned. "That's one way to put it, I guess. Not a very flattering one, but true enough. I don't manage the place. I'm just a silent partner."

"Well," Rhodes said, "let's go take a look at your investment."

CHAPTER 20

Clement hadn't wanted to go, but Rhodes had persuaded him by saying it would be good to have one of the owners around when he searched the place.

"Search the place?" Clements asked as they headed out of the office.

"There've been some more problems," Rhodes said.

As they drove the three blocks to the center, Rhodes told Clement a little about what had been going on. Clement claimed to have no idea about any of it. He said he didn't even know Al, but Rhodes wasn't sure he believed him.

When they got to the center, the gate was closed and the warehouse was shut. Rhodes wondered what had happened to Al. He might have decided to move on to another part of the state or the country. For that matter, he might have gone to Mexico with Frankie.

"Let's check the warehouse," Rhodes said. "There's a room I want to look at."

Clement didn't want to look at it, but Rhodes took him along. Although the warehouse door was closed, it wasn't locked. Rhodes flipped the hasp back and slid the door open with a metallic squeal.

"After you," he said.

Clement didn't move. "I'm not going in there."

"Why not?"

"I don't know what might be in there."

"There might be rats," Rhodes said. "In fact, I think I can promise you there are rats. They'll probably leave us alone, though."

"I don't like rats," Clement said.

Rhodes thought about Buddy. "Who does?"

"Probably nobody. You go on. I'll just stay here."

Rhodes asked Clement if he wanted to see the warrant.

"No. I don't care if you ransack the place. I'll wait for you."

"If that's the way you want it," Rhodes said and went inside.

He had his flashlight with him, and he turned it on. There must have been a light switch somewhere, but Buddy hadn't found it, and Rhodes didn't see it. He shone his light at the roof and saw some dusty fixtures dangling down. He still couldn't locate the switch that turned them on, however.

It was hot in the warehouse. The sun had been heating up the tin roof all day, and Rhodes started to sweat. He walked on back to the locked room, thinking that he could hear rats scurrying around behind the metallic junk. He told himself that he was just imagining it.

The locked room wasn't locked anymore. The door was wide open. Rhodes pointed his flashlight inside. He saw a couple of short bits of copper wire glint on the floor, but that was all. Rhodes had come too late. Al must have cleaned the place out as soon as he'd left the jail. Maybe Guillermo and Jorge had come along to help.

Rhodes thought that the other materials in the center had been obtained more or less legally and didn't need to be moved. If they'd been stolen, it would be hard to prove.

Rhodes looked around the room. He suspected that besides copper from various sources the room had held a few catalytic converters and maybe even some aluminum gutters ripped from houses, but there was no sign of them now.

He didn't need to look anymore. He knew he wouldn't find anything even if he did, so he went back outside. Clement was standing by the county car, and Rhodes went over to him.

"You need to get in touch with your partners," Rhodes told Clement. "You need to tell them that I know what they've been doing here."

"I don't know what you're talking about."

"That's what I'd say if I were in your position. It might even be true, not that I'm accusing you of anything. You just need to let them know that if there's another battery or catalytic converter or piece of copper wire stolen in this county, I'll find a way to trace it to them, and from them to you."

"I'm the mayor," Clement said, but Rhodes could tell his heart wasn't in it. "You can't talk to me like this."

"You might be the mayor, but you're also involved in a criminal enterprise."

"Now just a minute," Clement said. "That's slander."

"Only if I repeat it to someone else," Rhodes said.

"You don't dare repeat it because you don't have any proof of it."

"Not yet," Rhodes said, "but I'm working on it."

Clement stood up a little straighter. "Until you have some proof, you'd better watch what you say. Now take me back to my office."

"You sure you want to ride with me?"

Clement looked back toward the city hall. It was only three blocks, but it was a long three blocks.

"If you'll let me," he said.

"Get in, then," Rhodes said.

Rhodes dropped Clement off and drove straight to his house. It was in the part of town where some of the wealthy residents had built homes years ago, the same era that had seen the construction of the mansion that was now Ballinger's Funeral Home. These homes hadn't been turned to commercial purposes, however, and were all still occupied by people with a little money to spend.

Clement's house was big and imposing and one of the best looking in the neighborhood. The driveway was in the back, and Rhodes saw a big black Lexus SUV parked there. If he'd had any money to invest, Rhodes would've let Clement handle it, because he was obviously doing very well for himself.

Rhodes went up the sidewalk in front, feeling as if he should be looking for the servants' entrance. Lonnie Wallace's yard had looked good, but this one was perfect. The grass looked as if not one single blade was higher than any of the others. The flower beds were so perfect that a weed would have withered and died of embarrassment if it had dared to intrude into them.

Rhodes rang the doorbell, half expecting to be greeted by a butler dressed to perfection. Instead, Fran Clement opened the door. She was short, about five-four, and wore a white blouse and blue jeans with the cuffs rolled up to show her Nike walking shoes. She had dark eyes and short, very black fluffy hair. Rhodes wondered if she had it done at the Beauty Shack.

"Hello, Sheriff," she said. "Welcome to my humble abode. Won't you come in?"

Rhodes thought he got a faint whiff of liquor. "Thanks. I wanted to talk to you if you have a minute."

"A minute?" Fran gave a little laugh. "I have all day. Nobody's here but me. My husband's never around, but then you probably know that. You probably know all about him."

"Not much," Rhodes said. "Maybe you could tell me a few things."

Fran turned and walked down the hallway.

"I certainly could," she said, without turning around. "Come along, Sheriff. I'll tell you all."

Rhodes followed her into the den, a big room with a tile floor, lots of throw rugs, and one of the biggest flat-screen TV sets Rhodes had ever seen. There was plenty of seating in front of it: a leather-covered couch and two leather-covered recliners. A plate-glass sliding door looked out onto a concrete patio and another impossible lawn.

Fran sat on the couch. She curled her legs under her and said, "Sit down, Sheriff, and I'll unburden myself to you. I'll tell you all my sad little secrets."

Rhodes sat in a recliner. He wondered if she watched a lot of old black-and-white movies to get her dialogue. It sounded that way to him. He looked around the room but didn't see any bottles or glasses on the coffee table or end tables. Maybe he'd just imagined the smell of liquor. This room smelled more like some kind of flower. Lilacs, maybe. Rhodes had trouble putting a name to air-freshener odors.

"I don't need to know all your secrets," he said. "Just a few of them."

"My husband doesn't understand me," she said.

"That's not a secret I need to hear."

Fran leaned back on the couch and rested her left arm along the top. "You're not a bad-looking man, Sheriff. Has anyone ever told you that before?"

"Often," Rhodes said.

His answer threw Fran a bit off her stride. "They have?"

"Not *they*," Rhodes said. "It's usually my wife who tells me that."

"Oh." Fran frowned. "Your wife. We don't have to talk about her, do we?"

"No. I came here to talk about you and your husband."

"Who doesn't understand me."

"You mentioned that, but that's not the problem. The problem is Lynn Ashton."

"She's not a problem." Fran's frown changed to a smile. "Not now."

"I take it you're not grieving over her passing," Rhodes said.

Fran removed her arm from the back of the couch, curved the fingers of her left hand inward, and examined her nails. "Not a lot, no."

"Would you like to tell me why?"

"You know why or you wouldn't be here. She was trying to steal my husband from me."

"Just your husband? Or did she plan to

steal something else?"

"Well," Fran said, "him and his money. Cliff didn't think I knew about the money, but I did. Sometimes I wonder which one I'd miss the most."

Rhodes had an opinion about that, but he didn't express it. He looked out at the patio, where there was a white table with a furled green umbrella protruding from the middle.

"Cat got your tongue, Sheriff?"

"I was just thinking," Rhodes said.

"About me?"

"Sure enough, I was. Where were you the afternoon Lynn was killed?"

Fran gave her head a little toss. "Why, Sheriff. If I didn't know better, I'd think I was a suspect."

"Don't feel special," Rhodes said. "So is everybody else who knew Lynn."

Fran didn't want to hear it. "I like feeling special."

"You shouldn't," Rhodes said. "Not in this case. Where were you?"

"You're mean, Sheriff, and I think you're trying to trick me. I don't know where I was for sure because I don't know when she was killed."

"Let's say it was around six o'clock."

"Then I was here, the faithful wife, preparing a delicious evening meal for her wayward hubby."

"A sandwich?" Rhodes asked.

Fran laughed. It sounded forced. "You're a very funny man, Sheriff. Good-looking, too. My, my." She fanned a hand in front of her face. "Is it hot in here, or is it just me?"

Rhodes was tired of the act.

"This isn't a scene from a bad movie, Ms. Clement," he said. "This is about two murders that you're involved in whether you like it or not. You can't joke your way out of it. Now tell me where you were."

Fran took a breath and looked down. When she looked back up, she said, "I'm sorry. I know it's not a joke. I was here, like I said."

"Was anyone here with you?"

"You mean Cliff? The wayward hubby? I hardly see him in the evenings. He usually eats somewhere else, at the Dairy Queen for all I know. Then he runs around with his young floozies."

"Saucy" and "floozies" both in the same day. Maybe the old words were coming back. If they were, Rhodes was behind the curve.

"Floozies?" he asked. "He had more than one?"

"I don't know. I didn't even know he had

265

one for a good while. The wife is always the last one to know, they say. I only found out about the money because he forgot and left his checkbook here one day. So I looked at it."

"You have separate accounts?"

She nodded. "Yes, but I didn't know that. This was a secret separate account."

"It must have made you angry to find out about that."

Fran flared up. "Of course it did. I was furious. I told him that if he didn't break it off with her and give me half the money in that account, I'd . . . I didn't know what I might do."

She'd stopped herself just in time, but Rhodes had a pretty good idea of what she'd been about to say. Whether she said she'd kill Lynn or Clement was an open question, however.

"It would help if you could prove you were here when Lynn died," he said.

"I watched *Wheel of Fortune*. Does that help?"

"Not a lot."

"I can tell you what the final puzzle was."

"DVR," Rhodes said.

"What . . . ? Oh. I see what you mean. Are you going to arrest me?"

"Not yet. I'm going to think about it."

Fran cheered up at that. "You really are very attractive, you know."

"Don't start that again," Rhodes said. "It's just not going to work."

"I'm not trying to flatter you," Fran said. "I really mean it."

Rhodes smiled. "That's good. I'll be sure to tell my wife you said so."

Rhodes went back to the courthouse office. He needed a Dr Pepper, and he needed to think. A package of cheese crackers wouldn't hurt, either.

Rhodes knew that a lot of people who watched TV bought into the idea that crime-solving in the twenty-first century was purely scientific. Forensic wonders abounded. A drop of blood, a single hair, a particle of dust, a partial print, or a fingernail paring was all that was necessary for the modern crime-buster to bring a culprit to justice.

It didn't work like that in Blacklin County. It probably didn't work like that anywhere.

What worked for Rhodes was talking, asking questions, and weighing answers. Sometimes he even found a clue.

Not this time, however. He bought a Dr Pepper from the machine and got some of the yellow crackers with peanut butter because the machine didn't have the ones with cheese. He went up to his office and thought things over while he snacked.

What he came up with was a number of possibilities, starting with the simple fact that Lynn Ashton had been killed. Then Jeff Tyler had been shot. Lynn's purse was in the trash bin behind Jeff's store.

How it had gotten there? And why was it there? Rhodes came up with an answer that hadn't occurred to him before. What if Jeff Tyler had killed Lynn, taken her purse, and buried it in his trash, knowing that Frankie and his friends would come along, find it, and remove it? If they were caught with it, they'd be under considerable suspicion. Tyler might have intended to turn them in, but the killer had stopped him.

Another possibility was that someone who found out what Tyler had done got revenge for Lynn's death by killing Tyler. Maybe that person had even been the one to put the purse in the trash.

If that was the sequence of events, Lonnie was the one Rhodes liked for Tyler's death. Lonnie had shown a temper, and Tyler might have panicked and confided in him.

Rhodes saw a big problem with that version of events, however, and the problem was motive. Tyler didn't have one as far as

Rhodes knew. Maybe more digging would reveal one.

Or not.

Fran Clement was another good candidate, at least for Lynn's death. Say that Tyler had been sitting out in front of his store and had seen Fran's SUV at the Beauty Shack. The Lexus was a hard vehicle to miss. The fact that Jorge had said there was no car there didn't really mean much. He'd also said he hadn't been keeping watch and wouldn't have known.

If Tyler had seen Fran, it might have been his turn to try a little blackmail, but instead of paying him, Fran had shot him. Or Clifford had. That would mean that Rhodes had two killers to bring in.

Or maybe something else entirely was at work. Sharon Lawless had a good alibi, but what about Randy? Abby and Eric weren't in the clear yet, either, even though Rhodes had liked them and couldn't believe they'd killed Lynn or Tyler. Still, something had been said that nagged at him. He couldn't quite remember what it was, however. He wasn't worried about that. It would come to him.

Something else that Rhodes still wasn't clear about was the connection that Clement had with the reclamation center, and that was something he'd like to find out. Clement claimed not to know anything about the day-to-day workings of the place, but Rhodes didn't quite believe him. Surely he must know Al, even though he said he didn't.

Rhodes had Jennifer Loam's cell number, so he called her from the phone on his desk. He hoped she'd use that number rather than his own cell number the next time she called.

She answered on the third ring, and Rhodes asked if she had any new information for him.

"A little," she said. "I was just about to call you. This is going to be a great story for me to start my new online news with."

"What did you find out?" Rhodes asked.

"It's not so much what I found out. It's what I saw."

Rhodes wondered if everybody in the county had been taking lessons from Hack and Lawton. It wasn't the first time that this had occurred to him.

"What did you see?" he asked.

"I decided that I should have a look at the center, so I drove by there. You remember that you told me it was closed?"

"I remember."

"Well, it wasn't when I went by."

"When was that?"

"About an hour ago."

Rhodes would have been leaving the Clement house about that time. It was getting awfully late in the afternoon for the center to be open.

"I thought it would be a good idea to see who was there," Jennifer continued. "So I stopped and went into the office. The person in charge wasn't the one you called Al. It was a man called Mike. I told him I was doing a story for the paper on the environment and that I'd like to know about the center and all the good things it did. He was glad to tell me all about it. He even showed me around."

Rhodes could imagine Mike's delight at a reporter being there. Then he remembered that Jennifer wasn't just a reporter. She was also an attractive young woman. Rhodes suspected that Jennifer might have used some floozy wiles to get him to talk to her.

"What did you see?" he asked.

"A bunch of junk," Jennifer said. "I learned all about wearing gloves and safety glasses to handle batteries. I always thought people just threw them away."

"Not anymore," Rhodes said. "They're worth a little money to recyclers. People can even sell old ones that other people have thrown away." Which was another reason for Frankie, Guillermo, and Jorge to be checking out the alleys, he thought. "Surely that's not all you found out."

"No. While Mike was showing me around, I saw some men going into the office. There were four of them. I've never seen those four you arrested, but I'll bet they were the ones. Do you think they're running a theft ring there?"

"I don't know," Rhodes said, "but I think I'll try to find out."

CHAPTER 21

Rhodes met Buddy at the Beauty Shack parking lot.

"Hack said you needed some help," Buddy said. "What's going down?"

"I don't know for sure," Rhodes told him, "but I need some backup at the reclamation center."

Buddy paled. "Is this about the rats?"

"Just the human ones," Rhodes said.

"Oh. Good. I can handle those. I can handle the other kind, too. It's just that . . ."

"I know what you mean," Rhodes said. "Let's get up there and see what's going on before they close the place for the day."

When they got to the center, Rhodes drove through the open gate. Buddy drove in right behind him. They parked in front of the office and went inside.

The man called Mike was at a desk, looking over some papers. He might have been Al's brother, or at least a close cousin, though maybe just a little bigger.

Rhodes and Buddy waited until he looked up.

"Yeah?" he asked.

"Did you and Al study elocution together?" Rhodes asked.

The big word threw Mike. "Huh?"

"We're looking for Al," Rhodes said. "Also Guillermo, Frankie, and Jorge."

"Who?"

Rhodes repeated the names.

"Never heard of 'em," Mike said.

"You must've heard of Al. He works here."

"Not anymore, he don't. Had to let him go."

"Okay. Have you heard from Clifford Clement today?"

"Who?"

"You must've been taking owl lessons," Buddy said.

"Huh?"

Rhodes looked at Buddy. "It was over his head."

"You makin' fun of me?"

"Not us," Rhodes said. "You're the one who's having a good time, telling us you don't know Al, who's probably right there in the other room, along with the other fellas I mentioned."

"I'll have a look," Buddy said.

274

Mike moved from behind the desk and stood between Buddy and the door to the back room of the office.

"You can't go in there," Mike said. "It's not allowed."

"Sure it is," Rhodes said. "I have a search warrant."

"Then lemme see it," Mike said.

"It's in the car."

Mike crossed his arms. "Nobody's going in until I see the warrant."

Rhodes shrugged. "Wait here," he said to Buddy and went out to get the warrant.

As he reached out to open the car door, he realized he'd made a mistake. He pulled back his hand and ran around the office building just in time to see four men leaving by the back door.

"Hold it," he said.

They didn't hold it. All four started to run.

Rhodes felt tired. Dealing with those four was like training for the Olympic track team. As much as he hated it, there was nothing to do but to go after them. So he did.

They ran single file between heaps of junk with Jorge in the lead. He made an abrupt right turn, and Rhodes thought he was heading toward the building where he'd had the encounter with the bucket, but Jorge made another turn, dodged between a couple of rusty tractors, and disappeared behind a mountain of used tires. Guillermo and Frankie followed him.

Al wasn't so lucky, or so agile. When he tried to edge between the tractors, he stumbled and slipped. He fell against a tractor tire, bounced, and hit the ground. Before he could get up, Rhodes was right there with him.

Al wrapped his arms around Rhodes's legs and jerked. Rhodes fell backward, grabbing at the tractor to break his fall. He still hit the ground hard, and most of the air in his lungs whuffed out.

Al slid between the tractors. Rhodes stuck out a foot and tripped him.

Struggling to get his breath, Rhodes rose to his knees and lunged forward, managing to get hold of Al's foot. Al kicked at Rhodes's hand with the other foot, but Rhodes held on.

Al continued to kick, stirring up the dirt. Rhodes tasted grit and smelled dust. He sneezed and then pulled himself forward and got his other hand on the foot.

Al snorted like a bull and stopped kicking. He sat up and twisted around. Rhodes couldn't see very well from where he lay, thanks to the dust in his eyes, but he could see well enough to tell that Al had something in his hand, something heavy and hard, maybe a short length of pipe. That couldn't be good.

Al started to swing whatever it was at Rhodes, but Rhodes didn't let go of the foot.

Al didn't complete the swing, either, because Buddy said, "You better drop that pipe, punk, being as I'm holding a .44 Magnum, the most powerful handgun in the world, which if I pulled the trigger would blow your head clean off."

Buddy had been watching *Dirty Harry* again. Maybe Al had seen the movie, or maybe not, but he dropped his piece of pipe. Rhodes let go of his foot, stood up, and brushed himself off.

As he did, Jennifer Loam snapped his picture.

"Where did you come from?" Rhodes asked.

"I just happened to be passing by."

"I'll bet."

"When you said you were going to check things out, I thought I'd see what you were up to. So I just happened to be passing by." Jennifer gave Buddy an admiring glance. "I got here just in time. This is going to be the best possible break for me and my Web site."

"I can see how that might be. By the way,

that's a .38 Buddy's pointing at my friend Al, not a .44 Magnum."

Buddy grinned. "I know it, Sheriff, but .44 Magnum sounds a lot better."

"You have a point," Rhodes said.

Al was cowering on the ground between the tractors. The caliber of the pistol didn't seem to make any difference to him.

"Come on out of there, Al," Rhodes said.

Al crawled out from between the tractors. Buddy kept the .38 pointed at him, and Jennifer snapped more pictures.

"Stand up and put your hands behind you," Rhodes said.

Al stood up, but instead of putting his hands behind him, he dodged to the side so that Rhodes was between him and Buddy. Then he swung his big right fist at Rhodes's head.

Rhodes blocked the punch with his forearm and sent a short jab into Al's stomach, which wasn't as hard as Rhodes thought it would be. Or maybe Al just hadn't had time to prepare himself. At any rate Rhodes's fist sank a few inches into the stomach, and Al stumbled back until he hit the tractor, where he stood trying to suck some air.

"This is great, just great," Jennifer said. "I wish I'd put on the video setting, Sheriff. You'd be all over YouTube."

"It'd be like the screen test for the Sage Barton movie," Buddy said. "Have you read the Sage Barton books?"

"They're a lot of fun," Jennifer said. "Sage is a great character."

"Just like the sheriff here," Buddy said.

"In case you two have forgotten," Rhodes said, "I have an arrest to make. Turn around, Al, and put your hands behind you."

Al, still gasping, did as he was told, and Rhodes cuffed him. Buddy holstered his pistol. Jennifer took even more pictures.

"You won't be getting out of jail quite so soon this time," Rhodes told Al.

"Yeah," Al said.

They walked back to the office, where Mike was seated behind the desk. He was bent over and cuffed to the leg of the desk. Jennifer took a picture. Rhodes looked at Buddy.

"When I heard all the noise outside," Buddy said, "I thought I'd better see what was going on."

"I appreciate the help," Rhodes said.

"You're welcome," Buddy said. He gestured at Mike. "I couldn't just leave him here."

"I guess not," Rhodes said. "You can let him go now, though."

"We're not going to arrest him?"

"Can you think of a reason?"

"Harboring fugitives?"

"They were out on bail," Rhodes said.

"Suspicion of running a theft ring?"

"That's a good one," Rhodes said. "It might even stick. Let's haul him in."

Mike and Al didn't say anything at all. Buddy uncuffed Mike, then cuffed his hands behind him.

"Ready?" Rhodes asked.

Buddy nodded, and they took their prisoners outside, put them in the county cars while Jennifer photographed them, and took them to the jail.

"What about those other fellas?" Buddy asked Rhodes after Mike and Al had been booked and printed. "You know they must've been working with those two, stealing things for them and such."

"We suspect, but we don't know," Rhodes said. "We'll keep looking for them, but surely this time they won't come back."

"They seem to like it here," Hack said. "Blacklin County must be like home to 'em now."

"Here's what I think," Rhodes said. "I think Buddy's right. They were part of a theft ring, and they thought Al, or whoever really runs the reclamation center, would take care of them. It's different now. We've pretty much put them out of business, and they don't have any support. They aren't likely to stick around any longer. If they do, though, we'll arrest them the next time we see them."

"So they're not involved with the murders?"

"I don't think so," Rhodes said. "The purse is a connection, and the fact that a couple of them were squatting across from the Beauty Shack is a connection, but that's all we have. It's not enough to convince me. I think the thefts are all they've been up to."

"You want me to put out an APB anyway?" Hack asked.

"Good idea. Maybe we'll get lucky."

Rhodes smiled, thinking of Buddy's Clint Eastwood impersonation.

"What's so funny?" Hack asked.

"Nothing," Rhodes said.

Rhodes got home barely in time to give Speedo and Yancey a little exercise in the backyard before dark. After they'd romped for a while, Rhodes and Yancey went back inside.

"You're walking funny," Ivy said when he came into the kitchen.

"You think so?" Rhodes asked. "I've been

thinking I might give up sheriffing and try stand-up comedy."

"Not that kind of funny. You know what I mean."

"I had a little tussle this afternoon. I might be a little stiff."

Rhodes was sore, too. Rolling around on the ground didn't agree with him.

"Are you all right?" Ivy asked.

"I'm fine. Ready for anything."

"I didn't cook tonight. I thought we could go out. Is that okay?"

It sounded good to Rhodes. It meant no vegetarian chili.

"How about Max's place," he said.

Max was Max Schwartz, who'd moved to Clearview and opened a music store and a barbecue restaurant. The restaurant had been successful, and the music store had closed.

"That sounds all right," Ivy said.

"Wait a second," Rhodes said. "Tonight's Friday night."

"So?"

"So it might be a live music night at Max's Place. Seepy Benton might be singing. If you can call what he does singing."

"I like his singing," Ivy said. "Your deputy does, too."

"Ruth is . . ."

282

Rhodes stopped. He'd been about to say *mistaken*, but that might have led to a discussion of Ivy's own musical taste, and Rhodes didn't want to get into that. It was a losing proposition.

"Go on," Ivy said. "Finish the sentence."

"I was going to say Ruth likes him."

"I'll bet you were. Anyway, I like him, too. Shall we go?"

Rhodes was willing to put up with even Seepy's vocalizing as long as he didn't have to eat vegetarian chili again, so he said, "Race you to the car."

CHAPTER 22

Rhodes liked the way Max's Place smelled. The odor of smoked meat mingled with the odor of freshly cooked cobbler, and while Rhodes knew he wouldn't eat any of the cobbler, he could at least think about it.

Max Schwartz had been involved in a couple of Rhodes's investigations and had gotten to know the sheriff well enough to seat him far away from the tiny stage in the rear of the restaurant when Seepy Benton was performing. However, as Schwartz was leading Rhodes and Ivy to a table near the front, Rhodes spotted Ruth sitting with Benton near the stage.

"When's the next show?" Rhodes asked.

"In a few minutes," Max said.

"We'll sit with Seepy, then," Rhodes said.

"You sure about that?"

"I'm sure. I need to talk to him."

"Most of my customers really like his singing."

"There's no accounting for taste," Rhodes said.

Max didn't say anything to that. He just led them to the table.

"Mind if we join you?" Rhodes asked.

"Not at all," Seepy said, rising to his feet as Max pulled out Ivy's chair.

Ivy looked at Rhodes as if to say, *See what nice manners Seepy has?*

Rhodes pretended he didn't notice the look. He said to Benton, "Are you performing tonight?"

"Yes," Benton said. "I have a new math joke that I was just about to try out on Ruth. You got here just in time."

No, Rhodes thought, *I got here about three minutes too early.*

"Here it is," Benton said. "Why wouldn't the icosahedron go on a date with the dodecahedron?"

"That's a riddle," Rhodes said because he couldn't think of anything else to say, "not a joke."

"It's the punch line that makes the joke," Benton said. "Are you ready for it?"

"As ready as I'll ever be," Rhodes said. "Let me have it."

"Because their relationship was strictly Platonic!" Benton said and started to chuckle.

285

Rhodes didn't chuckle. He looked at Ruth and Ivy. They weren't chuckling, either, which made him feel a little better.

"What's the matter?" Benton asked. "Too esoteric? A little too inside for nonmathematicians?"

"That's it," Rhodes said. "Too inside."

Benton looked thoughtful. "I guess I won't use it, then. Anyway, I have a new song I'm debuting tonight. I don't want to hit my fans with too much new material at once."

Rhodes kept his mouth shut.

"The song's about Gandhi," Ruth said. "I've already heard it, and it's great."

"I'm sure it is," Ivy said, taking a menu from Max.

Rhodes waved away the menu. "I already know what I want."

"I'll send over a server," Max said, taking Rhodes's menu and leaving the table.

"Isn't anybody else eating?" Rhodes asked.

"I'm waiting until after the performance," Ruth said. "Seepy can't eat before he sings."

"It affects my voice," Benton said. "Not for the better."

"Oh," Rhodes said.

Ivy kicked him in the ankle as she studied the menu.

"How's our case going?" Benton asked. "Ruth tells me she hasn't been able to find out much by questioning the Beauty Shack customers."

"It's not that nobody wants to talk," Ruth said. "It's just that they don't seem to know much about Lynn. It's funny that she was talked about so much but nobody really knew her. The murder of Tyler complicates things a lot because the two just have to be connected some way or the other."

"Who did Lynn and Tyler both know?" Benton asked. "Find their mutual friends and acquaintances, and you'll find the killer."

"Seepy learned a lot of investigation skills in the academy," Ruth said.

Rhodes couldn't think of anything to say to that, but he didn't have to. He was rescued by a young woman who informed them that her name was Myra and that she would be their server. As if they didn't know.

Rhodes ordered the three-meat plate, the one with barbecued ham, beef, and ribs. That was a lot of food, so he ordered the small plate instead of the large one, feeling quite virtuous about his restraint. Ivy decided she'd just go to the salad bar. Rhodes wasn't surprised. He made it a point to stand up when she left the table, but so did Benton, so Rhodes wasn't one up on him.

"The thing of it is," Benton said as they sat back down, "people don't like the idea of a crazed killer walking the streets. They want to be able to sleep at night without having to worry about things like that. They want the killer brought to justice."

"First of all," Rhodes said, "we're not dealing with a crazed killer. We're looking for someone who acted in anger once and with deliberation once. I don't think there'll be any more killing."

"Why not?" Benton asked.

"Because of what he just told us," Ruth said. "The second killing was a result of the first one, but now it's over."

"How do we know that?"

"Experience," Rhodes said, "and it's the only thing that makes sense."

"So the second murder was to cover up the first one?"

"That's the way I see it," Rhodes said. "Tyler knew something that someone didn't want him to know. Now he can't tell anybody."

"What if he'd already told somebody?"

Rhodes didn't want to get into that. If Tyler had told Lonnie, Lonnie might be in danger if the killer knew, and Rhodes's experience might be leading him to a wrong conclusion. On the other hand, Lonnie might *be* the killer. Rhodes was still trying to work that out.

"There are other things, too," Ruth said. "We have clues, but we don't know what to make of them."

Rhodes didn't want to talk about that, either. The business with the purse still bothered him.

"What about those three men?" Benton asked. "The ones I helped you capture."

Before long, Benton would be taking all the credit just to impress Ruth. That was okay with Rhodes.

"They didn't have anything to do with it," Rhodes said. "Killers don't hang out across the street from the place where they killed somebody."

"They return to the scene of the crime, though, don't they?"

"He's joking," Ruth said. "I think."

"I'm a great kidder," Benton said.

He was, but Rhodes wasn't convinced he'd been kidding about the killers returning to the crime scene.

Ivy returned to the table with her salad plates on a tray. Rhodes and Benton stood up.

Ivy grinned and set her tray on the table. "And they say that chivalry is dead."

Rhodes helped her with her chair, and

everybody sat down again. The salad bar was bountiful, and Ivy had plates heaped with lettuce, pasta, cheese, and a lot of different kinds of vegetables, including broccoli, carrots, cauliflower, and tomatoes. Not that it all didn't look good, but Rhodes was glad he was getting meat.

The meat arrived even as he was thinking about it, along with a side bowl of sauce, three pieces of bread, and a couple of extra napkins. Rhodes and Ivy ate while Benton and Ruth talked about the murders.

Benton's opinion was that the Environmental Reclamation Center was somehow involved in the crimes, but Rhodes thought Benton was saying that only because he'd helped out a little there. Rhodes stopped eating long enough to tell them a little about his adventure that afternoon and the arrests of Mike and Al.

"They're guilty of something, all right," Rhodes said. "Theft, mainly, and employing those three fellas to steal for them. But that's all. They aren't killers."

"What about Jeff Tyler being Lynn's last appointment?" Benton asked. "Is there any connection between him and the men from the center?"

"I thought about it," Rhodes said, remembering the purse. "It's possible, but I'm still working on it."

Benton looked at him. "It looks like you're eating."

"I'm trying to. Even a sheriff deserves a break and a good meal now and then."

"No offense," Benton said.

"None taken," Rhodes told him and continued to eat.

He was just about finished when Benton looked at his watch and stood up.

"Time for my performance," he said. "I'll sing the new one first."

He walked over to the little stage, where there was a chair and a microphone. Benton's guitar case was there, too, leaning against the back wall of the restaurant.

"He's really good," Ruth said. "I think he could sing professionally if he weren't so dedicated to his teaching."

"Mmfff," Rhodes said, pretending his mouth was full.

Ivy kicked him in the ankle again.

Benton got his guitar, got seated, and tuned up. When he was satisfied, he said, "Good evening."

A couple of people applauded. Ruth was one. Rhodes was wiping his mouth and face. Eating ribs could be a messy business.

"I'm going to play a new song tonight," Benton said. "Let me tell you a little of the history behind it."

Rhodes hoped they weren't going to get a lecture about Gandhi, and they didn't. Benton told a story about going for a job interview wearing jeans, a shirt, and his hat. The hat was by the chair. Rhodes hadn't noticed it before, and now Benton put it on.

"When they asked me why I wasn't wearing a suit," Benton said, "this is what I told them. Gandhi wore a loincloth." He strummed a couple of chords. "If any of you are wearing loincloths tonight, feel free to wave them around in time to this song."

That got a few chuckles, though not from Rhodes, and Seepy launched into his song. Rhodes couldn't quite make out all the words, but he caught most of the chorus.

"I said Gandhi wore a loincloth.
He did not wear a suit.
Gandhi wore a loincloth,
When he went to see King George.
Gandhi wore a loincloth,
He never wore a suit.
And if it's good enough for Gandhi,
Then it's good enough for me."

The song was followed by polite applause. Rhodes looked at Ivy, who was looking at

Ruth. Ruth was applauding loudly. She had a big smile on her face, so Rhodes applauded, too, not loudly, while he wondered when songs had stopped rhyming. He was far out of the loop when it came to currently popular songs, so maybe rhymes had gone out of style some time ago.

On the other hand, maybe it was just a Seepy Benton quirk. It was a toss-up, and it didn't really matter. Either way, it was going to be a long evening.

After Benton had finished his set, he stood and gave a little head-tilted bow while the diners who were left in Max's Place applauded his performance. Rhodes thought that even Ruth's applause was a little less enthusiastic than it had been at the beginning, but that might have been only his imagination.

When the applause had died, which didn't take long, Benton returned to the table, looking pleased with himself and his show.

"I think I was in good voice tonight," he said as he sat down.

"You sure were," Ruth said.

"I thought the new song went over well, too."

"It sure did."

Rhodes made a noise that could've been

taken for assent by an optimistic person, which Benton emphatically was. Rhodes waited for a kick from Ivy, but it didn't come.

"I've been thinking," Benton said.

"Always a dangerous thing," Rhodes said, and this time Ivy did kick him. His ankle was taking a real beating.

"I can sing and think at the same time," Benton said, as if Rhodes hadn't interrupted. "Not many people can do that. I mean, I can sing and think about completely unrelated things. Like cell phones."

That got Rhodes's interest. Maybe Benton had come up with something useful.

"Tell us what you thought," Rhodes said.

"You had me look for Lynn Ashton's appointments on her phone," Benton said, "but not for anything else. That might have been a mistake."

"Why?"

"You could be underestimating Lynn. She could have put other things on the phone that would help you."

"I thought you looked."

"I looked for what you asked me to look for," Benton said. "It was so easy to find that I didn't stop to consider what else she might have put on the phone. I just stopped when I found what you wanted. I'd have kept looking if I hadn't had to get back to the college. I was distracted by my duty to my students."

As much as it galled Rhodes to admit it, Benton had a point.

"I could look at it tonight," Benton said.

As soon as the words were out of his mouth, he gave a jerk and got a funny look on his face. Rhodes grinned. It was about time someone else got his ankle kicked.

"You and Ruth must have plans for the evening," Rhodes said. "You can come by tomorrow and take a look."

"Saturday?"

"You don't have to make it early," Rhodes said.

"All right. I'll be there."

"Don't bring the guitar," Rhodes said.

Nobody laughed, but at least Ivy didn't kick him.

CHAPTER 23

"You need to behave better when you're out in public," Ivy told Rhodes as they drove home from Max's place.

They were in Rhodes's Edsel, which he'd bought on a whim during the course of an investigation. He thought it was a great car for one that was over fifty years old, but it had maintenance issues. It was running a little rough, and Rhodes thought it needed new spark plugs. Not to mention a major motor overhaul, which it wasn't likely to get anytime soon.

"I'll try to mind my manners from now on," Rhodes said.

"I'll bet," Ivy said.

As they got near the house, Rhodes saw two vehicles parked in front. There was a streetlight on the corner, so Rhodes could see them well. One was a black Cadillac Escalade. It was big, but not that much bigger than Rhodes's Edsel. Unlike the Edsel, however, it was polished to a high sheen. It looked like it was covered with black ice. Parked right behind it was a green Buick LeSabre.

Rhodes pulled into his driveway and stopped.

"Who's that?" Ivy asked, looking at the cars with suspicion.

"Don't know," Rhodes said. "You go on in."

"I don't think so," she said.

"When you don't know who might be waiting on you, it's better not to take any chances."

"You're with me," Ivy said. "I'm not worried."

Maybe she wasn't, but Rhodes was. He looked over at the two cars and saw Clifford Clement get out of the Buick.

"That's the mayor," Ivy said. "I wonder what he wants."

"I'll find out," Rhodes said. "You stay in the car."

This time Ivy didn't argue with him. He got out of the Edsel, and Ivy got out at the same time. He hadn't really expected her to stay inside it. She disappeared into the shadows, and Rhodes walked over to meet Clement.

"I didn't want to bring them here," Clement said as he neared Rhodes.

"Bring who?" Rhodes asked.

Clifford looked over his shoulder at the Escalade. "Them."

"I guessed that much," Rhodes said. "What I mean is, who are they?"

"Some men from Houston."

Rhodes didn't know a lot of men from Houston, so he didn't think they were there on a social call.

"Your business partners?" he asked.

"I never even met them before," Clement said. "When I invested in the reclamation center, I just thought it was a good deal, like I told you, something that would bring me a fair return on my money. I didn't know I'd be dealing with people like this."

Before Rhodes could ask what the people were like, the doors on the Escalade opened, and four men got out. Rhodes noticed that the interior lights didn't come on when the doors opened. He didn't think that anything had gone wrong with the Cadillac. Some people just didn't like much light, and they made sure it didn't bother them.

All four men walked over to where Rhodes and Clement stood. Three of them wore shirts that Mikey Burns might have envied. The fourth wore a black Western shirt with

298

a string tie held together by a turquoise slide.

"You the sheriff?" the one wearing the tie asked.

"I am," Rhodes said. "Who are you?"

"Name's Nolan."

"Ryan?"

Silence.

"It's a joke," Clement said after a few seconds. "Nolan Ryan's famous around here. He pitched for the Texas Rangers."

"I don't follow football," Nolan said.

Rhodes didn't know if he was putting them on, so he didn't laugh.

Nolan continued without giving the rest of his name. "What I'm here for is to look after my business interests at the Environmental Reclamation Center."

"That's good," Rhodes said. "Somebody needs to look after them."

"I hear that you've been spending a lot of time there," Nolan said.

"You've had some problems," Rhodes said.

He looked at the other three men, all of whom looked a bit like Mike and Al. Rhodes wondered if they all came from the same family. Cousins, maybe. The men looked back at him, saying nothing.

"Problems," Nolan said. "I guess you

could say that. Mike and Al, they don't know a lot about how to run a business. They could've made a mistake."

"Or two," Rhodes said.

"Sure. Or two." Nolan spread his hand. "Anyway, I wanted to talk to you personally to tell you that you don't have to worry about that kind of thing happening anymore. I've been to your jail, and I had a little talk with Mike and Al. They told me they were sorry they'd caused you any trouble. They won't do it again."

"They might not be in a position to do it again," Rhodes said.

"I think they will. I got 'em a good lawyer. They'll be out on bail tomorrow."

"A good lawyer. Let me guess. Randy Lawless."

"Yeah," Nolan said. "Lawless. Funny name for a lawyer if you ask me, but they tell me he's the best one around here."

"He is," Rhodes said. "That doesn't mean he wins every time."

"I think he'll win this time."

"Let me ask you something," Rhodes said.

The three men in the Hawaiian shirts moved a step closer to him. Nolan held up a hand, and they stopped.

"Sure," Nolan said. "I got time. Ask me."

"What about Frankie, Guillermo, and Jorge?"

"Never heard of 'em."

"Why don't I believe you?"

Nolan tensed. The other three took another step forward.

Rhodes looked at them. "Are these your minions? They must come in handy. Sometimes I wish I had some minions myself."

"You're not funny, Sheriff," Nolan said.

"Neither are you. You come to my house, you more or less tell me to mind my own business because I'd better stay out of yours, and you bring these three goobers with you to back you up. I don't know how people down in Houston do business, but people here don't act like that."

Clement, who'd kept quiet so far, put out a hand and touched Rhodes on the arm.

"Sheriff . . ." he said.

"Mr. Mayor, you'd better go on home," Rhodes said. "If I were you I'd sell out my interest in Mr. Nolan's business tomorrow if I could find anybody to buy it."

"Good idea," Clement said. "I'm leaving now."

He walked away and got in his car. Nobody said anything until Clement had driven away.

"You take a lot of chances, Sheriff," Nolan

said when Clement turned the corner at the end of the block.

"That's why the county pays me so well," Rhodes said.

"Maybe they don't pay you enough. You got good insurance?"

"Good enough. Now tell me about Frankie and his friends."

"Like I said, I never heard of 'em. I mean it. What Mike and Al did, that was on their own hook. I'll find out. If they went against my business practices, they'll get their pay docked, and I might even fire 'em, but I don't know anything about those people you mentioned. Hell, I couldn't even say the names right if I tried."

Rhodes didn't believe a word of it.

"We're gonna leave now, Sheriff," Nolan said. "You have a nice night."

"You, too," Rhodes said. "But before you go, I have one more question."

Nolan had already started back to the car, but he turned back. All three of his minions turned, too.

"What?" Nolan asked, with only a little edge in his voice.

"Do your minions get to take the pistols out from behind their backs when they ride in the car? Having a gun rub against you can be uncomfortable on a long drive."

"You have good eyes, Sheriff. My associates are licensed to carry, of course."

"I never doubted it," Rhodes said.

"Is that all you wanted to know?"

"That's all."

"Good. See you around, Sheriff."

Rhodes watched as Nolan and the minions got into the Escalade.

One of the minions was the driver.

When the SUV was out of sight, Rhodes walked over to the corner of the house near the driveway where Ivy stood in the deep shadows. She was holding the 12-gauge shotgun that Rhodes kept in the bedroom closet just in case he ever needed a little home defense. The shotgun pointed at the ground.

"Nolan's minions can't see as well as I can," he said. "They never even knew you were here."

"You didn't look over here," Ivy said.

"No, but I knew where you were going."

"How did you know?"

"I'm a careful observer and a keen student of human behavior."

Ivy grinned. "Plus you know me all too well."

"That, too. Did you load it?"

"Are you joking? The box of shells is right there on the shelf. How could I forget?"

"Just asking," Rhodes said.

"I would have used it, too," Ivy said.

"A shotgun?" Rhodes asked. "I was standing right by them. You'd have hit me, too."

"I thought just the sound of the pump was supposed to discourage them."

"It would've discouraged me, all right. I'd have hit the ground fast."

Ivy laughed. "Next time I'll just release Speedo on them."

"Speedo would just want to be friends. Yancey, too. Release Sam on them. That might do the trick."

"I hope there won't be a next time," Ivy said. "Do you think they'll be back?"

"Maybe not back to the house," Rhodes said, "but I have a feeling I haven't seen the last of them. Nolan's not happy with the way things are going at the reclamation center."

"Who's Nolan?"

"The one who did all the talking. He owns the place, or at least speaks for the owners. He says he's straightened out Mike and Al, and maybe he has. Or maybe he'll just move them somewhere else. There used to be another fella in charge of the place, but he's gone now. Maybe he retired."

"Or maybe he's sleeping with the fishes."

"You've been watching *The Godfather* again."

"I don't think they ever said that in *The Godfather*, or on *The Sopranos*, either."

"Well," Rhodes said, "they should have if they were trying to be authentic."

"Right," Ivy said. "All the real gangsters talk like that."

"Let's go in the house and put the shotgun in the closet," Rhodes said.

"Good idea," Ivy said.

CHAPTER 24

The next morning, Rhodes got to the jail early, but Mike and Al were already gone.

"AAA Bail Bonds again?" Rhodes asked Hack.

"Yep. Those two didn't seem to be bothered much by their night in our accommodations. I don't think they expected to be around long."

"You remember what you said yesterday about powerful friends?"

"Yep," Hack said.

"You were right," Rhodes told him.

"You know who they are?"

"That's my job," Rhodes said. "To know things like that."

"I don't see how you coulda found out."

"I'm the sheriff," Rhodes said. "I have lots of sources."

He liked to give Hack a little dose of his own medicine now and then just to let him know how it felt.

Hack looked hurt, as if he knew what was going on. "You ain't gonna tell me?"

Rhodes sat down at his desk and started to go through some papers. "Maybe later."

"You're gettin' mean in your old age," Hack said.

"Mean? Me?"

"I notice you didn't say anything about *old*?"

"That's because I know you're joking."

"That's what you think," Hack said. He might have gone on, but the door opened, and Seepy Benton came in.

"I'm not interrupting anything, am I?" he asked.

"Not a thing," Rhodes said. "We were just having a conversation about something or other. I'm not sure exactly what."

"Hmpf," Hack said.

"I came about the phone," Benton said.

He was wearing his hat, a white shirt, blue jeans, and jogging shoes. He sounded eager to get started with his work on the phone.

"You're a little early," Rhodes said.

"I thought it might be a good idea for me to come as soon as I could. For all we know, Lynn might even have named her killer. All we have to do is find it."

"You don't really think that," Rhodes said.

"Why not? Anything's possible."

307

Rhodes didn't believe that, but he liked Benton's optimism and enthusiasm.

"You have a seat," Rhodes said. "I'll get the phone."

When Rhodes returned from retrieving the phone, Benton was sitting at Ruth's desk, talking to Hack. Benton was explaining his new exercise program. Rhodes didn't think Hack was interested, but Benton taught college students. Lack of interest was no deterrent.

"I was just telling Hack about the benefits of walking," Benton told Rhodes. "It's easy, it's safe, and it's really good for you. I've lost five pounds since I started walking every morning."

"Really," Rhodes said, handing him the phone.

"I feel better, too," Benton said. He turned on the phone, ignoring any sarcasm in Rhodes's tone. "It's great to get out there in the morning air. It smells great before the day heats up, and Bruce likes to go with me. It's good for him, too."

Hack was shaking his head, but Benton had turned to Rhodes and couldn't see him.

"So the real reason you got here early," Rhodes said, "is because you'd finished your morning stroll."

"That, and I wanted to help out." Benton

was looking at the phone while he talked. "The sooner I get started, the sooner I might find something that will help find Lynn's killer."

"I don't think you'll find anything," Rhodes said.

"Do you know about the dog in the night-time?" Benton asked, continuing to work with the phone.

"You mean Bruce?" Rhodes asked.

"Ha," Hack said.

Rhodes looked at him. "*Ha*? What does that mean?"

"It means you don't know about Sherlock Holmes, that's what it means."

"I know about Basil Rathbone and Nigel Bruce."

"That's because you watch a lot of old movies," Benton said. "Everybody knows that Jeremy Brett was much better than Rathbone."

"I'm the sheriff," Rhodes said. "I could shoot you and Hack would swear it was an accident. No jury in the world would convict me after the prosecutor told them what you said."

"You wouldn't do that," Benton said, not looking up from the phone. "Would you?"

"He might," Hack said, "but I wouldn't back him up in court. Anybody ought to know about that dog."

"Which dog?" Rhodes asked.

"In the nighttime," Hack said. "The one that didn't bark."

"Oh," Rhodes said. "That dog."

"That's right," Benton said. "That was the curious incident. The dog didn't bark. Holmes knew it wasn't what happened that mattered, at least in that case. It was what *didn't* happen. So maybe it's not what I found on the phone that matters. It's what I didn't find."

Rhodes was glad they'd finally gotten around to the point of the discussion.

"What was it that you didn't find?" he asked.

"I still haven't found it," Benton said. "If Lynn had so many men friends, she'd have their numbers in her phone. They're not here."

"She might have had another phone for that," Rhodes said. "If it was a big secret."

"You really think she was that complicated?"

"She was smart," Rhodes said. "She was able to keep things pretty well hidden. Nobody knew how many men she was dating." He wasn't going to mention her blackmailing. "There were a lot of things people didn't know."

"If she was smart, all she had to do was hide the numbers somewhere. I can't find them, so she didn't hide them."

"You think you're that good?"

"Sure," Benton said. He held up the phone. "She has her appointment book here. She has a list of contacts, too, but it's just people you'd expect. People at the shop, other people who are all on the client list. No boyfriends, no nothing."

"What you need is some time with her home computer," Rhodes said.

Benton couldn't believe it. "You haven't looked at the home computer?"

"I'd planned to have Ruth do that, but she's been busy. I don't have enough deputies to do everything that's needed around here."

"You haven't looked at her Facebook page or checked to see if she had a blog?"

Rhodes knew about those things, and it occurred to him that the first place he should have checked was Facebook. It seemed as if that site was helping law enforcement more and more often because of the kinds of things people posted there.

"What about Twitter?" Benton asked. "Did you check to see if she'd been tweeting?"

Rhodes admitted that he hadn't done

311

those things. "But Ruth would have as soon as I got her started on it."

"I know that it's her job," Benton said. "I don't want to interfere."

Rhodes kept a straight face, but it wasn't easy. Things must be getting serious between Benton and Ruth if he was that thoughtful of her. If it had been Buddy's job to look at the computer, Benton wouldn't have hesitated.

"You won't be interfering," Rhodes told him. "She needs to be out on patrol anyway."

"If you say so." Benton stood up and took Rhodes the phone. "I'm ready when you are."

Rhodes returned the phone to the evidence room. This time when he came back, Jennifer Loam was talking to Benton. She was telling him about her Web site.

"It's called *A Clear View of Blacklin County*," she said.

"That's a great name," Benton said. "What about your job with the paper?"

"I'm no longer an employee of the *Clearview Herald*," Jennifer said. "I'm on my own. I already have some advertisers lined up, so I'll be okay."

Rhodes hoped she was right. She didn't sound overly confident.

She turned to Rhodes. "I'm here to see if you have any more scoops for me. Have you found Lynn Ashton's killer?"

"Not yet," Rhodes said. "Have you found out any more about the owners of the reclamation center?"

"Yes, but before I tell you, let me say that those pictures I took yesterday are great."

"What pictures?" Benton asked.

"You'll see," Jennifer said. "Just log on to the Web site. I haven't officially opened it, but it's already live. Sheriff Rhodes is doing his best Sage Barton impersonation."

Rhodes sighed.

"I'm sold," Benton said. "I love Sage Barton."

"You, too?" Jennifer asked. "I've just finished the latest book. Claudia and Jan sent me a copy. It's great."

"They sent me one, too," Benton said. "I've read about half of it. I don't see much resemblance between Sage Barton and Sheriff Rhodes, though."

"It's about time somebody admitted that," Rhodes said, though oddly enough his feelings were a little hurt. "I'm nothing at all like him."

"I might feel differently when I see the pictures," Benton said. "What's that URL?"

Jennifer told him, and then she told

Rhodes what she'd found out, which was that the reclamation center was indeed owned by people from outside the county and maybe even from Houston but that it would be next to impossible to find out who the real owners were.

"It's all hidden in various corporate names," she said. "It would take a long time to untangle."

"I met one of the principals last night," Rhodes said, "or at least he claimed to be. I have a feeling we might be having more trouble with that place, but our mayor won't be involved. He'll be selling his share as soon as he can."

Rhodes went on to tell Jennifer and Benton about his visitor of the previous evening. Hack listened in, too, though he pretended not to.

"You can't use any of that on your Web site," Rhodes told Jennifer when he'd finished. "It's off the record."

She looked disappointed but agreed.

"Now Dr. Benton and I have a little investigating to do," Rhodes said.

"About the murders?"

"Yes, but you can't come along. This is coply business."

Benton puffed up a little at that. He liked being a part of the coply business, which was why Rhodes had used the phrase in the first place.

"You'll let me know when you crack the case, won't you?" Jennifer asked.

"When *we* crack the case," Benton said.

"Right," Jennifer said.

"You'll be the first one to hear," Rhodes told her.

Jennifer left, but Benton wasn't ready to go anywhere. He was leaning forward, looking at the computer.

"This is great, all right," he said. "You're more like Sage Barton than I thought."

"What are you talking about?" Rhodes asked.

"These pictures that Jennifer took. They're right here in high res and full color. You're going to be famous when these go viral."

"Viral?"

"That means they'll be all over the Internet. Come look."

Rhodes looked at the computer, where Benton had called up Jennifer's Web site.

"See?" Benton asked. "Look at you, punching that guy right in the gut."

"Yeah," Hack said. Rhodes hadn't even heard him leave his chair and join them. "That's a Sage Barton move if I ever saw one. Look at that one where Buddy's holding his gun on the fella. Buddy's gonna love that. What's that writin' under 'em say?"

Benton read it aloud. "Blacklin County Sheriff Dan Rhodes battles miscreant with bare hands."

"Miscreant?" Rhodes asked.

"Means somebody who breaks the law," Hack said.

"Thanks," Rhodes said. "I just wondered why she'd use a word like that."

"Kinda gussies things up," Hack said. "Makes it more interestin'. I gotta bookmark that site."

"Everybody in the county will bookmark it," Benton said, "as soon as they find out about it."

"Great," Rhodes said. "Just great."

"We could've just used the computer at the jail," Benton said when he and Rhodes arrived at Lynn Ashton's house.

"For the Facebook stuff, sure," Rhodes said, "but not for anything else. The personal things, remember? The things you were talking about last night. Besides, we spent too much time looking at nonwork-related stuff. We needed to get busy."

Benton grinned. "I see what you mean."

Rhodes didn't grin back.

"I'll look at the social networking things first," Benton said, suddenly all business.

"That will be easy to find."

"If she used her real name and not a screen name," Rhodes said.

"Nobody uses screen names for Facebook and Twitter," Benton said. "Well, hardly anybody. Even if she did, I could find them on the computer."

They went inside the house, and Rhodes showed Benton the computer.

"It's not a Mac," Benton said.

"Does that make a difference?" Rhodes asked.

"Macs don't get viruses, Macs can run for weeks without rebooting, Macs have great customer support, Macs —"

Rhodes was sorry he'd asked. He held up a hand. "The computer in your office isn't a Mac."

"That's the college's fault. I don't understand why so many educational institutions bought into the PC market. They'd have been so much better off with Macs that it's hard to explain. If I were in charge —"

"Well, you're not," Rhodes said, "and this is a PC. Will that make a difference in what you can do with it?"

"No. I can work with any platform."

"Then it's not a problem, so I'll let you get started. I'm going to poke around some while you do the technical stuff."

Benton sighed, nodded, and sat down at the computer. Rhodes went on into the bedroom to take another look around. He didn't know what he thought he might find. A secret compartment in the closet? A wall safe hidden behind a mirror? If it were that simple, life would be sweet.

He wandered around, not seeing anything of interest, berating himself for not having thought of the social networking things earlier. That was a rookie mistake, or the mistake of someone who'd grown up in a different era. It was also a mistake he wouldn't make again. Benton would never let him live it down if he found something on a Facebook page or in a tweet.

If there was something in her e-mail, Rhodes would feel bad about that, too. He should have had Ruth check it immediately. It might have saved Jeff Tyler's life.

Rhodes was still trying to figure out Tyler's place in the whole thing when he thought about something that should have occurred to him much earlier. Maybe it didn't mean anything at all, but it was something that would bear looking into. He filed it away for the moment and got down on his knees to look under Lynn's bed, the only place in the room he hadn't looked on his previous visit. He didn't see anything other than a few dust bunnies.

There was a chair over by the dresser, and when Rhodes was through looking under the bed, he got up and went to sit in it. Looking around the room, he thought about Lynn Ashton. All that was left of her was here in this house, in the closet, under the bed, on the computer. Well, there was her little red car, but there hadn't been much of her left there, either. Someone had killed her, and before long all traces of her would be gone.

Jeff Tyler had owned his store, but soon enough the people who had put things there on consignment would come and get them and take them away. Tyler's own things would remain until either his heirs took them or someone broke in and stole them or they just mouldered away inside the old building.

Lonnie was likely to be Jeff's heir, and Rhodes wondered what Lonnie would do with the store. Sell it if he could, maybe, or go into business for himself. That thought reminded Rhodes of something else he needed to consider. Things were starting to come together in his head, the way they sometimes did. He didn't necessarily like everything he was thinking, but at least he had the illusion that he was making progress. That was something, he supposed.

CHAPTER 25

Rhodes went back to the room where Benton was working at the computer. Benton turned around in the chair and said, "She didn't have a Twitter account. She must not have had time for that since she worked all day. I didn't really expect to find one since it wasn't on her phone."

"What about Facebook?" Rhodes asked. "Wouldn't that have been on her phone, too?"

"Not if she couldn't get to it at work. She'd have had it here, where she could update it in the evening."

"So did she have it here?"

"Yes," Benton said, but he didn't look happy about it.

"What's the matter?" Rhodes asked.

"She didn't ever update it. She just had the account. Now and then someone would post on her wall, but she never responded. She must not have had much interest in social media."

Rhodes thought about it. "No wonder. She worked all day most days, and she had a pretty active social life. What about e-mails?"

"She didn't do much e-mailing, either," Benton said. "She had an account that's not even password protected. She got a lot of spam, like everybody does, but she doesn't have much personal e-mail, just an occasional joke from Lonnie Wallace. She didn't even bother to respond to most of them."

"Who else e-mailed her besides Lonnie?"

"Nobody. She must not have given out her address to any of her clients or boyfriends."

"What about an address book?" Rhodes asked.

"Nothing," Benton said. "No diary. No YouTube channel. No blog that I can locate."

"You have a YouTube channel?" Rhodes asked.

"I showed you in my office. Seepybenton. All one word. I have a few videos of my singing on it. You should check it out."

"I'll do that the next time I'm on YouTube," Rhodes said, which wasn't a lie since he didn't expect he'd ever be on YouTube.

"I don't think Lynn ever even looked at YouTube," Benton said.

He shook his head as if he couldn't understand how anybody could live a life that was so unplugged. Rhodes could understand, though. He wasn't any more plugged-in than Lynn had been. It was easy enough to live like that if you didn't ever get into computers in the first place. For his part, Rhodes couldn't imagine what it must be like to tweet or to have a Facebook page.

Rhodes believed that most people in Blacklin County, at least the ones over forty, were like him. They watched television, and they might use computers in their work, but that was the extent of their electronic experiences. Rhodes thought that was enough. Sometimes it was more than enough.

"Did you find anything at all?" he asked. "Anything out of the ordinary, anything that might give me some help?"

"No," Benton said. "I looked for things that might be connected to the reclamation center, but if there's something there, I couldn't find it."

The implication was that he'd have found it if it had been there.

"I'm not surprised there's nothing about that," Rhodes said. "There's no connection between the murders and the center."

"You sound pretty sure about that."

Look who's talking, Rhodes thought.

"I'm sure," he said. "I could be wrong, but I don't think so."

"You still don't know who killed Lynn and Tyler, though."

"I'm getting closer," Rhodes said, but he didn't explain what he meant. "Did you find anything else?"

"I wish I could tell you that I did," Benton said, "but I didn't, so I can't."

"Don't feel bad," Rhodes said. "It was something we had to try. I should have thought of it sooner. In this case it didn't matter, but it might the next time. I need to think more like the people who are wired into things. People like you."

"Nobody's like me," Benton said.

"Truer words were never spoken," Rhodes said.

Rhodes dropped Benton off at the jail, where he'd left his car, and drove by the Beauty Shack. It was still closed, so Rhodes decided to pay a visit to Lonnie Wallace.

Lonnie's neighborhood was noisier than it had been the last time Rhodes had been there. Saturday morning was the time for working in the yard. The noise of lawn mowers and leaf blowers filled the air, and Rhodes enjoyed the smell of freshly cut grass that he hadn't had to mow.

Lonnie was kneeling at a flower bed, looking for weeds to pull. Rhodes didn't think he was going to find any.

"Hey, Sheriff," Lonnie said, looking up from his work. "What's going on?"

"Nothing much," Rhodes said. "I just wanted to talk to you some more."

Lonnie stood up. It was easier for him than it would have been for Rhodes. He wore khaki shorts, a blue polo shirt, and a straw hat with a wide brim.

"I've been trying to keep busy," he said. "Since . . . you know. I can't seem to concentrate on anything. Working in the yard takes my mind off . . . you know."

"I know," Rhodes said. "You want to talk out here?"

"Let's go around back," he said, and Rhodes followed him around the house.

In back, Lonnie had a covered patio. A pitcher of lemonade sat on a small table between two flimsy-looking green plastic lawn chairs. Condensation ran down the side of the pitcher and pooled on the table. There had been ice in the pitcher, but most of it had melted. The lemonade would be watery. A glass stood by the pitcher. Rhodes

325

thought about Jeff Tyler and how he'd sit outside and drink lemonade in front of his store. Something he and Lonnie had in common.

"You sit down," Lonnie said to Rhodes. "I'll run in and get you a glass."

"No, thanks," Rhodes said. "You go ahead and have a drink. I don't need one."

"You're sure?"

Rhodes said he was sure and sat down, hoping the chair would hold him. It sagged under his weight, but it didn't crumble. Lonnie poured himself some lemonade and sat in the other chair.

"I can't stop thinking about Jeff," Lonnie said after he'd taken a sip of lemonade. "I don't know what it's going to be like here without him. You probably think this is selfish, but there's nobody else like me in town, nobody I can talk to now that he and Lynn are both gone."

"You might be surprised," Rhodes said. "There are plenty of people around here who'd talk to you."

"Name one," Lonnie said, setting his glass on the table.

Rhodes looked out across the perfect lawn at the board fence enclosing the yard. A sparrow lit on the fence, then flew away.

"Well," he said, "there's Nora Fischer."

Lonnie smiled a sad smile. "She's a friend, and I enjoy her company, but she's so much older than I am. It's not quite the same."

"And there's me," Rhodes said.

"You're only here because I'm a suspect in Jeff and Lynn's deaths." Rhodes started to interrupt, but Lonnie didn't let him. "No use to deny it, Sheriff. How often did you drop by before they died?"

That was an easy one to answer. "Never," Rhodes said.

"That's okay," Lonnie said. "I didn't ever drop by your house, either."

"You need to get out more," Rhodes said. "You should go to Max's place for dinner some Friday night and see what you think of Seepy Benton's performance. He's a guy you might like to talk to."

"I've heard about him. He teaches math at the college. I was never very good at math." Lonnie's voice quavered. "Jeff was. He was good at lots of things, but people didn't know because they didn't know him like I did. They thought he was some lazy goober with an antique store."

"Nobody thought that."

"You're just being nice. They did think it, but he wasn't like that at all. He read books. He liked ghost stories. His favorite TV show was *Firefly*. I'll bet you didn't know that."

Rhodes shook his head. He'd never even heard of the show.

"Jeff liked Dean Martin better than Frank Sinatra. He liked Westerns, and he didn't like musicals." Lonnie looked at Rhodes. "Who's going to remember those things besides me?"

"You'll do," Rhodes said. "One person who remembers is more than some people have. What about Lynn? Who's going to remember her?"

"I will," Lonnie said. "I'll remember both of them." He gave Rhodes a weak smile. "She didn't like Dino or Sinatra, either one. She liked Madonna and Blondie. She liked quiz shows on TV. *Jeopardy!* was her favorite."

"Did she and Jeff get along?"

"They didn't really know each other. She cut his hair, and they talked then, but that was all. She knew about me and Jeff, and she didn't care, any more than I cared about what she did in her personal life."

Now the conversation was getting around to what Rhodes was interested in. It was time to find out what Lonnie had been keeping from him if he could.

"You never did tell me if Lynn had someone special. She must have mentioned that to you."

Lonnie had denied earlier that Lynn had said anything about her romances, but Rhodes thought something was missing from the denial.

"I didn't tell you because she didn't tell me," Lonnie said.

"I've talked to three or four men who said she broke up with them because she had someone special."

"Then I don't know who it could've been." Lonnie picked up his lemonade glass and took a sip. "Maybe they were mistaken. Maybe they were lying to you."

"Either one is possible," Rhodes said. "They were all getting uncomfortable in their relationships with her because she'd asked them for money."

"She asked them for money?"

"That's what they told me. She threatened to tell their wives they were dating her. It didn't work. Or so they told me."

"It's not like her," Lonnie said. "She never asked me for money. If she wanted to blackmail somebody, I'd have been a good candidate."

"She must have needed the money for something."

"The little red car, maybe," Lonnie said after a slight hesitation. "That's another thing she loved. She liked to drive it with the top down, even when it was too cold or too hot to do that."

"Didn't she make enough money to buy the car without help?"

"I think so, but none of us made that much. People don't get their hair done as often as they should when money's tight like it is now, and Sandra always got her share. She made more than any of us."

"She owns the shop," Rhodes pointed out.

"Sure. It's only fair that she make more than the rest of us. I'm doing okay, and Abby has a husband with a job, so they're all right."

"Lynn, though," Rhodes said. "Lynn needed money."

Lonnie looked away. "She liked nice things."

Rhodes tried to think of nice things in Lynn's house. There weren't many. She had a flat-screen TV, and the furniture was okay, but there was nothing fancy anywhere. Her clothes and shoes came from shops in nearby cities and not from Walmart, but they weren't from Neiman Marcus.

"Did Jeff need money?" Rhodes asked.

"What? Why would you say that?"

"I was just wondering. You said you talked to him the day Lynn was killed. You were the one who told him about it."

Lonnie looked as if he were trying to recall what he'd said and not succeeding. "I did?"

"That's right. I've been wondering about that."

"If I said I called him, I guess I did."

He wouldn't say any more, so Rhodes said, "Back to the money question."

Lonnie shuddered as if a chill had hit him. "Jeff? He didn't need money. That's another thing about him nobody knew. He had money. Not a lot, but enough to live on. He just did the antiques thing for the fun of it. He liked old stuff that most people would consider junk. He liked being around it, so that's why he had the store, not because he needed the money."

Rhodes hadn't known about the money, though he'd have found out eventually. At any rate, it didn't seem likely now that Tyler would've been engaging in any form of blackmail. Rhodes brought up Lynn again, but Lonnie was stubborn. He continued to insist that he didn't know why Lynn might have asked anyone for money.

Rhodes continued not to believe him, but that was all right. As soon as he got everything worked out to his satisfaction, Rhodes would come back and talk to Lonnie again. He thought Lonnie would be ready to talk by then.

"I still think those men living across the street killed her," Lonnie said when Rhodes stood up to go.

"No," Rhodes said, "they didn't."

"Are you sure?"

"I'm sure."

"Are they still there? In the hotel, I mean?"

"I haven't checked today, but I figure they're long gone from Blacklin County."

"Bail jumpers?"

"Somehow I don't think the people who put up the money for them are going to care," Rhodes said, "and the bondsman will be taken care of. Everyone will be glad to have them gone."

"I hope you're right and they're really gone," Lonnie said. "I didn't feel safe with them around."

"They wouldn't hurt you," Rhodes said. "They might steal your car battery or cut the catalytic converter off your car, but they wouldn't hurt you."

"I don't believe that."

"Lonnie," Rhodes said, "remember what you've said about how people wouldn't like you if they knew you were gay?"

"Well," Lonnie said, "it's true."

"No, it's not. Everybody knows already, and everybody likes you. You're just another guy who lives in Clearview to them, and they'd be your friends if you'd let them."

Lonnie didn't appear to be persuaded. "What does this have to do with those men living in the old hotel?"

"Think about it. You're acting the same way about them that you claim everybody's acting about you. You don't know them or anything about them, but you're willing to believe they're murderers."

"Well, they . . ." Lonnie stopped. He looked down at the concrete patio. "You're right. I shouldn't judge people I've never even met. Maybe I'd like them if I knew them."

"I wouldn't go that far," Rhodes said, rubbing the place on his head where the bucket had hit him.

CHAPTER 26

After leaving Lonnie's, Rhodes drove to the reclamation center. He wanted to see if it was open, and if it was, he wanted to see who was in charge. He thought Nolan might have sent Mike and Al away.

The gate was open, so Rhodes drove inside and parked in front of the office building. He got out of his car and looked around the piles of metal. The sun glinted off an old car bumper, and Rhodes could almost feel the heat coming off the twisted chrome and steel. He remembered what the place had been like when he was a boy. There had been no stacks of salvage. The now vanished cotton gin had been in full operation, and the place hummed with activity.

Rhodes had occasionally walked there on a slow Saturday morning to watch the farmers bring the cotton wagons in. The wagons would be positioned under a big tube that hung down from the gin, and the cotton would be sucked out of the wagon and up into the tube. After the cotton was in the gin, the cotton would be separated from the seeds before it was pressed into the heavy bales that had been stored in the warehouse that still stood across the street.

The cleaned seeds were sent to the seed mill, which was also on the property, and turned into cottonseed oil. Rhodes imagined that he could still smell it, though now there wasn't a trace of it left.

He got out of his car and went into the office. Mike and Al were both there. Neither was pleased to see him.

"You again," Mike said when Rhodes walked in.

"Yeah," Al said.

"What d'you want?" Mike asked. "Me and Al don't want any more trouble. You already like to got us fired. Ain't that enough for you?"

"I don't think I'm the one at fault here," Rhodes said. "I'm not the one who's been stealing car batteries, copper wire, and catalytic converters."

"Hey, we never stole anything," Mike said.

"Yeah," Al said.

"You're right," Rhodes said. "I'm sorry if I hurt your feelings. You never stole a thing.

You had somebody else do that for you."

"I don't like you much, Sheriff," Mike said.

"Yeah," Al said.

Rhodes was starting to admire Al's use of the language. He might not have a big vocabulary, but he had a good control of his tone of voice. He got a lot of meaning into the one word he seemed to prefer over any other.

"I like you fellas a lot," Rhodes said. "I like your friends, too. You know. Guillermo, Jorge, and Frankie. They been by here today?"

Mike and Al looked at each other. Then they looked back at Rhodes, crossed their arms over their chests, and said nothing at all.

Rhodes thought they'd probably win a staring contest if he got into one with them, so he said, "If you see them, tell them I'm still looking for them. If you see Nolan, tell him I said hey."

Mike and Al looked at each other again. They didn't ask who Nolan was, and they didn't look happy that Rhodes had mentioned the name.

"It's been nice talking to you," Rhodes said. "I hope I don't have to put you in jail again."

"You won't," Mike said, uncrossing his arms and dropping his hands to his sides.

"Yeah," Al said, doing the same.

Rhodes left them there. He wondered how long it would be before they got into trouble again. Two weeks, tops, he figured.

Rhodes went back to the jail. He thought he had things worked out now, but he needed to get Lonnie to talk to make sure he was right. Give him a little more time, and it would come out, or at least Rhodes hoped it would. Rhodes didn't think Lonnie was in any danger, but you never knew about that kind of thing.

Rhodes went in the jail and told Hack to have Buddy drive by Lonnie's house now and then to be sure everything was all right.

"Any reason why things wouldn't be all right?" Hack asked.

"Two people are dead, and he knew both of them," Rhodes said.

"So you think somebody might kill him just because he knew the other two?"

"Never mind," Rhodes said. "Just let Buddy know."

Hack muttered something about being mean, but he made the call. Rhodes sat at his desk and started writing things down, including all his speculations about the sequence of events from Lynn's death up to Tyler's. Everything fit.

Lawton came in just as he was finishing up.

"You ever eat raccoon?" he asked.

"Never did," Hack said. "I've had 'possum, though."

Rhodes hadn't heard any culinary discussions between the two of them lately, and he wondered what had brought this one on.

"Reason I ask," Lawton said, as if Rhodes had spoken aloud, "is I was talkin' to one of the prisoners back there. Ray Slade. Buddy brought him in this mornin'. You know him, Sheriff. He's been here before."

Rhodes was familiar with Slade, all right. He'd arrested him once himself. Slade had several bad habits, one of which was ignoring stop signs. He claimed he didn't see any use to stop if there was nobody coming. He didn't have much use for speed limits, either. Neither of those things would have been so bad if Slade had a driver's license, but that was something else he didn't believe in. He also didn't believe in liability insurance, which was yet another problem.

"He lives out on the old McCollum place," Lawton said. "Lots of 'coons in those woods, and he hunts 'em now and then."

"Wasn't brought in for that, though," Hack said.

Rhodes didn't bother to ask what Slade's offense was. He could just look it up if he wanted to know, which he didn't.

"He says a 'coon's real good if it's cooked right," Lawton said. "He says he can make a 'coon pie that'd make you think your mama cooked it. Says you have to be sure you get the meat tender. He soaks it in brine for eight hours or so and that does the trick."

"Reminds me of Clint Worsham," Hack said. "You remember him?"

"Sure," Lawton said. "Lived in the country outside of Obert. I know why you thought of him. He's the one —"

Hack cut him off. "Clint had what he called his annual marsupial supper. Invited nearly ever'body in Obert. I never went myself, but I heard he had 'possum fixed five or six different ways. You ever eat 'possum, Sheriff?"

Rhodes stood up. He didn't think he wanted to hear any more about gourmet cooking.

"I never did," he said. "Where's Buddy?"

"Prob'ly on patrol. You want me to call him?"

"Might be a good idea," Rhodes said.

"Tell him he can meet me at Lonnie Wallace's house."

It was a lot quieter in Lonnie's neighborhood than it had been earlier in the day. Nobody was mowing a lawn or blowing the grass off a driveway. Rhodes figured everybody was inside having lunch or off having a burger at the Dairy Queen. He was pretty sure nobody was having raccoon pie or a tasty 'possum dish.

Lonnie came to the door and let Rhodes in.

"I was just about to cook myself a hamburger," Lonnie said. "You want one? I can throw another patty on the grill."

"No, thanks," Rhodes said. "We have some things we need to talk about."

"I thought we'd gone over everything," Lonnie said. He looked a bit apprehensive. "I've told you all I know about Jeff and Lynn."

"Not quite all," Rhodes said. "There's one other thing."

"I don't know what it could be," Lonnie said.

"You can go ahead and grill that burger," Rhodes said. "I can talk while you do."

"Okay," Lonnie said.

They went through the house and out on

the patio. Lonnie had a little hibachi that he'd set near the table. Rhodes sat down in one of the lawn chairs while Lonnie put charcoal in the hibachi.

"You're sure you don't want anything?" Lonnie asked.

Rhodes said he was sure, and Lonnie put starter fluid on the briquettes. He put away the fluid, then touched a match to the charcoal. When he was sure it was burning properly, Lonnie sat in the other chair.

"It'll take a few minutes for the coals to get ready," Lonnie said. He looked out at his lawn. "Sometimes Jeff would come over, and I'd grill burgers for the two of us."

Rhodes was saved from having to respond to that because Buddy appeared from around the corner of the house.

"Who's that?" Lonnie asked.

"That's Deputy Buddy Warren," Rhodes said. "How'd you find us, Buddy?"

"Smelled the charcoal," Buddy said. "Thought you might be back here. Hope I'm not interrupting lunch."

"Lonnie was just about to grill himself a hamburger," Rhodes said. "I told him this wouldn't take long."

"What's going on here, Sheriff?" Lonnie said. "Are you going to arrest me? Is that what the deputy's here for?"

"We'll just see how it goes," Rhodes said.

"I don't think I'm hungry anymore," Lonnie said, looking at the charcoal.

Rhodes couldn't blame him for losing his appetite. "You've been holding out on me, Lonnie."

"No," Lonnie said. "I've told you everything you asked."

Rhodes shook his head. "Not quite. I think I know pretty much what happened, but there's still one thing I haven't quite figured out. I have a guess. You can tell me if I'm right. It's about the money. Lynn had a reason for wanting it, and you know it. Now's the time to tell me."

"I don't know. Not really."

"She must have talked to you about it. Here's what I think. I think she wanted to open her own shop. Maybe she even wanted you to go to work for her."

Rhodes was only half guessing. Everything he'd heard added up to the idea that Lynn might have been leaving the Beauty Shack.

Lonnie seemed to shrink in his chair.

"She didn't have anybody special," Rhodes said. "She didn't even care that much about the men she was dating. She just wanted money, and she was going to use it to go out on her own."

Lonnie straightened. "It wasn't her fault.

She tried to get a loan. The banks wouldn't even talk to her. They blamed the economy. They said it wasn't because she was a woman, but I'm sure that was it. Or part of it."

"So she tried to get the money from another source," Rhodes said. "I can understand that, I guess, but she should've found a better way."

"Name one," Lonnie said. "Money just wasn't coming into the shop the way it used to. She couldn't save enough to start her own place, and even if I'd gone in with her, she might not have had enough." He stopped and looked at Rhodes. "Anyway, I was scared to try. I've been with Sandra too long. I didn't want to take the risk."

Buddy stood by listening. He didn't say anything, but his hand stayed near the butt of his pistol.

"Lynn wanted to take the risk, though," Rhodes said. "What would've happened to the Beauty Shack without her?"

"Sandra would've lost a lot of business," Lonnie said. "Especially if I went with Lynn. But I wasn't going to."

"So Lynn had to keep it a secret," Rhodes said.

"She couldn't tell Sandra. If she had, Sandra would've tried to stop her. Lynn was a little paranoid about it. She even thought Sandra might have suspected something and talked to the banks so they wouldn't lend her any money. That's crazy, I know, but she mentioned it to me."

"She must have finally said something to Sandra," Rhodes said, "and Sandra didn't like it. Maybe she even lost her temper. Or maybe Lynn did. There was a fight."

Everything pointed that way. Sandra's nervousness was clear from the way she'd been smoking. She'd even been sure to tell Rhodes that she'd touched some of the things in the Beauty Shack, and she'd tried very hard to make him believe that Guillermo and Jorge had killed Lynn.

It also explained why the two men hadn't seen any cars over at the Beauty Shack when Lynn was killed. Well, that wasn't quite true. They'd seen cars, all right, but they hadn't noticed them because they were just the ones that were often there. Lynn's and Sandra's.

"I don't think Sandra would kill anybody," Lonnie said, but his voice wavered. "She liked Lynn."

Rhodes didn't doubt it, but he also knew what could happen when tempers got out of hand. A jab with a pair of scissors, a hair dryer swung at the end of a long cord. Bad things could happen, and had.

"One other thing you haven't told me," Rhodes said.

"What?"

"Jeff was Lynn's last appointment on the day she was killed. You said you were the one who called him to let him know."

"Yes," Lonnie said.

His voice was so low that Rhodes could hardly hear him.

"Somebody must have called him to cancel the appointment," Rhodes said. "I don't think it was Lynn. Was it?"

"No."

"He told you who it was, though, didn't he."

"Yes."

"It was Sandra, wasn't it."

"Yes," Lonnie said. It was no more than a whisper.

CHAPTER 27

Lonnie told Rhodes that he hadn't thought anything about it at first, not even after Jeff was killed. It was the usual way of things. Somebody couldn't keep an appointment, and Sandra would call the client to let him know.

"You can see why I didn't think about it," Lonnie said. "Can't you?"

"If you had, Jeff might not have been killed," Rhodes said.

"I know."

Lonnie started to sniffle. Buddy tore a paper towel off a roll that sat on the table and handed it to Lonnie. Lonnie took it and wiped his face.

"Sandra got worried," Rhodes said. "After she thought about it, she knew she shouldn't have called Jeff. She only did it because she didn't want him to come in and find the body. She hadn't decided what to do about that yet."

Buddy spoke up for the first time. "She just left Lynn's body there?"

"That's right," Rhodes said. "Then she worked out a plan. She'd come in the next morning, pretend to find the body, and call it in. She took the purse to make it look like a robbery, and she tried to put the blame on the men living across the street."

Rhodes thought that Sandra knew about Frankie and his friends' habit of looking through the trash for things and that she'd planted the purse behind Tyler's store in hopes that Rhodes would think they'd left it there or that they'd tossed it there after killing Lynn. She should've thought about taking things out of the purse first.

"If that was her plan, it didn't work very well," Buddy said.

"No," Rhodes said, "it didn't."

"She didn't have to kill Jeff," Lonnie said. "He wouldn't have said anything."

"He might have after he worked things out," Rhodes said. "You're the one who should have told, though. You knew all this, but you kept it quiet."

"I couldn't believe it was Sandra," Lonnie said. "I still can't believe it. I didn't want to say anything that might get her in trouble if she was innocent."

"You have to trust the system," Buddy

said, always ready with a cliché.

"Ha," Lonnie said. "Trust the system. Do you ever read the papers? Do you know how many death row inmates have been released in this state in the last few years because they shouldn't have been there in the first place?"

Rhodes stood up. "None of those were from this county."

"I don't care. I wasn't going to take a chance. I still don't think Sandra did it."

"I do," Rhodes said.

Rhodes parked in front of the Wileys' house. Buddy parked right behind him. When they started up the cracked walk, Buddy said, "You think Lonnie called 'em to say we were on the way?"

"I told him not to," Rhodes said.

"Maybe he did it anyway."

"I don't think so. He'd be too scared. He still thinks we might arrest him."

"Well, we might."

"Not likely," Rhodes said.

He rang the doorbell, and Jimmy answered it. He was dressed just as he'd been the last time Rhodes saw him. White shirt and jeans. He didn't look any healthier.

"What's up, Sheriff," he said.

"We're here to see Sandra," Rhodes told him.

"Take two of you to do that?" Jimmy asked. He didn't move out of the doorway.

"Don't make this any harder than it has to be, Jimmy," Rhodes said.

"Just kidding, Danny. Come on in."

Jimmy moved aside, and Rhodes went into the house. Buddy followed him.

"Sandra's in the kitchen," Jimmy said, "cleaning up a little. You two go in the den and I'll get her."

Rhodes and Buddy went into the den. Rhodes looked around the room, which if anything looked shabbier than before. He wondered how much money Jimmy and Sandra had spent on Jimmy's medical bills over and above what the insurance had paid. *A lot* was the only estimate he could come up with. It was a sad situation all around.

Jimmy and Sandra came into the room. Sandra was smoking a freshly lit cigarette, as nervous as ever. More nervous, if anything.

Jimmy said, "Have a seat, Danny. You, too, Deputy. No need to stand up."

Rhodes and Buddy sat in chairs in front of the coffee table. Jimmy and Sandra sat on the sagging couch across from them. Jimmy squirmed as if he couldn't get comfortable. Sandra blew out puffs of gray smoke.

"What's the big deal?" Jimmy asked. "Did you catch the people who killed Lynn?"

"Not exactly," Rhodes said. "We're getting close to making an arrest, though."

Jimmy gave a husky chuckle. "Cops always say that on TV. 'We're close to making an arrest.' Sometimes they are, and sometimes they aren't."

"We are," Rhodes said.

"Who you think did it?"

"Sandra," Rhodes said.

Sandra coughed as if she'd inhaled too much smoke and couldn't get it out of her lungs. Jimmy took the cigarette from her hand and crushed it in an ashtray that badly needed emptying.

"You ought not to joke about that kind of thing, Danny," Jimmy said. "Sandra's mighty upset over the whole thing, and you're not helping."

"I think she killed Jeff Tyler, too," Rhodes said.

Sandra had stopped coughing. She leaned back against the couch and closed her eyes.

"You say you *think* she did. You got any proof of that?"

"Not yet," Rhodes said. "I figured I'd ask her. Just a few things I have to say first. Or

I'll let Buddy do it. You have your Miranda warning, Buddy?"

Buddy pulled a laminated card from his shirt pocket and read out the warning.

"Thanks," Rhodes said. "That was for the two of you. Any questions?"

"You think Sandra's going to say she killed anybody?" Jimmy asked. "You must be crazy."

"I don't think so," Rhodes said.

"There's that *think* again."

"Let me tell you why I think it," Rhodes said, and he got out his own paper, the one on which he'd written everything down, and hit the high points for them.

Jimmy and Sandra didn't say anything when he finished. Sandra lit another cigarette.

"Doesn't prove anything," Jimmy said. "Just a lot of speculation."

Rhodes folded the paper and put it back in his pocket. "That's right, but it all points one way. I think that if I look hard enough I'll find somebody who saw Sandra's Suburban in the alley behind Tyler's place when he was killed. Believe me, I'll look hard enough. I think we'll find Sandra's fingerprints on Lynn's purse. I think —"

"Think, think, think," Jimmy said. "That won't cut it, Danny, and you know it."

"You're right," Rhodes said. "That's why I want Sandra to tell me what happened."

Sandra put out her cigarette and patted Jimmy's hand. "I knew you'd figure it out, Danny. You always were one of the smartest boys in our class. I'll tell you how it was."

"No," Jimmy said. "You hush. I'll tell him. I'm the one who did it, Danny. I killed them both." He reached behind his back and brought out a snub-nosed .38 revolver. "I sure would hate to kill you, though."

"I wouldn't like it a whole lot, either," Rhodes said. "You better put down the gun and let Sandra talk."

"She doesn't have anything to say. I was at the shop with her and Lynn. Lynn got smart about how she was going to quit and get her own place. She said she was tired of Sandra raking in all the money. Look around, Danny. Does it look like we were raking it in?"

"Takes a lot when you have doctors' bills," Rhodes said.

"You're damn right it does. Lynn didn't care about that, though. Just cared about herself. I told her she better not talk like that, and one thing led to another. She had her scissors in her smock, and she took a swipe at me with 'em. Came right at me. I snatched up that dryer and swung it."

Jimmy paused and looked Rhodes in the eyes. "What happened then was an accident. I never meant to kill her. I was trying to knock the scissors out of her hand, that's all."

"Maybe that's so," Rhodes said, "but Jeff Tyler's a different story."

"He got to thinking about Sandra calling him to cancel his appointment. That wasn't smart. I should've told her not to do it, but I wasn't thinking just then. Jeff wanted Sandra to come by and talk to him, but I knew what he wanted. Money. That's what everybody wants."

"He might have wanted to make sure she didn't do what he thought she did," Rhodes said.

"Well, he never got to talk about it. I shot him, and that's all there is to it."

"What about the purse?"

"I threw it away. Shouldn't have taken it from the shop in the first place, but Sandra . . . *I* thought you'd believe somebody killed Lynn for it and then ditched it. Those fellas across the street don't belong in this country anyhow. I figured they could take the blame."

Rhodes thought things had gone pretty much the way Jimmy had told it, at least in the case of Tyler's death. Jimmy was probably responsible for that one, all right, but not for the other. That one had gone the way he told it, too, but with Sandra doing the things Jimmy claimed he'd done.

"Things didn't work out like they were supposed to, did they," Rhodes said.

"No, but if you were any kind of sheriff, they would've. You shouldn't care more about a bunch of illegals than you care for somebody you grew up with and played football with, Danny. This country's just plain gone to hell when that happens."

"So now you're going to shoot me and Buddy?"

"Nope. Sandra and I are gonna leave, and you and your deputy can just sit here till we're gone. After that you can try to chase us down if you want to, but it won't do you any good. I know all the places to hide in this county, Danny. You won't find us."

Rhodes didn't think that was Jimmy's plan at all. He turned to Buddy.

"You ever hear of 'suicide by cop'?" he asked.

"Sure have," Buddy said. "Guy tries something that gets himself killed, and it turns out he planned it that way all along. You think that's what Mr. Wiley has in mind?"

"Might be," Rhodes said. "That way

Sandra might get off. Jimmy, has the cancer come back?"

"None of your business," Jimmy said. He stood up. "Come on, Sandra. Let's go."

"It won't work, Jimmy," Rhodes said. "We aren't going to shoot you."

"You will if I shoot first. Come on, Sandra."

"I'm not leaving, Jimmy. You sit back down."

Jimmy looked at her, and that was all Rhodes had been waiting for. He kicked the coffee table, and it smacked into Jimmy's shins with a *crack* like the sound of a branch breaking.

Jimmy yelled and fell back on the couch. He fired the pistol, but the bullet went into the ceiling. He tried to right himself and shoot again, but he was too weak. Rhodes stepped across the coffee table and took hold of the revolver. His hand grasped the cylinder so it couldn't turn.

Jimmy didn't let go of the pistol. He twisted and thrashed as he tried to break away. Rhodes pushed him into the back of the couch with his free hand. Jimmy tired quickly and stopped struggling. Rhodes pulled the pistol away and handed it to Buddy, who was standing nearby with his own gun drawn.

"You didn't use to be so tough, Danny," Jimmy wheezed.

"Like you said, times have changed."

"Not for the better, either. You might as well lock me up. I don't care. I confess to everything. Just leave Sandra alone. Can you promise me that?"

"Sure," Rhodes said. He looked at Sandra, who gave a slight nod. "I can promise you that, Jimmy."

"Thanks, Danny. You're doing the right thing."

"We'll see," Rhodes said.

Rhodes didn't have to break his promise. He left Sandra alone, but as soon as Jimmy was booked and locked up, Sandra asked Rhodes if they could talk. Rhodes took her to the interview room, where she admitted that she'd killed Lynn.

"It was just like Jimmy said," she told him. "An accident. I never meant to kill her."

Rhodes didn't know the truth of that, but he wasn't the one who had to make the judgment. A jury would have to do that. Maybe Sandra wouldn't spend too long in jail. She might even be able to work at the Beauty Shack again, though how many women would want her to dry their hair was an open question.

As for Jimmy, he'd get a long sentence if he was still alive to go to trial. Rhodes didn't think he would be. He looked worse every day.

Lonnie had opened the shop the day after Sandra's arrest. The parking lot was crowded, and Rhodes wondered if Lonnie and Abby could handle all the business. They might have to find someone else to help them out.

Rhodes hadn't become the star of the Internet, but Jennifer Loam's Web site was a big hit, and Rhodes was at least the star of the county for a couple of days. After that there had been a car wreck near Thurston, and the photos that Jennifer took of the mangled autos had replaced Rhodes as the main attraction.

The autos had wound up at the Environmental Reclamation Center, where Mike and Al were still running things. Rhodes stopped in every few days to check on them. Al remained a man of few words.

Jeff Tyler's business was still closed, but Lonnie had placed a "store manager wanted" ad on Jennifer's Web site. Rhodes thought the place might reopen any day.

One evening when Rhodes was playing ball with Speedo and Yancey, Ivy came out and sat on the steps with him. It was getting dark, and some of the heat had gone out of the air. Now and then a car would drive by on the street in front of the house, but other than that the neighborhood was quiet.

"I've been thinking about what Jimmy said," Rhodes told Ivy as Speedo rolled over Yancey and stole the ball from him.

"He said a lot of things."

"He said the times have changed."

"Of course they have," Ivy said. "That's what times do."

Yancey ran over with the ball and dropped it at Rhodes's feet. Rhodes picked it up.

"Do you think they've gotten worse?" Rhodes asked.

"They've gotten different, that's all."

Rhodes threw the ball, and Speedo and Yancey charged off after it.

"He told me I'd gotten tough," Rhodes asked.

Ivy laughed. The dogs stopped and looked back at her, then went for the ball. Yancey snatched it right out from under Speedo's nose and bounced off across the yard.

"You don't think I'm tough?" Rhodes said.

"You are when you have to be, and you had to be this time. Besides that, you're the star of the Internet."

Rhodes hadn't mentioned Jennifer's Web

site to Ivy.

"Who told you that?" he asked.

"I heard it at the beauty shop," she said.

ABOUT THE AUTHOR

Bill Crider is an Anthony Award winner and Edgar Award finalist. He lives in Alvin, Texas.

The employees of Thorndike Press hope you have enjoyed this Large Print book. All our Thorndike, Wheeler, and Kennebec Large Print titles are designed for easy reading, and all our books are made to last. Other Thorndike Press Large Print books are available at your library, through selected bookstores, or directly from us.

For information about titles, please call:
(800) 223-1244

or visit our Web site at:
http://gale.cengage.com/thorndike

To share your comments, please write:
Publisher
Thorndike Press
10 Water St., Suite 310
Waterville, ME 04901